A MEAN SEASON

A DOM REILLY MYSTERY

MARSHALL THORNTON

Published by Kenmore Books

Edited by Joan Martinelli

Cover design by Marshall Thornton

Images by 123rf stock

ISBN: 979-836804606-8

First Edition

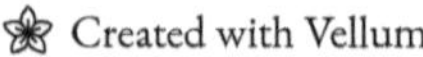 Created with Vellum

ACKNOWLEDGMENTS

A heartfelt thank you to Joan Martinelli, Nathan Bay, Danielle Wolff, Ben Thompson, Jenna McGrath, Shanee Edwards, Chris Carter, and Lemise Rory.

PROLOGUE

April 1976

Larry Wilkes always hung at the back of the pack. There were twenty-one boys in his gym class, not enough for any of them to escape notice but enough to break into distinct groups as they ran around the track. The jocks in front, the nerds in the middle and the stoners at the rear. Larry couldn't ever figure out where he belonged. Sometimes he was a nerd, and sometimes he was a stoner. He could even run fast if he wanted, but he was never a jock. Figuring that out was easy.

It was a bright, comfortable morning. The sky clear and the pollution low, blown away by the last of that year's Santa Anas. The white-capped San Gabriel Mountains were postcard clear, but the boys paid no attention as they ran the track. Even from the back, Larry managed to keep his eyes on Pete Michaels. Blond and freckled, with a smile that melted the hearts of teachers and cheerleaders alike, he ran up at the front with his brother Paul. Pete had been kept back a year because he'd had some horrible illness in grade school. Larry could never remember which illness, though.

The school sold gym uniforms, but no one bought them. Larry ran in a pair of cut-offs and an old tie-dyed T-shirt. The other boys were just as ragtag. Pete wore a pair of gray sweatpants and a cut-off football jersey with the number 69 on it.

As he ran, Pete giggled like a possessed child. Larry couldn't see the reason until he noticed that the back of Pete's sweatpants would flop down and show his ass and the thick waistband of his jockstrap, then flop up, then flop back down. Pete had loosened the string that held the pants up and was holding them up from the front.

Every few seconds his smooth, pink ass cheeks would be exposed, mooning the boys behind him. Then they disappeared behind the grass-stained gray cloth. Pete kept giggling while his brother rolled his eyes in exasperation. They were, after all, running extra miles because Pete had made the gym class crack-up one too many times. Larry could barely breathe. And not because he'd run for too long, though they had been running far too long.

Looking back over his shoulder, Pete saw Larry watching the sweatpants flop up and down. Then he grinned and, with a glint in his eye, winked.

CHAPTER ONE

April 1, 1996
Monday

"Do we have a problem?" Lydia asked. In the time I'd known her, which was only a few months, I'd noticed she had a very casual way of asking important questions.

We were sitting in a teal-colored vinyl booth at the Park Pantry, my favorite breakfast place. She munched on a veggie skillet, while I worked my way through a San Francisco Joe. When she asked her question, I stopped eating and looked out at the traffic rolling along on Broadway.

Did we have a problem? She knew who I really was. Something I'd been trying to keep secret for a long time. So, yeah, we had a problem. I just wasn't sure how big a problem it was.

"Is that the setup for an April Fools' joke?" I asked.

"It's a serious question."

About a month before, we'd gotten a kid named Danny Osborne out of prison for a murder he didn't commit. I say we, but it was mostly Lydia and her not-for-profit, The Freedom Agenda. All I did was some basic investigation. She'd hired me despite my lack of visible experience, which at the time hadn't made much sense. But then, eventually, she admitted knowing a journalist named Richland Keswick. He'd written a book called *Operation Tea & Crumpets* about the Chicago Outfit in which I had a supporting role. Lydia had known who I was all along and had hired me for the experience I'd attempted to hide.

"Are you good at keeping secrets?" I asked.

"Really?" She scowled, and said, "Fine. Pay me."

"What?"

"Give me a couple of bucks."

I knew what she was doing. I didn't mind the formality of it. I pulled a five out of my wallet and gave it to her.

"Great. Now we have attorney-client privilege. I can't tell anyone anything you don't want them to know. Okay?"

"Okay," I said. I knew I could trust her. I just didn't want to.

"Fabulous. Now that we have that out of the way, you know I'm dying to ask you questions," she said, with a spec of spinach floating on her front tooth. I decided not to mention that.

For the last few weeks, Lydia had been focused on pulling together Danny Osbourne's file for his civil attorneys. There was likely to be a large settlement, a small portion of which would come back to The Freedom Agenda as a donation. From Danny, of course. My understanding was that it could have come as a referral fee, but most civil attorneys were loath to reduce their take.

I'd spent March with my nose buried in a stack of files, reading letters from prisoners claiming their innocence and hoping we'd get them out. I had to decide which ones might have merit. It was a gruesome job. Dull and dispiriting. Most of the letters were from desperate men who were guilty as sin but had nothing to lose by writing a letter. The thing was, no matter how hard they tried, they never managed to hide their guilt.

"All right," I said. "I'll answer your questions on one condition."

"Which is?"

"I want you to give me Richland Keswick's address and phone number."

"You don't have it?" It was a logical question. I had been one of the primary sources on a book he wrote, after all.

"Apparently, he's moved."

A large, brown leather tote sat next to her. She dug into it and pulled out her thick black Day Runner. A little more than three months into the year, and it was already bursting with sticky notes and beginning to fray. She flipped to the section that held her addresses.

"What phone number do you have?" she asked.

I rattled it off by rote.

"That's the old one," she said. Pulling out one of her business cards, she flipped it over and wrote his number on the back. Then she added his address. "He's in the Valley now. If you go to his apartment, you'll need to ring Winchell."

"He's changed his name?"

The hair on the back of my neck stood up. The guy who'd written about the Chicago Outfit, who'd written about me, was living under an assumed name. That couldn't be good.

"It's not what you're thinking," Lydia said. "Winchell is the name of the previous tenant. He just hasn't changed his bell."

"But he's had trouble, after the book?"

Our waitress, Cindy, who was tall and linear, came by and refilled our coffees.

"How is everything?"

"Great," I said, though my breakfast had gotten cold while we talked. Cindy finished filling our cups and took off.

"Tell me how you did it, how did you become Dom Reilly?" Lydia said.

I put more ketchup on my breakfast to make up for its being chilled. I took a bite to put off answering her.

"You gave me your driver's license for the I-9 when I hired you. It looked real."

"That's because I got it at the DMV."

"How did you manage that?"

"I found a guy in Reno. For five thousand, he sold me a birth certificate, a social security number and a Michigan driver's license with my picture on it."

"So, Dominick Reilly is a completely made-up person?"

I shook my head. "The real Dom Reilly disappeared in eighty-two."

It didn't take her long to figure out what that probably meant. "Aren't you afraid someone will try to find him?

"No. Anyone who liked him knows better than to try and find him. Anyone who didn't like him knows where he is, which is probably the bottom of Lake Erie."

She raised an eyebrow at me.

"I was told he was peripheral to the Detroit Partnership and crossed the wrong person."

Lydia's hobby was organized crime, so I didn't have to explain the Detroit Partnership. Or what it meant to cross the wrong person. And yes, I did fly into Detroit for a long weekend once to nose around. I was right. No one was looking for the real Dominick Reilly.

"Still, I try to keep off the grid. I don't have a bank account. I use Ronnie's credit cards."

Ronnie Chen was my boyfriend and the person who'd introduced me to Lydia. He'd sold her a cute little house on Orizaba. He was a good real estate agent and I wished that was why she'd hired him.

"But you and Ronnie own two houses."

"Ronnie owns two houses."

"You're not on the deeds?"

I shook my head.

"Isn't that risky? I mean, people do break up."

I decided it was a good time to take a few more bites of my breakfast. After a moment, she said, "I guess that's none of my business."

When I didn't respond to that either, she said, "Well, we should get down to *our* business." She reached again into the leather tote. After moving a few things around, she pulled out three files which were each about an inch thick.

"These are three separate cases. All rape. We've tested the DNA, twice, and it doesn't match the men sitting in prison."

"You're grouping them together?"

"Yes. Same police officer, same prosecutor. Each conviction

was made primarily on witness identification. We crack one we've got them all." She slid the files over to me saying, "Read through these, then I want you to talk to the victims."

"That's sounds pretty awful," I said. "They're not going to want to hear that the man they think raped them didn't."

"And you won't be telling them. The LAPD will have gotten there first."

"They'll say we're trying to get their rapists out on a technicality."

"And you'll explain what a DNA test is."

I can't say I was looking forward to dealing with three traumatized women armed only with science. I flipped open one of the files, glanced at the top document—an incident report from the late eighties.

"Silverlake," I said, recognizing the street name. "Are these all out of Rampart?"

She nodded. "Detective Brenda Wellesley. She made detective in eighty-seven. She was just thirty. Apparently fast-tracked under The Blake Consent Decree."

"Explain."

"The Blake Consent Decree sets hiring and promotion goals for the LAPD. As a woman, she probably benefited from that."

"So, you think she was out to impress and screwed up?"

"Yes and no. Prior to DNA, a blood typing test was used on sperm. Unlike DNA, it could only exclude suspects. It was either their blood type or it wasn't. A certain portion of the population is what they call nonsecretors. People who don't secrete the antigens needed to perform the test. These three gentlemen are nonsecretors."

"But there was more evidence than that."

"The witness statements are all strong. Almost too strong."

"You think Wellesley coached them?"

"That's what I want you to find out. Subtly."

I nodded, then said, "There's something I'd like in return."

"Aside from your paycheck?" She seemed annoyed by my proposed negotiation.

"We got a letter from a kid named Larry Wilkes. I'd like to follow up on it."

Lydia frowned deeply. "I'm guessing there's no DNA angle," she said. Something to test for DNA was a requirement for a file to advance in our offices.

"No. It's not that kind of case."

Sipping her coffee, she stared me down. Finally, she asked, "Why?"

"He's accused of killing one of the other students at his high school right after graduation. He says he didn't do it. I believe him."

"More."

"He says he was in love with the guy."

"That's not evidence of anything."

"No. But it's a reason to look for evidence."

"I didn't realize you were such a romantic."

"Me neither."

Cindy came over and picked up our plates. "I'll get your check in just a minute," she said, before she sped off to the kitchen.

"When you go to see Richie, don't tell him I'm the one who gave you his address. I wouldn't have, but I know you'd have found him eventually."

"I think he'll figure it out, don't you?"

Lydia didn't have time to answer. Cindy was back with the check and she grabbed it. "This is on me. It was a work breakfast. Mostly."

She handed Cindy her American Express. Then looked back at me and asked, "Was it lonely? Becoming someone else?"

"Sometimes."

CHAPTER TWO

Summer 1990

"You ever go by Nick?"

One night that summer, I was bartending at the Gauntlet, a leather bar in Silverlake. The guy looked completely out of place. He was wearing a leather jacket, but it was the wrong kind. Brown and blousy. If you told me his mother bought it for him, I'd have believed you. He looked to be in his late twenties, attractive but nothing to write home about. He'd ordered a tequila sunrise, meaning he didn't know where he was. I only had half the ingredients, which meant he got a shot of tequila with a Bud Light.

"I've always been Dom," I said, giving him my most charming smile. It wasn't the first time I'd been asked, but I always hated it.

"It's Domi-*nick*, though, right?"

"It is."

"So, you could go by Nick."

"But I don't. Like I just said."

"I'm looking for a guy named Nick."

"Most of the guys in here aren't that specific. Wait, I take that back. They're specific, just not about names."

"I need to find this Nick because I'm writing a book and he

knows the people I'm writing about. I'm a journalist."

I had a Johnny Walker Red on the rocks under the counter, so I pulled it out and took a sip. It was about my third that night. It might have been a Wednesday, or a Thursday. It wasn't that busy. I wasn't drunk, but I might have been a little stupid.

"You know I think you'd be better off playing the Lotto. Your odds would be better."

"Oh, I don't think so. The guy I'm looking for was a private detective in Chicago, but he sometimes worked as a bouncer or a bartender. And he's gay. See, I figure he's going to be doing something familiar, like bartending, in a place he feels safe, like a gay bar."

"It's a good thing for you there's only two or three of those in the world."

"I spent three weeks in New York and two in San Francisco. Now I'm in L.A."

"Where to next?"

He just smiled. "So, this guy, Nick Nowak, was involved with a gangster named Jimmy English. Kind of a henchman type, you know?"

That wasn't true. I was never a henchman for Jimmy, but I declined to say so. He was baiting me. He wanted me to slip up. He kept doing it, too.

"There are rumors he's connected to a murder at a construction site in the North Loop."

Okay, that was basically true. But I let it run off my back like water, and asked, "So, he's dangerous?"

"Something tells me he's not."

"Like a little birdy?"

"Like my intuition."

"You want something from this guy, so what are you offering?"

"A chance to put the record straight."

"Good luck with that."

"I can't offer money. It's not ethical and I don't have any."

"Yeah, well, you'd better think of something. You know, just in case you find him."

I went off and waited on some other guys for a while. Eventually, I glanced over and noticed that my journalist friend had finished his beer. I held off for a bit hoping he'd leave. He didn't.

Finally, I walked back down and asked him, "You want another?"

"No, I'm fine." After a moment, he said, "My name is Richland Keswick."

"Is that supposed to mean something to me?"

"No. But I'm hoping you'll remember it." He took a white card out of this jacket pocket. Laid it on the bar. "This might help."

I left it sitting there.

He leaned in, and said, "So this is what I can do for Nick. I can write that he's dead and then I'll be the last person who comes looking for him."

I wished him luck and said goodnight. He left me a two-dollar tip. Even as I promised myself I'd never see him again, I put his card into my wallet. A week later, I called him.

Giovanni Agnotti, AKA Jimmy English, was a high-level member of the Chicago Outfit. He was born sometime around the turn of the century and died in the summer of 1985. I did a few odd jobs for him in the early eighties—again, I was never a henchman—and then later I was deeply involved in a sort of sting he pulled on the Chicago PD, the Feds and the state's attorney. They were investigating him, so he slipped them false information and then pulled the rug out from under them at trial. He did it so that they'd never get their hands on his assets. Little known fact: When the government gets their hands on someone like Jimmy, they don't just send them to prison, they take their stuff. In the end, it worked out well for Jimmy. For others, not so well. Three people ended up dead and another permanently injured. It wasn't pretty.

I was lied to. A lot. And I played my part somewhat blindly. I didn't appreciate being a pawn in the whole thing, but I guess I shouldn't have been surprised. Jimmy English was a nice old man who did terrible things. And let's be honest, the world is full of nice old men doing terrible things. It's kind of the way of things.

I met Richland Keswick at the American Burger on Hollywood Boulevard. I think it was a Tuesday afternoon. American Burger was a cheesy place, a relic, a fast-food joint that wasn't part of a giant chain. The burgers weren't bad but not a lot of people went there. I'd neglected to ask if anyone in the Outfit knew about the book he was writing, so I made it my first question.

"They might have some idea," he admitted. "I met with Jimmy's granddaughter, Deanna Hansen."

"Then they know."

"No, she's out of it. She went legit."

"I wouldn't believe that if I were you. Crime is a hard business to leave. If only because it's so lucrative."

"I'll keep that in mind." He ate a few French fries, then said, "Tell me about Owen Lovejoy."

"He was my lawyer. He was also one of Jimmy's lawyers. I wouldn't believe a word he says. He kind of double-crossed me."

"I wasn't able to talk to him."

"Attorney-client privilege?"

"No. He passed away last year. AIDS."

That hit me like a hard slap in the face. It took a few moments for me to pull it together. I mean, he wasn't always my favorite person in the world, but I hated that he was dead. Dead people never apologize for their bad behavior.

"Tell me about Operation Tea & Crumpets," Richland said, sipping a giant Coke.

I spent the next three hours telling him everything I knew. We ended up getting four more sodas and three more orders of fries so they wouldn't throw us out. He took notes the whole time in an imitation leather journal. When I ran out of things to tell him, he said, "I'll have questions. Let me dig into this and we can—"

"Call me," I said. "It's probably better if we don't get together again." Telling the whole story reminded me of how many people might enjoy dumping my dead body into a large body of water.

I stood up, ready to leave, but I had one final thing to say.

"Don't forget. I'm dead."

CHAPTER THREE

April 1, 1996
Monday

I spent a lot of that Monday reading the three files Lydia had given me. Immediately, I saw that the rapes were not likely to be connected. I hadn't expected them to be, but it was a good thing to verify. Locations, victims and modus operandi were all different. The only thing they seemed to have in common were the investigating detective, Brenda Wellesley, and that I happened to be familiar with all the locations.

The first rape I looked at took place August 22, 1987, on the Los Angeles City College campus. It happened at eleven-thirty at night after classes were over and most students had gone. A young woman named Selma Martinez was walking to her car after a late conference with her professor. The car was parked on North Heliotrope, but before she got there she was beaten and raped behind the theater building. When she regained consciousness, she drove herself to the emergency room at County USC.

The second rape occurred on November 12, 1987, in a private home at 2145 Avon Court in Elysian Heights. The rapist broke in through the back door of the house around two in the morning and raped thirty-six-year-old Joanne Yardley, a props person for Lorimar Studios. She was blindfolded and tied to her bed. She remained tied there for ten hours until her neighbor came over to complain about Joanne's howling Chihuahua.

The third attack happened January 29, 1988, at five-thirty in the morning. A twenty-seven-year-old jogger on the running track around the reservoir was pulled into a small, wooded area near Earl Street. Cammy Wainright was punched in the face until she passed out. She was raped while unconscious. Another jogger discovered her two hours later when he heard moaning.

Those were the basics.

The files also contained wince-inducing Polaroids of the victims' injuries, statements collected by uniformed officers from potential witnesses, and the blood tests Lydia had talked about. Then there were the descriptions; long, detailed descriptions in each file. I felt like the descriptions of the rapists should have been included on the incident reports, but for some reason they were not.

Selma Martinez described her assailant as a young Black man in his early twenties, about six-foot-two and a hundred-and-seventy pounds. She said he was very dark-skinned and had Jheri curl in his hair. Detective Wellesley found Alan Dinkler, who took a history class that met an hour earlier in the classroom across from the one where Selma took American Literature, Part II. Even though Dinkler's mother said he was home and in bed by the time of the rape, he was convicted on the strength of Selma's identification. A photograph of Dinkler showed that he was very dark-complected and wore Jheri curl in his hair.

Joanne Yardley's attacker wore a ski mask during the rape. She didn't see him, though she knew he was around six-feet tall, white and wore Aramis. Her ex-husband had worn the cologne, so she was familiar with it. The stronger description came from Joanne's neighbor—a woman named Candy Van Dyke—who had seen the man, later identified as Stu Whatley, coming out of the house without the mask. She added blond hair, blue eyes and muscular build to the description.

Detective Wellesley did a search of the area for sex offenders and found Whatley. He'd been arrested for felony rape, but not charged. Instead, he'd pled to a misdemeanor assault charge and had gotten probation. Wellesley put him in a lineup. Joanne didn't recognize him until he was asked to speak; then she knew him. They searched his apartment and found that he wore Aramis.

Despite being beaten to unconsciousness, Cammy Wainright remembered quite a lot about her attacker. Somewhere in his early twenties, he was white with light brown hair, dark eyes. He was several inches taller than she was—five-seven—and strong. Very strong. Wellesley focused on a list of men Cammy had met through a classified ad she'd placed in the *LA Weekly*. Her assailant was not one of the men she'd dated. He was, according to Wellesley, a man named Peter Linder who was the roommate of one of the men she'd gone on a date with. Linder had an arrest for assault stemming from a bar fight he'd been involved in while in college.

Once I'd read through the basics, I took a break. Getting this far had taken most of the day. Something was bothering me. Around four, I went for a walk around the neighborhood. The Freedom Agenda occupied an old storefront in a not-so-great neighborhood between Long Beach's gay ghetto—a neighborhood called Alamitos Beach—and the downtown area. There was an art supply store on one side and a record store—a relic of a bygone era—on the other. Nearby was a Vons nicknamed Ghetto Vons, a Jack in the Box with bulletproof glass, and an empty shopping mall. Not exactly urban blight but well on its way.

On that afternoon, I wasn't paying much attention. Something nagged at me about the rapes and I couldn't quite put my finger on it. Their only connection was Detective Brenda Wellesley. She had solved three rapes in three months. Not just solved but made arrests that led to convictions.

And that's what was bothering me. I'd read an article in the *Los Angeles Times* that said very few rapes led to convictions. I probably should have known that from my time on the job in Chicago back in the seventies, but things like rape didn't matter in the same way then. Nobody bothered to count.

So how does it happen that one brand-new detective manages

to hit three in a row out of the park? That's what I needed to find out.

****

I would have gotten home sooner, but I stayed an extra half hour talking to Karen, Lydia's assistant/office manager, about Dr. Jack Kevorkian. He was on trial for assisting in the suicides of two different women. She thought he should go to prison; I thought he'd get off, as he had before. I didn't say whether I thought it was right or wrong. In all honestly, I wasn't sure.

"I don't think you should call murder a personal favor or a kindness," was her point.

Having killed a couple of people in self-defense, I thought it might not be so terrible to kill someone who wanted to be dead. I didn't say that though. Instead, I said, "I don't know. We kill animals when we know there's no hope. We think of that as being kind. Why can't we be kind to each other?"

"So you think doctors should just kill anyone who asks?"

I could see all the ways that might go wrong, so I said, "I guess it would be a tough thing to make work."

"A lot of people would knock off their parents given the chance."

"Yeah, that's true," I said.

And it was, but it also wasn't. It did seem like a good place to end things though, so I said good-bye. I promised Ronnie I'd bring home dinner, so I hurried out, jumped into my forest green Jeep Wrangler, and stopped at Star of Siam to pick up two pad thai, a green curry with shrimp, and a beef and noodle dish. The two of us didn't need four entrees, but we lived with two room-mates and I never knew who was going to be around for dinner. Plus, the leftovers were better than you'd think.

While I waited, I began thinking about Owen Lovejoy, Esquire. When had Richland told me he was gone? Six years ago? I had one friend from my days in Chicago who still sent me cards. Unmarked by agreement. I wondered if he knew. He might not. I couldn't remember if they'd ever even met.

Memory was a crazy thing. Sometimes it punched you in the gut like a heavyweight champ, other times it was as ethereal as smoke. Owen, his body, his voice, his betrayals, all of that was a punch in the gut. Who knew who and when they knew them, that was smoke.

Thinking about the old days made me wonder if I was being ridiculous. Maybe after eleven years I could relax and not be so careful about people knowing who I was.

But then I remembered that when I left Chicago I owed Deanna Hansen a hundred thousand dollars by my estimation—though I hadn't asked her for the money—and a quarter of a million by hers. A quarter of a million that would have grown substantially over a decade. I didn't remember her as the sort to forget a debt like that.

And then there was the small matter of the man I killed. That wouldn't matter to Deanna, but it might matter to the Chicago Police. Sure, it was self-defense, but I ran so I didn't expect to be believed. In fact, I ran because I didn't expect to be believed no matter what.

And it would matter to a nasty piece of work named Rita Lundquist. She'd already tried to kill me once. I didn't see why she wouldn't try again if she knew where I was. No, it didn't feel safe for me to let people know my true identity. Not at all.

Our house was on 2nd Street, a nearly century-old, two-story, five-bedroom Craftsman with a partial wrap-around porch. We'd had it painted sage green with cream and purple trim. The colors were architecturally correct. Ronnie was working on getting us a historical plaque, which he figured would up the value of the house by at least twenty thousand.

Walking through the front door, I found him, my lover, sitting in the living room with both of our roommates: Junior Clybourne and John Gallagher. They were each drinking a cosmopolitan. Ronnie had bought new over-sized martini glasses at the Crate & Barrel Outlet downtown and was desperate to use them. He jumped up off the loosely slipcovered white sofa and came over to me.

"Thank God, you're here. We're starving."

He stood on his toes and kissed me. Small, Eurasian and much younger than I was, there were times when I could barely take my eyes off him—and that night was one of them. He took the bags from me and scurried out to the kitchen. I followed him like a puppy.

As I reached our kitchen, I heard Junior say, "Hello, Dom! Nice to see you too."

"Hi, Junior," I called out but didn't turn around. I watched as Ronnie got the dishes out and set them next to the bag of take-out. I took the boxes out of the bag.

"This smells amazing," he said. "How was your day?"

"We're starting a new case. Three, actually. Rapists."

"Three rapists? Yuck."

"Well, not rapists actually. Sorry, I shouldn't say it that way. The DNA doesn't match. So they're not rapists."

"Of course. You don't actually defend real criminals. I like that about your job."

"How was your day?"

"Busy, busy, busy. I got an offer on my listing in California Heights. One-ninety-five." He began dumping the boxes into big bowls. The food was still steaming.

I knew the house he was talking about. It was a Spanish-style three-bedroom in desperate need of an update. The offer was good. Maybe the market was picking up.

"Good for you. Is that all that happened today?"

There was something unspoken hanging between us. His mother had walked out of his life more than a month before. I was sure she'd come back; he was sure she wouldn't. I'd asked if he'd heard from her a few too many times. Now I just asked leading questions.

"I got a call about joining the board at The Center."

"Don't you have enough to do?"

"I do, but it's such a good way to meet potential clients."

"You have clients."

"I could always use more." He blinked his eyes flirtatiously. "Notice the dollar signs in my eyes."

"There's nothing wrong with liking money," I said, because I knew he did. "It's just not worth killing yourself for."

"I'm young. Being busy isn't going to kill me."

"Or sacrificing your youth."

He called out, "Come and get it." In a moment, John and Junior were in the kitchen.

"This looks fabulous," Junior said. "Dinner is on me next time."

He always said that and somehow next time never rolled around. It was okay though. He had AIDS—or had had AIDS. He was on some kind of 'cocktail' of drugs which was supposed to make things better. And it did seem like that was the case, though with Junior it was hard to tell if he was really getting better. He was around my age, though he looked and acted ten years older. I never thought I'd get to a time where I wondered if someone had AIDS or was just getting old. There were so many things about my life I hadn't expected.

I didn't know John's status and didn't want to ask. Maybe he was HIV positive, too. He was in his mid-thirties, thin, blond and eternally in light blue scrubs. He was an ER nurse, probably worked sixty hours a week, and always seemed to be just returning from the hospital or about to leave.

"John, talk to me about rape kits," I said, the idea suddenly occurring to me.

"My God," Junior said. "Over dinner?"

"I don't mind," Ronnie said. "I've heard the term, but I don't really know what it means. It sounds interesting."

"Well, I do have—" John started.

"Can we at least get settled," Junior said. Heading into the dining room. "And I'm going to need a glass of wine."

Ronnie grabbed a bottle of the pinot grigio from Trader Joe's that we liked out of the fridge, then followed Junior into the dining room. John rolled his eyes at me.

When we were all settled, wine poured, napkins passed around, soy sauce packets ripped open, I looked at John hoping he'd—

"I heard the most appalling thing about Hillary Clinton," Junior began.

"No, you're not going to change the subject," I said. "John, you had some kind of rape training, right?"

"I was trained in Sexual Assault Examination. I don't do it often, most victims, most female victims prefer a woman. I mean, I let them know I'm gay right off the bat, but the state they're usually in, it doesn't matter much. I'm still the person called if the victim is male."

"Oh, well, *that* doesn't happen," Junior said. "You can't rape the willing."

That didn't sit well with John. He frowned, and said, "One in ten rape victims are male. And that's only what's reported. Everyone thinks the number is higher."

"Ha! April Fool," Junior nearly yelled.

John visibly winced. "Rape is violence, not sex."

Junior shook his head, unwilling to give up his point. "You need an erection, so it's sex."

"You don't need an erection at all."

"You don't need—" Junior did his best to look appalled. Then, discomfort filled his face as he realized what that meant. "Oh. Well, yes, I suppose there are always foreign objects."

Finally, he was sufficiently cowed.

"So when a victim comes into the ER, what happens first?" I asked, trying to get back on track.

"I try to reassure them that they're safe. And then I tell them what's going to happen. When I've done that, I'll ask them to stand on a large piece of paper that comes in the kit. While they're standing there, they take their clothes off. I'll bag their clothing, for evidence. Meanwhile, the paper collects anything that falls off them. Hair, sand, dirt, whatever."

"And they're standing naked in front of you? After they've been raped?"

"I know. It's hard. I work as quickly as I can. I have to label the bags that hold their clothing. Then I take a comb from the kit that's similar to the kind used for lice. Using a different piece of paper I comb the victim's pubic hairs, then their head. Some loose hairs might land on the paper on the floor, but that's fine. That's what it's there for. If there are bruises or abrasions, I take pictures with an old Polaroid One-Step. Those go into the kit. At this point I give them a paper smock to wear during the rest of the exam."

He looked at his dinner as though he might have a bite, but then changed his mind.

"In the kit, are four long swabs. I have to swab all the orifices. Mouth, vagina, anus. I need to do it even if the victim says there's no need. You can't trust everything they say. They might not be ready to talk about some of the things that happened to them. So they don't always acknowledge that they even happened. Later, when they're ready to talk about specific acts, you'll want to have swabbed everything. There's a nail pick to scrape under the victim's nails. Again, I ignore them if they say they didn't scratch their rapist. It's possible they might not remember, and you don't want to not have a sample if they do remember. The kit also contains vials for blood and urine. Unfortunately, they have to give a urine sample in front of a nurse, me. Otherwise, it technically breaks the chain of evidence."

He stopped and took a long breath, then went on,

"At this point I get the victim onto the exam table. I fold up the paper they've been standing on and put it into the bag provided. Then I do the internal exam, noting any injuries. This is usually the hardest part. Before they leave, I get them a prescription for antibiotics. Their blood will tell us if they've picked up any STDs. but we go ahead and treat first."

We had all stopped eating. It was a lot to take in. Finally, I asked, "And then they talk to the detective?"

He shakes his head.

"That usually happens before we collect the evidence."

"But that can take hours."

"Yes."

Somehow that seemed the worst part. Talking with detectives is an ordeal all on its own. Having to go through that before you've gotten out of the clothes you'd been raped in, while you're still covered in your assailant's semen... Well, I can see why so many victims choose to take a shower.

"Thank you. I have to interview three rape victims. It helps to have some idea what they went through."

"I don't know about anyone else, but I need another drink," Junior said. That seemed to break the tension. More wine was poured, dinners were eaten, and at eight o'clock we were in the living room watching *Melrose Place*.

I stayed pretty quiet, thinking about the three women I needed to interview. After what they'd been through—the rape, the statements, the exams—I could see how much they'd want someone to be caught. Otherwise, the whole thing, the whole ongoing trauma of it, wouldn't make any sense. It must have been so satisfying when their rapists were convicted. And now that was being taken away.

When the show was over, Ronnie turned the television off, saying, "Such a dreadful show."

"Why did we just watch it then?" I asked.

"It's a cultural phenomenon. We don't want to be left out."

"All I have to say is that Heather girl is no Bette Davis," Junior added. "She's not even a Joan Crawford."

"They're both dead, aren't they?" I asked. It did prevent their auditioning for the role.

"Of course, they're dead. Bette died in Paris. Chic right to the end. I met her, you know. Did I mention that?"

He had. Several times.

"She had the top floor of this apartment building, four stories, brick. I can see it like it was yesterday. I swear it was on Franklin and Sierra Bonita."

I was fairly certain it wasn't, but we'd had that conversation. Bored with this, John said, "My favorite thing about *Melrose Place* is the boys. They're all so sexy."

"I'd kill to live in a courtyard building like that," Junior said.

"There are a couple just like it on 3rd Street. I can check and see if they have anything coming up," Ronnie said. He wasn't all that fond of Junior.

"Oh, but I love it here with the two of you. You're so wonderful."

"Then I guess you wouldn't kill to live in a building like that. Would you?" I pointed out.

"You're so literal."

"Well, I suppose it's time for bed."

"It's nine o'clock," Junior started but then stopped. "Oh, I see. Well off you go. Have a lovely time."

"Good night, John," I said.

"Good night," he said, with a slight smirk.

Ronnie and I went upstairs. Outside our room, he tucked his fingers into the waistband of my 501s bringing me to a stop.

"What?"

"What if it was just us?" he asked. "Would you like that?"

"I'm not unhappy." And I wasn't. I genuinely liked John, and I found Junior to be as amusing as he was annoying. "Are you unhappy?"

"We could rent our room. Buy something smaller. Maybe a condo even. For just the two of us."

"It's up to you. You're the real estate baron."

"I just need, maybe, around ten thousand dollars. I should have it in six months, or a year."

"Okay, we'll talk about it then."

"You have something else on your mind?"

I gave him my filthiest leer, and said, "You know I do."

CHAPTER FOUR

April 3, 1996
Wednesday morning

Cammy Wainwright was now Camille Eggleston. She lived south of Ventura Boulevard on Davanna Terrace in Sherman Oaks. The address wasn't far from the 405, but I knew better than to take that route. I came up the 710 to the 5 and took that to the 134 going west. That merged with the 101 and I got off onto Ventura Boulevard almost immediately. Even though I didn't leave until ten, hoping rush hour would die down, it took well over an hour.

Mrs. Eggleston lived in a gray clapboard house that would have fit right into a tony suburb outside of Boston. Only the bright sunshine and the neighbor's palm trees gave it away. There were matching bay windows on the first floor, dormer windows on the second, a brick walkway to the front door. The lawn was brilliant green and there were well manicured boxwoods forming a border around it. Though I didn't see any evidence of it, I assumed there was an expensive sprinkler system buried beneath the lawn to keep it from frying in the scorching heat of the Valley. Even in April it was seventy degrees, what most of the country called summer.

I knocked on the front door, a tasteful charcoal gray, and

waited. After a moment I reconsidered my decision and rang the doorbell. She knew I was coming; I'd spoken to her on the phone. She'd asked to do the whole thing on the phone, but I'd pressed her until she'd finally agreed to my visit. I was beginning to wonder if she'd changed her mind when the door opened.

She was around thirty-six-years-old, though she already had the ultra-thin, dried-out look that well-preserved, upper-middle-class women often take on. She probably weighed less than she had in college, was personally trained, professionally manicured and pedicured, waxed, trimmed, highlighted and styled on a monthly basis. She wore just enough make-up to look like she didn't wear any at all.

That day, she wore a crisp lemon-yellow shirt with the collar turned up and a pair of mint-green capris with a pair of white strappy sandals.

When I introduced myself, she said, "I'm afraid I don't have much time. My daughter gets out of preschool at 2:30, but it's in Northridge and I need to make a couple of stops first. I absolutely must leave by 11:45. I'm sure you understand."

I did understand. She didn't want to talk to me.

"I'll do my best to make this quick."

More than an hour up and at least an hour back for a half an hour conversation? Yeah, I was thrilled.

She led me out to a patio next to a built-in pool. There was a tray with iced tea sitting on a wrought iron table. She poured me a glass and I sat down. At least I wouldn't get dehydrated.

Slipping the file I'd brought onto the table, I said, "As I told you yesterday on the telephone, we represent Peter Linder. Evidence has come to light that proves his innocence. I'd like to ask you some questions about the investigation and trial."

"Yes, I remember what you said."

"Can you tell me about Brenda Wellesley?" I asked.

If this had been a deposition, an attorney would advise her to answer yes or no. I do my best to make that difficult.

After a long moment that included a sip of the ice-cold tea, she said, "It's been seven years since it happened, and I can't tell you how many times I've thought 'Thank God for Brenda.' Until you've been raped you don't realize how often the subject comes up, on television, in the news, in conversation even. Do you remember the Central Park Jogger case in New York? That happened almost two years before my rape. There was a little press attention because of the similarities. I was jogging. There was a park. Normally a rape like mine doesn't even make the news. Luckily my rapist was caught quickly so it died down."

She stopped for a moment. I waited. She hadn't really told me much about Wellesley. I hoped she might if I just kept silent.

"I think the fact that Brenda's a woman helped. She was kind, patient, helpful. She's *always* been helpful. She came herself to tell me that the case might be reopened. That my rapist might go free."

"When he goes free, it will be because he's not your rapist."

She tilted her head and looked at me curiously. Obviously, that was not how Wellesley had explained things.

I continued, "DNA testing has already shown he's not the man who raped you."

"But we all know how easily that can be faked. I mean, look at the O.J. trial."

"Well, I wouldn't say it was conclusive that evidence in that case was faked," I said—everyone in L.A. had an opinion about that case. "And, even if you believe that, in the case of O.J, it would have been the police faking the evidence. Not the accused."

She looked confused for a moment, then seemed to reject what I'd said, "Either way it's a relatively new science. It's not reliable."

From the file, I pulled out a thick packet. "My office put together some information on DNA and DNA testing for you. It's actually *very* reliable science. There's only a one in a million chance the test is wrong."

Taking the packet from me, she set it on the table without looking at it. She smiled, a little smugly, and said, "There's a small chance the test is wrong, provided there's no mix-up at the lab."

"Is that what Brenda told you? That there was a mix-up at the lab?"

"She said it was possible. Actually, she said it was likely." Her look was defiant. She'd bought whatever Wellesley said, hook, line and sinker.

"Did you ask Detective Wellesley how often she's using DNA evidence to convict in her current cases?"

"No. I'd have no reason to ask that."

That seemed to pierce the veil, though. I had the strong feeling much of what Wellesley had said to Camille was lifted from defense experts who tried to dismiss DNA evidence. Experts who were rarely believed.

"Did she tell you we're handling three of her cases? Three cases where she got the wrong guy."

If the first question pierced the veil, this one ripped it to shreds. Camille took a moment to rearrange her face.

"No. She didn't say anything about that."

"I'd like to know more about the identification process."

"Don't you already have that? Brenda said you'd been given everything they have."

"I know what's in the file, yes. You were shown a photographic lineup and you picked out Peter Linder."

"I did."

I slipped a hand into the file a second time and brought out a Xerox of the photo lineup used. It was in black-and-white. It would have been better if the LAPD had popped the extra few bucks and sent us a color copy. I held the sheet of paper up in front of her.

"Is this the lineup?"

"It appears to be," she barely looked at it.

"And you identified which photo?"

There were six photos in two rows of three. Reluctantly, she looked at the sheet of paper. Very quickly, she chose the middle photo in the bottom line, as she had previously. She looked away, out over her pool.

"He fit your description perfectly."

Camille shrugged. She got up, walked over to a lounge chair with a beach towel spread across it. She folded the towel and left it at the foot of the chair. She returned to where I was sitting.

"Do you notice anything about the others?"

"What others?"

"The men you didn't choose."

"Well... they don't look like my rapist," she said. I could see she was trying hard not to get angry.

"Exactly. They don't fit your description. They don't even come close."

And they didn't. Three looked to be what you'd called dishwater blonds, nearly brunette. And two were actually brunette. In the copy five of them seemed like clumps of toner, while Peter Linder almost glowed.

"Did you remember meeting Peter Linder?"

"No. I don't think I ever did, actually."

"You were answering personal ads during this period?"

"No. I placed an ad. *LA Weekly*. I paid for a mailbox. Men would send me letters. I got dozens. I think I answered less than ten."

She was back to being defiant, this time for herself. I hadn't read the trial transcript yet, but I imagine the defense tried to make something of her using the personals. A rape trial could be an awful process for the victim. If she appeared to like sex at all it made it seem like she'd asked for what happened to her.

"I'm not here to judge you."

"Why are you here?"

"Peter Linder didn't rape you. You do want to see him released, don't you?"

"Yes, of course. *If* that's true."

"Do you remember anything about Tony Albom?"

"Yes, he's one of the men who answered my ad. His letter was funny and clever. He looked kind in the photo he sent with the letter."

"He was Peter Linder's roommate."

"Yes. But I didn't know that then. When we had our date we met at the restaurant, so I wouldn't have met his roommate."

"How was it? The date?"

"Um, we had dinner at an Italian place on Vermont. He wasn't quite as charming as he had been in his letter. In fact, I wasn't entirely sure he'd written the letter himself. He tried to get me to go home with him, but I had a rule about first dates. The fact that he tried it... well, that alone took him off my list."

"Did Detective Wellesley aid you in your identification in any way?" Beside the fact that only one of the men fit the description she'd given.

"She was supportive. But I don't think she influenced my identification. That's what you're asking, isn't it?"

"It is, yes."

"Then the answer is a definite no. She didn't influence me, or coach me, or tip me off or in any way suggest which of the men I should identify."

"Except only one of the men fit your description."

"I don't think you'd act this way if we were talking about a male detective."

I wanted to snap back at her, to make it clear how wrong I thought she was. But then I remembered everything she'd been through. I took a long draft of my iced tea and then stood up. "I'll let you get on with your day."

As she walked me to the front door, I said, "It's nice to see you've done well for yourself." Immediately, I regretted it. Was I minimizing her rape? Was I insulting other rape victims who hadn't done so well for themselves?

She took it at face value though, saying, "Thank you. I've had a lot of therapy, and my husband is wonderful. About a year after I was attacked, my therapist thought I should date again, so I thought if I'm getting back on the horse I should really get back on. My husband had sent a letter in response to my ad. I hadn't answered it, but I'd kept it. Despite its being a year later he wanted to meet me. I spent half of the date sobbing in the restroom. Dennis, my husband, was exceptionally kind. I laughed out loud when he asked me for a second date, I thought it had gone terribly. He told me he couldn't imagine anything better than making me laugh."

Thanking her for her time, I stepped through the front door she was holding open. I was only a few feet away when she said, "Mr. Reilly. I'm sorry if I got angry about Brenda. It's just that she made me feel like I mattered. And that's not how most women feel after a rape."

****

Since I was in the Valley, I decided to drive over to Toluca Lake and drop in on Richland Keswick. His apartment was on smoggy Vineland Avenue right where the 101 and the 134 crossed. The building was a creamy white box. One of those places that were going up everywhere, the ones that seemed to be made of cardboard and paste. They looked like they'd come apart in a heavy rain.

I rang the bell for 204, which said Winchell, and waited. After a bit, a man's voice said, "Yeah?" over the intercom.

"Richland Keswick?"

"Who is this?"

"Nick Nowak."

"Oh."

The security door buzzed, a sound that reminded me of an electrocution, and I grabbed it. I walked through a tiny lobby to the elevator. Getting in, I pressed the button for the second floor. The inside of the building seemed as cheap and flimsy as the outside. It wasn't the kind of place I'd want to be in an earthquake, although the building materials might be light enough that you could just shake them off after the place fell down.

When I got off at the second floor, I turned and saw that 204 was at the far end of the hallway. I walked down, and before I could knock the door opened and there stood Richland Keswick. He was older, of course, his hair had started to turn gray, and a few extra pounds clung to his middle.

"Long time no see," he said.

I punched him square in the nose.

CHAPTER FIVE

April 3, 1996
Late Wednesday morning

Richland's living room looked like something out of one of those newspaper flyers that arrives in the mail. The ones that sell a complete room full of cheesy furniture for $999. There were three matching black leather pieces: a sofa, a loveseat and an occasional chair. The coffee and end tables were glass and brass. There was an Erté print on the wall. It was the home of a single, straight man. One who thought he had taste.

He was sitting on the sofa with a wad of paper towels shoved up against his nose and a cold can of beer tucked up against the back of his neck. He didn't seem too happy.

"You didn't have to do that."

"I didn't do it. I'm dead, remember?"

"You're mad because I told Lydia Gonzalez who you are."

"That's a possibility."

"She promised she wouldn't tell you she knew."

"She broke that promise."

"Yeah, I figured that out the moment your fist found my face."

"You shouldn't have told Lydia where I was."

"You're right, I shouldn't have. But... I mean, she's Lydia. I've never been able to say no to her."

"You did a lot more than that... tell me how it came up."

"She told me she and Duncan were moving to Long Beach and I told her you were there. I might have had a drink or two. I might have been showing off."

"You don't like Duncan?"

"I don't like any man she's with who's not me. I mean, have you ever really looked at her? She's so—I guess you wouldn't appreciate her that way."

Great. My whole life was on the line because this dickwad wanted to impress a girl.

"So after the book came out, nothing happened?"

"There was a little interest in a movie, but that died down."

"That's not what I mean. You've moved and there's someone else's name on the doorbell."

"Well, yeah, there were some threats. Nothing that I'd call credible."

"Have you gotten threats here?"

"No. At my old place."

"What kind of threats?"

"Phone calls, mostly."

"What did they say?"

"That I needed to mind my own business. Stuff like that. I heard from a source in Chicago that Deanna Hansen wasn't happy about the book. But what can she do about it? She claims she's gone legit and that's what I put in the book. If I end up dead no one will believe she's left the Outfit."

"I don't think anyone believes that in the first place. She may not have as much to lose as you think."

The color went out of his face.

"And..."

"And what?"

"The FBI may be investigating her."

It was not a fun thing to hear, but I tried staying calm so I could think. "That can't have anything to do with what you wrote. The statute of limitations is five years. Nothing in the book can be prosecuted."

"Except, they're looking at conspiracy, conspiracy to protect Jimmy's assets from seizure. They're arguing that it's an ongoing conspiracy. They've been to court about it several times."

"Are you saying Operation Tea & Crumpets is still alive?"

"Basically, yes."

That was a lot to take in. If they figured out I was alive, they'd want me as a witness. That meant there might be someone else after me. Someone I hadn't even thought of.

"A couple of phone threats. Is that all?"

"I don't know. Weird things were happening. Some of my friends said a woman was asking about me. My editor got mugged in New York. My mail was stolen a couple of times, but I don't think that has anything to do with the book."

I wasn't as sure.

"Tell me about the woman."

He shrugged. "I didn't talk to her, so I don't know anything about her."

"Call your friends and find out."

"Now?"

"Soon. Call me and tell what you find out."

"And if I don't want to do that?"

"I'll punch you in the nose again."

He pulled the paper towels away from his nose to see if it had stopped bleeding. They went right back on.

"Something else happened."

"Yeah, what?"

"I got a call from a police detective in Chicago. He wanted to know when I talked to you and why I thought you were dead."

"What was his name?"

"White, I think."

"Monroe White?"

"I think that was it."

"What did you tell him?"

"Nothing. I gave him my lawyer's number. Through my

attorney we told him that I had researched the book in New York and that I might have heard the rumor there about your death."

"How'd that go over?"

"Not well. In the book I said you were dead. Period. Definitive statement. To say something like that based on a rumor would have been very sloppy journalism."

"I hope you told him you're a shitty journalist."

"Through my attorney, I said I can't reveal my sources."

"When was this?"

"After the book came out."

That was a long time ago. Well, nearly two years. It certainly seemed like they weren't following the lead.

"I shouldn't have talked to you in the first place."

"Is that the big thing you came here to tell me?"

"No, I came here to call you an asshole."

"And you decided at the last minute to let your fist do the talking?"

"Something like that."

"You're fine. It's just Lydia. I haven't told anyone else."

"Somehow that's not reassuring. If you can't keep your mouth shut when a good-looking woman is in the room, what's going to happen if someone shows up and pushes you around a bit? You're going to squeal like a stuck pig. And that's not going to be good for me."

Instead of attempting to deny that, he weakly said, "Fuck you."

****

I got back to Long Beach at almost three. I'd taken a detour to Studio City for a quesadilla from Poquito Mas. I mean, why not? I'd just had a conversation that kind of scared the crap out of me. Good Mexican food seemed as good a remedy as any.

I sat in my Jeep eating the quesadilla trying to work things out. The book had come out in 1994. Two years and nothing had really happened. Well, nothing I knew about until today. Deanna Hansen wasn't happy about the book, but that didn't mean she knew anything about me. I didn't have any reason to think she didn't believe I was dead. Or that she'd do much about it if she didn't believe it. I wasn't thrilled the FBI was still looking at her. That could prove to be a big problem. A very big problem.

Monroe White worried me. I knew him, of course. He worked the 18th district in Chicago, which happened to be where I'd killed a guy named Possum. Or at least I was pretty sure I'd killed him. It was dark and I was in a hurry to get out of there.

Possum's real name was Mike Mazur. I'd done a couple of newspaper searches trying to find out if he was dead. I hadn't found much. Which didn't mean anything. People died every day in Chicago. Not everyone made the papers. Not everyone got identified. However, the fact that White was calling around looking for me suggested Possum might be dead. And they might have connected him to me.

White would be close to retirement. I doubted he'd stop looking for me until he retired. Like most cops, he'd want proof I was dead, concrete proof, like an actual death certificate. I was tempted to buy one and send it to him in the mail.

When I walked into The Freedom Agenda office, Karen was sitting behind her desk reading a copy of *George* with a tall Black man dressed in a white wig and parts of a revolutionary war uniform.

"I didn't know you were a fan of politics," I said.

"I'm not. I'm fan of Charles Barkley."

"Baseball?"

"Basketball."

"Clippers?" I guessed. I think that was the L.A. team.

She rolled her eyes at me. "Suns. Phoenix."

I decided to quit while I was behind, and asked, "Is Lydia in?"

"She's on a call, but she'll be done in a—oh, there you go. She's off." I don't know how she did that. I'm sure it had something to do with the lights on her phone and what she could hear through the paper-thin wall, but still. It always seemed like magic.

I walked around the corner and stood in Lydia's door. She looked up at me, flipping her hair out of her face as she did. It was the kind of move that would have driven Richland Keswick crazy.

"I saw Camille Eggleston. She has a very high opinion of Detective Wellesley. She's adamant that Wellesley didn't try to influence the identification. Of course, there's still a problem with the lineup. The only person who fit the description is the person Camille picked."

Lydia nodded, taking it in. Then she called out, "Karen?" A moment later Karen was standing next to me.

"Karen, would you make Dom a copy of your file on Detective Wellesley?"

"You wanted to return calls this afternoon."

"After that," Lydia said.

"Tomorrow is fine," I said.

Karen went back to her desk.

Then to me, Lydia said, "Could you write up your notes on Camille Eggleston? We'll go over it again if we need to depose her."

"Sure. So, this is unusual, isn't it? Grouping three cases like this?"

"Yes. I'm not sure I'll be able to get a judge to go for it. If I can get the DA to relent and join our petition for release, a judge can approve them together or separately, it really makes no difference."

"So the grouping is really a pretrial thing."

"Yes. It's better on our end and it's better for LAPD in the long run."

"I can't imagine it's good for Brenda Wellesley."

"Well, no, but then it wouldn't be no matter how we did this."

"Do you think there are more bad cases that she worked?"

"Yes. They'll turn up eventually."

"How'd you find these three?"

"After we won Jimmy Claxton's case there was a lot of publicity. We got an avalanche of mail from prisoners. Karen noticed that these three cases were all out of Rampart, all around the same time, all one detective. I was intrigued, but I put them aside while we did the Danny Osbourne case."

I nodded. "Um, change of subject. Yesterday, I made arrangements to see Larry Wilkes at Corcoran."

Actually, I'd had to ask Karen enough questions that she eventually just did it for me. "I'm planning to go up on Monday, if that's okay."

"All right. Keep track of your mileage and get a receipt for lunch. But that's it. You need to come up with a good reason to move forward on his case. Otherwise, no expenses."

"Okay," I said, not sure I'd be able to do that.

Before I was able to walk away, she said, "And Dom, you shouldn't have punched Richie in the nose. He could have you arrested for that."

"Point taken."

Tail between my legs, I walked over to the antiquated coffee machine and got myself a cup of bad coffee. As I walked over to the makeshift desk I'd put together for myself, I heard Karen call out, "Edwin is on the line." She'd begun going through Lydia's call sheet.

I sat down in the open area behind the two offices. There were a couple of banquet tables filled with files, each file started when a letter arrived. I was meant to go through them on my down time. That's how I'd found Larry Wilkes. It was also where I kept Larry's file. Other than his letter and a couple of newspaper articles there was nothing much in it yet.

Dear Sir, the letter started. *My name is Larry Wilkes. I am serving a sentence of twenty-five years to life for the murder of Pete Michaels. Maybe you hear this a lot, but I'm innocent. I am. I did not kill Pete Michaels. I could NOT have killed him; I loved him. I still love him even though it's been almost twenty years since he died.*

Pete was killed on September 28, 1976. I'd been living in Santa Barbara at the university. I'd enrolled as a freshman but did not attend many of my classes. I missed Pete. I'd tried calling him. There was a payphone in my dorm. I didn't have my own phone. They were so expensive. He never seemed to be at home. I don't think his family gave him my messages. Kids were supposed to answer the payphone when it rang but that didn't mean they'd give you the message. I hadn't talked to Pete in so long. I was getting frantic.

So I went home. Took a bus from Santa Barbara to Downey. When I got to my parents' house I kept calling Pete, but he didn't call me back. Something was wrong. I just knew it. Finally, I took my mother's car and went to Pete's house. When I got there, the door was open. I called out but no one answered. I stepped into the living room and saw Pete on the floor. He'd been shot. I hurried over to him and took him into my arms. There was blood everywhere, but he was already cold. I couldn't stop crying.

Pete's parents came home and found me with him. The police came. They pulled me from him. I don't remember a lot of what happened. I didn't really care. They arrested me, asked me a lot of questions. I didn't say much. They told me they'd found the gun I used.

I couldn't afford an attorney, so they got me one. He wanted me to plead guilty. But I couldn't. I couldn't stand up and say I'd killed Pete when I hadn't. I loved him. I would never hurt him.

At the trial they made a big deal out of the fact that I'd wiped off the gun so there were no fingerprints. Except, I hadn't done that. I told my attorney it didn't make sense. If I'd wiped off the gun, I'd have run away. And I didn't, I couldn't, I couldn't leave Pete alone like that. Whoever shot him did.

Anyway, for a long time it didn't matter that I was in prison. I was so sad about what happened. I should never have gone away to school. I should have stayed. I think if I'd stayed nothing would have happened to Pete. So, in a way, I thought it was my fault he died.

But now, well, you see I've fallen in love again. His name is Brysen. He was another prisoner here. He didn't do very much. Just took credit cards that weren't his. Anyway, he got out a while ago and it would be nice if we could be together again. So if you think you can help me...

Okay, so yeah, I'm a romantic sucker.

CHAPTER SIX

April 4, 1996
Thursday morning

The next morning, I skipped going into the office and drove out to Hemet. It took only a tiny bit longer to get there than it had getting to the Valley, though it was twice as far. Driving against traffic has its advantages, I'll give you that.

Selma Martinez lived in a very ancient Airstream. It was at least a big one, but the silver travel trailer was dusty and scorched by the sun. It was surrounded by potted plants, yucca and other succulents. Sitting among them was the Virgin Mary caught in prayer. She was probably praying to move to a better neighborhood.

Sitting next to the Airstream was a fifteen-year-old Dodge Aries. Even if Selma wanted to travel with her Airstream, she didn't own a vehicle that could pull it. I knocked on her door. While I waited, I listened to the hum of the air conditioner attached to the top of the trailer. It was eighty-two degrees at 11 a.m. and the little machine was already straining.

The door opened and Selma smiled at me. She was close to thirty with long black hair she'd pinned up into a bun. She wore a pink and white waitress uniform with a nametag pinned up high over her left breast. It said Selma underneath the logo for Polly's Pies.

"Hi. I'm Dom Reilly. I called you the other day."

"I remember. Come in," she said, stepping out of the way. I climbed inside. Even though there were four or five inches between the top of my head and the ceiling I still felt like slouching.

"One of the other waitresses called in sick, so I have to get to work by noon."

I was beginning to sense a theme. No one wanted to talk to me and they'd use any excuse to get out of it.

"I'll try not to take up much of your time. Do you mind if I sit down?"

She shook her head, and the two of us sat at the dinette which folded down into a bed. I set the file I was carrying on the table, then glanced around. The trailer was neat, orderly and very clean. There wasn't much counterspace in the kitchenette and what there was had been given over to a small collection of figurines depicting Catholic saints. I couldn't tell you which ones they were. Partly because there are thousands of saints and partly because I'm a bad Catholic.

She didn't offer me tea or coffee or even a glass of water. I could have used a glass of water.

"I believe the LAPD has contacted you and explained that the man convicted of your rape, Alan Dinkler, could not possibly have raped you. We represent Mr. Dinkler. We've done testing and his DNA does not match the sample. Do you understand all that?"

As I took out the information we'd put together about DNA and slid it over to her, she said, "I've forgiven him."

"I appreciate that, but Mr. Dinkler didn't rape you. If you read through the materials—"

"I forgave him years ago. I wrote to the parole board and told them that. I don't understand why he's still in prison."

I was about to explain that parole boards don't parole people who maintain their innocence. Remorse is the get of jail free card even if you did nothing. Selma stood up and took one of the saints off the counter. She set it in front of me. It was a young girl wearing a pink shawl and holding flowers tight to her chest.

"St. Maria Goretti, the patron saint of rape victims. Maria was eleven when the neighbor boy wanted to have sex with her. She said, 'No, it's a sin.' He tried to force her, and she fought. She would rather die than sin. She tried to get away from him, but he stabbed her with a knife, over and over again. They tried to save her, but they couldn't. As she lay dying, she forgave her rapist. She wanted to see him in heaven with her. I forgive my rapist."

"We don't know who raped you."

Confusion overtook her face. *How do you forgive someone if you don't know who they are?* I could see her struggling with that.

"Is that all you came to say?"

"No. I need to ask you about Detective Wellesley."

"Brenda? What about her?"

"Did she influence your identification of Alan Dinkler in any way?"

In a very small voice, she said, "She was so certain."

"He was at home with his mother."

"Mothers lie for their sons."

"Is that what Brenda told you?"

She nodded. "She's still sure it was him. She says the science is wrong. Science is often wrong."

I was tempted to suggest she read the materials for a second time. Instead, I said, "Tell me about the identification. How was it done? Were you brought into a room with the men or were you able to—"

"She had photographs, I mean copies. Copies of photographs. There were six of them."

That was interesting. The photographs, copies or otherwise, were not in the file. If they were not provided to the defense that would be a big problem.

"Tell me about the photographs. Were they mug shots?"

"What is that?" Her voice was small again, she seemed frightened of making a mistake.

"You know, when you're arrested, they take a photograph. Were their lines behind them?"

"I don't think so," she said, tears welling in her eyes. "No, they were normal pictures."

I knew I should ask more questions about the photos. Were they all African American? How many times did it look like the sheet had been copied? Did Wellesley tip her off in any way as to which photo she wanted her to choose? I couldn't ask though. How could I?

I sat there quietly for a bit. It was all so clear to me. Selma had been a hopeful, optimistic young college girl hoping for a better life. But that had been derailed and now she was a waitress in a pie shop relying on a child-saint to protect her.

Pressing her, making her understand clearly that she'd helped put an innocent man in prison. It didn't feel right adding that to her burden. I had what I needed; she'd admitted that Detective Brenda Wellesley had influenced her identification of Alan Dinkler. And she'd inadvertently tipped me off that Wellesley, or someone, had withheld evidence.

Selma seemed not to want to lie, which fit her general character. Lydia would easily be able to get her to tell the truth. Lydia might feel it necessary to make her understand she'd put an innocent man in prison, either in the deposition or at trial, if it came to that. That was her job. To do what it took for her client.

It wasn't mine, though. I'd gotten the information Lydia would need, so I thanked Selma for her time and left.

****

The first case I'd worked for Lydia, the victim had been raped and murdered more than a decade before. So I didn't have to interview her. I felt bad for her, but she seemed very far away. And her pain was long gone. She was almost abstract, a puzzle to work out, nothing like a real, living person. Talking with these victims, opening wounds, turning over what justice they'd found, was more difficult than I'd expected. I was happy there was only one more victim to interview.

I found an In-and-Out Burger in the Moreno Valley and stopped for lunch. I had a double-double with fries and a chocolate shake. I sat in my Jeep and ate my lunch looking out at some mountains in the distance. I was all turned around so I couldn't tell you which mountain range it was.

After I finished the burger, I picked up Larry Wilkes's file and poked through it while I finished my French fries and the shake. He wasn't a client yet, so we hadn't much. I'd imposed on Karen to find me what she could on Lexus Nexus. That gave me a few short newspaper articles to read.

A couple were from small-time local newspapers, the kind that burn out after a year or two. Larry Wilkes had been an honor student. Pete Michaels had been on a high school tennis team that placed second in the state. There was an initial account of the murder from the Downey Daily News:

On Saturday, police were called to a home at 7815 Via Amorita where Larry Wilkes (18) was found next to the dead body of Pete Michaels (19), the murder weapon, a Colt handgun, less than six feet away. Despite having made no attempt to hide his crime, Wilkes became uncooperative and refused to speak with the police. He was taken into custody and is now being held at the Los Angeles County Jail.

Nothing in the article conflicted with what Larry had said in his letter. At first, I didn't think the story told me much at all. But then I wondered, maybe it did. The police thought Larry did it right from the start. They'd conveyed that to the reporter. It was bad journalism to say, 'no attempt to hide his crime' but probably not something the reporter made up on his own. Important because it means the police did little in the way of looking for another suspect. There could easily be evidence they rejected because it didn't fit with the solution they'd already decided upon.

The article included a final sentence: "No motive has been given for the murder, though a source mentions that the victim had recently become engaged."

That was interesting. Larry hadn't mentioned it in his letter. Was I wrong to pursue this? The letter said his boyfriend hadn't been returning his calls. If he'd gotten engaged that would explain why. It was also a motive. For Larry.

There were only three articles concerning the trial, none of which came from the bigger papers. It turned out to be a very uninteresting case. At least to the press. There were articles stating that a jury had been chosen, that the trial had begun, and that Larry had been convicted of first-degree murder and was to be imprisoned for twenty-five years to life.

First-degree meant that the prosecution had proven premeditation. That must have to do with the gun. But how did they link the gun to Larry? Obviously, the killer—if he wasn't Larry—could have brought gun, killed Pete, wiped it off and left. But why hadn't it been traced back to them? And why leave it?

The fries where gone and I'd slurped down the last of the shake. I started the Jeep, stopped at a garbage can to get rid of the wrappings, and got back on the highway.

I reached Elysian Heights around two-thirty. Joanne Yardley lived on Avon Court, a tiny slip of a street that wound up a hill. On the other side of the hill was Dodger Stadium.

Her house was a tiny Craftsman built into a steep rise. At the curb, there was a five-and-a-half-foot tall retaining wall running across the front of the property. Beyond that a sloping front yard covered in tiny succulent plants that were putting out pink blooms.

A heavy, iron gate crossed the driveway. An intercom with a keypad was attached to one side. Beyond the gate, sitting in the driveway was a very dusty bronze Camry from the eighties. The tires looked soft, and if you looked closely at the windows you could see streaks made by the last rain we had. And maybe the one before that.

I went ahead and pressed the button on the intercom. As soon as I did, I could hear at least two dogs begin barking in the house. Nothing happened. I found myself staring at glass shards that had been embedded in the top of the retaining wall. If you tried to climb passed the gate, you'd end up sliced and diced. You needed to be about six foot tall to see that the glass was even there.

The barking continued.

And then, suddenly, the gate began to creep to one side. When there was enough room, I slipped through. As I walked up the driveway, I noted that there were bars on the windows. Through the heavy metal screen door, I could see a small woman looking out at me. At her feet, a couple of small dogs bounced up and down, jockeying for position.

"Hello," I said.

"Are you Dom?"

"I am, yes."

I climbed onto the front porch as she held the heavy metal door open. It turned out to be three dogs, chihuahuas, or mixture of chihuahua and something else. Two were black-and-brown, the third was tan. The tan one looked old and grizzled and I suspected he might have been with Joanne when she was raped. The way he was barking, he seemed determined it wouldn't happen again.

I maneuvered into the house, trying very hard not to step on a dog. Joanne herself was a small, round woman with short spikey hair she'd dyed flat black. She wore a black cotton sweater and black jeans. Closing and locking the door, she offered me a seat on a sage green sofa with beige piping and went to make tea.

Maybe *went* is too strong a word. She stepped over to the kitchen area, which was basically part of the living room. The rooms had originally been tiny. At some point, the kitchen and living room had been combined into one small room with barely enough space for the sofa, a table and the kitchen cupboards. To my left was another small room, which clearly served as an office. Somewhere toward the back of the house I guessed there was a bedroom and bathroom.

I sat on the sofa. The tan dog jumped up next to me and curled his lip to keep me in my place. None of the dogs had stopped barking since I walked in.

"They'll calm down in a minute," Joanne said. I can't say I

believed her. She was getting out a couple of mugs, when she said, "You're here about Stu Whatley, aren't you?"

"I am. You've probably heard that DNA testing has made it impossible for him to have raped you?"

"Yes, Brenda was here. She explained it all."

"She may have made it sound less conclusive. I have some information—"

"Don't worry. I looked up DNA on the world wide web. I found a lot of information. I also called a friend who's a scientist."

I'd started to take the information out of her file but slipped it back in. Then I asked a question I probably should have asked the other victims. "How do you feel about Stu Whatley getting out of prison?"

"It appears he's innocent so he should be released as quickly as possible."

"Do you feel like Detective Wellesley put pressure on you to identify Stu Whatley as your rapist?"

She was very quiet. I hadn't noticed, but the dogs had quieted down. The tea pot began to whistle.

"I hope you don't take milk," she said, pouring hot water into the cups. "I ran out yesterday and my groceries aren't delivered until tomorrow."

"A little bit of sugar is fine."

She nodded. A few moments later, she shooed the tan dog away, her name was Muffy—I'd guessed male but was wrong—and sat down on the sofa next to me. I took the cup of tea from Joanne and held it on my lap. I was about to try asking my question again, when she said, "I didn't see him, you know. My rapist."

"But you identified him by voice."

"That wasn't used at trial. I—uh... about a week after the rape, I was brought to a room with six tall men. No two-way glass, no separation. The men were asked to say, 'you like it, bitch, don't you,' which is what my rapist kept saying. It was awful. By the time we reached the fourth guy I was coming apart. Brenda told them to stop, and she said to me that... we didn't have to continue if I'd heard my rapist's voice. I could tell she wanted me to pick number four, so I did. I regretted it, and before the trial I told Brenda that. But it didn't matter. By then she had Candy Van Dyke's statement."

"Who is that?" I asked, even though I remembered the name from the file.

"My neighbor, across the street. She got a good look at him. Or at least she said she did. I suppose the DNA test proves she was wrong, too."

"Do you think she'll mind my stopping by after this?" I asked, though I would no matter what she said.

"She doesn't live there anymore. She moved away shortly after the trial, about three months. I don't know where she went. We weren't friendly."

"Why didn't you move?" I asked, an obvious question.

"I was going to. I had the house on the market for two months in 1990. I even had an offer. It's just, it felt like surrendering. He took so much from me. I didn't want him to take my home. And there were practical reasons. It's an inexpensive house and that has allowed me to make significant security upgrades."

I nodded. It made sense. Logical sense. I still had trouble with the emotional sense.

"Do you have any idea who your attacker might really be?"

She shook her head. "When I was researching DNA, I found an article about the databases being developed. So, maybe someday."

"You did a lot of research."

"I design websites."

"For AOL?"

My understanding of computers was woefully limited. I did notice that Ronnie and I got a blue plastic floppy disc with free hours from AOL every week or so. I think he might even have signed up. If he tried to show me, I'd blocked it from my memory. I knew there was some real estate database that he worked with and that he had a laptop he hooked up to the phone line. I knew that mainly because I couldn't make calls when he did it.

Joanne was chuckling. "AOL is a browser and a rather primitive one. I use Navigator to access the web. AOL is proprietary. People will move away from it soon enough."

Honestly, I didn't know enough to have an opinion.

"Well, I should go." I'd barely sipped my tea.

"I appreciate what you're doing. I do want to say, though, I don't think Brenda did anything on purpose. I think she really believed she had the right guy."

"I'm sure she did."

CHAPTER SEVEN

April 5-7, 1996
The weekend

Friday through Sunday I worked at The Hawk on Broadway. In the gay rags it was listed as a leather & Levi bar, but it wasn't that rigid. For about four hours on Friday and Saturday nights it was what you'd called an S&M bar —Stand & Model. Guys would stand around looking at each other trying not to look interested in whether or not they were going to pick each other up. The rest of the time—and often overlapping—it was just a neighborhood gay bar. I started work at six and finished around three in the morning.

Normally I try to sleep in on Fridays, since I'd be up so late. It almost never worked. That morning I woke up at nine. Ronnie was rushing around grabbing his keys, his wallet, his briefcase, his cellular phone, his sunglasses and his lip balm. I said good morning but was barely acknowledged. I didn't mind. The night before he'd told me he was going on an agents' open house tour. He'd be spending the morning driving around Long Beach stopping at open houses for agents only. He always wanted to know what was on the market the moment it became available.

As soon as he left, I got up and began pulling myself together. I was pretty sure John had worked all night, which meant he'd be sleeping most of the day. That basically left me alone in the house with Junior. I decided it would be a good idea to take myself out for breakfast.

When I got downstairs, I found Junior in the living room doing a workout routine with Jane Fonda. Their outfits were disturbingly similar. Before I could get out of the house, he paused the tape and asked, "You and Ronnie seem just frantic. Is there anything I can do? Anything at all."

Now I felt bad about my mental critique of his workout wear. Well, a little bad. I tried not to look at it. I said, "We could always use some toilet paper."

"Wonderful, I'll pick some up. Paper towels?"

"Knock yourself out," I said, slipping out the front door. I drove around the corner to the Park Pantry and had Cindy bring me biscuits and gravy with scrambled eggs and a double side of bacon.

I'd brought *Midnight in the Garden of Good and Evil* with me and read a few pages. I can't say I was enjoying the book, it seemed to wander all over the place. It was a true story and, of course, true stories were like that. Then Cindy was back with my breakfast. "You're a bartender, right?"

"Yeah. It's a little early though, don't you think?"

She brushed me away with a raspberry. "I don't want a drink. No, there was this guy come in. He was asking all sorts of questions about bartenders in this neighborhood. He kind of described you. I didn't say nothing. It's not my business."

Now that I'd completely lost my appetite, I sat back in the booth and asked, "Did he tell you who he was?"

"He said his name was MacBeth. No wait, Hamlet. Hamlet Gilbody. He said he was a private eye from Chicago. It was kind of like TV. Except creepier."

I shrugged. "I don't know anyone in Chicago."

"I do. You're not missing much."

"Did he leave his card?"

"I wouldn't take it. I said I didn't know anybody like that so what did I need his card for?"

I nodded. I wouldn't have minded seeing the card, but her way was probably better.

"I should leave you alone so you can eat your breakfast."

"Thanks, Cindy. A lot."

An hour later, I was in Downey. I crawled slowly past 7815 Amorita then pulled a U-turn and parked a few houses down in a way that let me get a good look at the house.

The first thing I noticed was that the mailbox said MICHAELS. The family still owned the house. They owned the house where their nineteen-year-old son had been murdered. They probably crossed the spot where he died a dozen times a day. It seemed every bit as odd to me as Joanne Yardley still living in her house.

But hey, maybe I was the one who was odd. Maybe the way to deal with tragedy was to hunker down and live with it. Maybe they were right not to budge. I was a runner. I thought I'd done it for people I cared about, but I could be wrong. I could have done it for me. I could just be a coward.

I shook those thoughts off and went back to staring at the house. In the driveway sat a Mercury station wagon from the eighties. It was beat up, with a lot of dents and peeling paint on the roof. There were two recent bumper stickers on the back. One said PAT BUCHANAN FOR PRESIDENT and the other HARVEST 95. The first I understood well enough; the second was some kind of Christian revival meeting. I'd never been to one. Just the idea was scary enough.

The house itself looked small and, like the car, was badly in need of new paint. The paint that was on there was so faded I couldn't quite tell what color it had started out as. There was a brightly colored, plastic Big Wheel sitting near the cement stoop that suggested grandchildren. Pete Michaels was nineteen when he was killed. His parents would be in their sixties or even seventies now. I didn't remember anything about siblings, but that didn't mean there weren't any.

I tried to imagine what the house had been like at the time of the murder. The paint job was probably fresh. There would have been a different station wagon. It would have had a FORD/DOLE sticker on the back. I glanced around the neighborhood. All the houses seemed to be about the same age. There were a lot of potential witnesses. I wondered if the police did a canvas.

Larry's letter said the murder happened September 28, 1976. What day of the week was that? Who might have been home? The letter said Pete's parents came home and found Larry there. They weren't working, so maybe it was a Saturday or a Sunday. I would need to figure that out.

Pete's real killer would have had to come and go before Larry showed up. It was possible one of the neighbors saw something. They could have seen someone and not thought anything of it— of course, if they didn't think about it then, they were unlikely to remember it twenty years later.

What about the gun shot? Someone could have heard that. And it would have happened before Larry arrived. I'd have to go over the witness statements carefully—if there were witness statements. If we took the case, we'd get them in discovery. I just had to convince Lydia to take the case.

Unexpectedly, the front door opened and out came a hard looking woman nearing forty with light brown hair tied back and a big floral top. She was at least nine months pregnant. Trailing behind her was a thirteen- or fourteen-year-old girl wearing pajamas. The girl looked flushed and unhappy. They were heading toward the station wagon when I decided it was probably best if I moved along.

Driving away, I kept an eye on them through the rearview mirror. They didn't notice me. I wondered who they were. They didn't fit the story I'd made up about Pete's parents keeping the house. Maybe they had, though. Maybe the pregnant woman was Pete's sister living there for some reason and the girl his niece. And somewhere there was a smaller child attached to the Big Wheel. This was all information I'd need to find out. It might mean nothing, but it might also mean something.

I drove back to Long Beach and made a quick stop at Ghetto Vons. Then I popped by The Freedom Agenda office. Karen was at her post in the reception area.

"It's Friday, what are you doing here?"

"Is Lydia in?"

She shook her head. "No, she's downtown with Edwin."

Edwin Karpinski was another attorney with The Freedom Agenda. Well, he wasn't really with The Freedom Agenda. He had an office there, but he did very little. I got the impression he had something to do with finding civil attorneys for our clients, then facilitating our getting some portion of the settlements. I also noticed he'd swoop in and seem to take credit for most of Lydia's work.

It was just as well she was out; I wasn't there to see her. I plunked a bottle of wine, still in its brown bag, in front of Karen. She eyed me suspiciously and opened the bag. She gave me a stern look, and said, "White zinfandel? Really? Because I'm a Black girl?"

I blushed, that was exactly why I'd chosen it. I'd heard that Black girls liked sweet wines—not that we got many of them at The Hawk.

"I can go back and get you a chardonnay."

"No, I like white zinfandel. I just don't like you knowing I like it."

"Okay. Next time I'll ask."

"No. Next time you'll bring me Courvoisier."

That was another alcoholic beverage supposedly enjoyed by Black people. I couldn't tell if she was ribbing me or serious. She set the bottle of wine to the side. "I'm guessing you want something. Something you're not supposed to have?"

"It's personal. I need you to find out what you can about a private detective named Hamlet Gilbody."

She shook her head, and said, "The things people do to their children. Is that all you know about him?"

"He said he's from Chicago but that might not be right."

"He could be lying about that name, too. I'll do a broad search."

"Thank you."

"Mmm-hmmm."

The way she looked at me, like she could see right through

me, made me wonder if she'd gotten bored one afternoon and done a search on me. Very little she found would match the things I'd said about myself. It might be a good idea to get her that bottle of Courvoisier.

****

Lydia came into The Hawk about seven that night. We were still in the thick of the afterwork crowd, the serious drinkers who didn't want to start at the nicer, more expensive bars down the street. There weren't any seats at the bar, so I raised a finger at her asking that she wait. I took a Bud Lite out of the cooler under the bar and poured a shot of tequila. I set them in front of a guy named Bucky.

"These are on me."

"Really, thanks!"

"Because you're going to give this nice lady your seat." I pointed at Lydia. Bucky glanced at her and then downed the tequila. He picked up the bottle of beer he hadn't finished and the one he hadn't started and moved away.

Lydia slid onto the stool. "Absolut martini, straight up, olive, dry as a bone."

"I remember."

I took down a martini glass. Honestly, I used them far more than I wanted to. The fad for appletinis was spreading like herpes. I made the drink quickly and set it down in front of her.

"What are you doing here?"

"I'm meeting Dwayne for a drink and then dinner at Nectar."

Dwayne was her husband, a rather tight-assed studio executive, which is why I asked, "And you thought a visit to a sleazy gay bar would be a great start to a romantic evening?"

"I have a couple of things I want to talk to you about. Two birds, one stone."

"Sip on that," I said. "I'll be right back."

I made the rounds, sold a few drinks, and was back about five minutes later. "All right, shoot."

"How were the interviews?"

"I'm going to write them up on Tuesday."

"In general."

"In general, Detective Wellesley coached the victims on their IDs. Selma and Joanne will very likely confirm that in a deposition."

"That's great."

"Maybe not. Camille is your strongest witness, but she's firmly in Wellesley's corner. Joanne... I don't think she leaves her house. Ever. That could a problem if you go back to court or if the district attorney insists on deposing her anywhere but her living room. And as for Selma, she's gotten religion and wants to forgive everyone. Which probably doesn't help her credibility."

Lydia nodded and sipped her drink.

"One thing about Selma though. She said she picked out a photo of Alan Dinkler from a photo array, but we don't have that."

She nodded. "A possible Brady violation. Good work."

"I didn't mention this the other day, but Camille seemed to think I was questioning Wellesley's work because I'm a man."

"Chip on her shoulder. Always helpful. Since you're going up to Corcoran on Monday, I had Karen set up meetings with Alan Dinkler and Stu Whatley for you."

"What about Peter Linder?"

"He's at Solano." Sensing that I might not know where that was, she added, "Near San Francisco. If it gets too late and you want to stay over, go ahead. Just bring a receipt—"

And then Dwayne was standing at her shoulder. "Oh hello," she said, kissing him on the cheek. To me she asked, "Do you have a decent red open?"

"I have red open. I don't know that I'd call it decent."

"That's okay," he said. "I'll wait until we get to the restaurant."

"Are you sure?" I asked. "I can manage a seat for you." All it would cost me was a Ketel One and tonic.

He shook his head, which was Lydia's cue to swallow the rest of her drink and stand up.

"See you Tuesday," she said, with a wry smile.

CHAPTER EIGHT

April 7, 1996
Sunday evening

Sunday was Easter. I worked at The Hawk until seven, having given half my shift to Robbie, the bartender who worked peak hours on Friday and Saturday. Since I was driving up to Corcoran on Monday, I didn't think it was a good idea to work until three in the morning. I also wanted to be home with Ronnie for at least some of the day.

Easter wasn't a big holiday. It wasn't Christmas or New Year's or Valentine's Day or even Halloween. But it was a holiday we—or more often he—typically spent with his mother. I thought it was a good idea to spend the evening with him.

I walked into the house around seven-thirty and found him sitting at the breakfast bar in the kitchen watching Junior turning our kitchen into a battleground.

"What's going on?"

"Junior offered to make Easter dinner."

"Was that before he demoed the kitchen?"

"Oh, you—" Junior said. "It's all going to be fine. Just you wait and see."

I was hungry. I hoped I didn't have to wait too long to wait and see. "What are we having?"

"A chilled melon soup, salad, beef Wellington, and a lemon soufflé for dessert."

I glanced at Ronnie and then asked Junior, "Do you have experience cooking?"

"You don't need experience to cook. Not if you have a recipe. I mean, I can follow instructions."

"What time do we eat?"

"Soon. Very soon. Have some wine."

"I don't drink."

"I can never remember that. You *seem* like a drinker."

"Is that a compliment?" Ronnie asked for me.

"Absolutely. Teetotalers are so dull, and Dom is anything but dull."

I had the feeling he expected to be thanked for the compliment. I decided not to. "What are you making now?"

"I'm making the beef." He'd stacked three steaks one on top of the other and then set them into the center of a crumbling pie crust. I was sure he was doing it wrong. It also seemed like we wouldn't be eating for a very long time.

"I hope you don't mind my taking over," he said. "You two have been so good to me and I want to show that I'm grateful."

"This must have all cost a fortune," Ronnie pointed out. Something of a double-edged statement since Junior paid a reduced rent—my fault.

"I'm a *good* little shopper."

I refilled Ronnie's wine glass and suggested, "Why don't we leave Junior to it." And then walked through the butler's pantry into the living room. Ronnie followed.

Under his breath, he said, "I don't trust him not to burn the house down."

"He could do that making toast. This way we at least have a chance of dinner."

Ronnie scowled, clearly wanting to complain some more. I distracted him by asking "How was your open house this afternoon?"

"Lonely. I don't understand people. Prices are low, which makes it the perfect time to buy; the problem is, no one else is buying so people think it's the *wrong* time to buy. They wait until everyone else is buying, which means they're going to pay top dollar."

I sat in one of the orange chairs, saying, "It's been two years since the Northridge quake. People will forget and then prices will go up so people will start buying again."

In the kitchen, something clanged loudly as it hit the floor. Before he could budge, I told Ronnie, "Just drink your wine."

"You don't know how hard this is."

I did but decided not to disagree with him. Normally at Easter, he and his mother would make a very traditional, American-style Sunday dinner. Spiral-cut ham, candied sweet potatoes, green bean casserole, crescent rolls from a cardboard tube followed by store-bought chocolate cream pie. Other holiday meals were more Asian-centric, but Mai, Ronnie's mother, had become a Christian shortly after arriving in the United States and spiral-cut ham with a gravy boat of honey glaze had been her way of showing both devotion and patriotism.

"Do you miss your mother?"

"No. Not at all. I wish it had been me, though. I wish I'd dumped her."

"You were patient. You gave her chance after chance. You should be proud of yourself."

"I guess so." A moment later he added, "The thing that makes things okay is you. I have you."

That made me edgy. Richland Keswick was acting suspiciously and someone with the first name Hamlet was looking for me. Neither of those things made me feel safe. It was always in the back of my mind that I might need to leave Ronnie, that it might become too dangerous for him if I stayed.

I knew he loved me, but I always felt like he'd be fine if I disappeared. Without his mother in his life, it felt like he needed me more. It felt like he might not be fine if I left suddenly. It was a feeling I hated. It meant that he was in danger if I stayed and in danger if I left.

"You have a serious look on your face," he said. "Are you regretting that you let Junior move in?"

"I don't know. He's a character, that's for sure."

"You wouldn't tell me if you did regret it, would you?"

"Probably not. Just focus on the fact that he's paying part of the mortgage for you."

"A small part."

"He's making this house possible."

I turned on the TV and convinced Ronnie to watch part of *Somersby*. That was probably a mistake, since it was the story of a man pretending to be someone he's not. That struck a little close to home. I shuffled around in my chair a few times.

Of course, in the movie the man is returning to his "wife." How it was that she didn't notice the man she was having sex with was *not* her husband was something Ronnie and I debated for about an hour. His position was that during the Civil War era no one cared if women enjoyed sex and it was always done in the dark. My position was that even if both men were selfish pricks, they'd be selfish pricks in different ways.

Starving, I snuck into the kitchen during a commercial break and asked Junior, "Did you plan any appetizers?"

"Oh God no. I should have, shouldn't I?"

"I'll get some cheese and crackers."

I found a small piece of brie and a chunk of cheddar. I put them on a plate and then added water biscuits. As I did, I peeked at what Junior was doing. The beef Wellington had come out of the oven a mucky mess, the crust pink and soggy from the blood oozing out of the steaks. On the stove was something brown and sunken which I guessed was the lemon soufflé.

"There's no shame in ordering a pizza."

"Oh my God, would you?"

I'd meant *he* could order a pizza but decided not to belabor the point. I called The Pizza Place for a pesto pizza and three tiramisus. Then Junior and I went out into the living room and broke the news to Ronnie.

"Fabulous," Ronnie said. "Let's watch *Crimes of Passion*."

So much for *Somersby*. *Crimes of Passion* was probably Ronnie's favorite movie. We'd nearly worn out the VHS tape and I wouldn't have been surprised if it broke when he put it into the

VCR. The movie starred Kathleen Turner as a fashion designer-slash-prostitute, but as interesting as that was, Ronnie was much more interested in the lead actor and Anthony Perkins' over-the-top performance as a crazy priest. It was directed by Ken Russell, which somehow made the 87 minutes of titillation art.

After the pizza arrived and was eaten, Junior said. "I can't watch anymore of this movie. It's the kind of film you have to be stoned on something to watch."

"You've had quite a bit of alcohol," I pointed out.

"Stoned as in something illegal," he said before toddling off to bed.

Ronnie and I watched the rest of the movie, and yes, it would have been better if we'd been just a little bit stoned. But it wasn't terrible. Afterward, we brought the pizza box and soda cups into the kitchen. Of course, Junior had not cleaned up.

Ronnie promised he'd clean it up in the morning, but I felt like we should get it out of the way. I began scraping the attempted dinner into the trash. I couldn't help saying, "It seems like such a waste."

"Hmmm," Ronnie said. "We should get a dog."

"Why would you say something like that?"

"Because then we'd have someone to feed this mess to."

"We're not getting a dog," I said. "No way."

"Well, that's definitive."

I might have been a bit strident, but I didn't want one more thing in my life I'd have to let go of.

CHAPTER NINE

April 8, 1996
Monday

I don't keep a lot of CDs in the Jeep. I have a little carrier strapped to the back of my sun visor. It holds just five albums: *Keith Jarrett at the Blue Note*, Willie Nelson's *Stardust*, *Chet Baker Sings: It Could Happen to You*, Ella Fitzgerald *Sings the Duke Ellington Songbook*, and Boz Scaggs' *Silk Degrees*. Someday I'll splurge and get a disc changer put behind the backseat. Meanwhile, those five albums contained enough music to get me halfway across the country.

Of course, a Jeep Wrangler—even with a hardtop—does not have the best acoustics in the automotive world. I kept the stereo going at top volume for most of the four-hour trip. This was my second trip to California State Prison at Corcoran and my first alone. I knew from my previous visit to wear khaki pants—jeans were forbidden—and nothing with metal buttons. I was allowed a legal pad and a see-through Bic pen. Files baked into layer cakes were not even remotely possible.

To keep myself entertained during the drive, I thought about The Freedom Agenda's basic strategy. I wasn't a lawyer, of course, so I listened closely and then tried to dumb things down for myself. Lydia's basic strategy was to do everything possible to avoid a retrial. Jurys could be fickle; she didn't want to risk one that might reject DNA evidence—as O.J.'s jury did. Her goal was always to get the prosecution to fold before trial.

The prosecution's goal was almost the opposite. They wanted to protect their convictions. One unraveled conviction could lead to many more. Typically, they also did everything they could to avoid a new trial, while at the same time dragging their feet as much as possible. Our goal was to provide as much evidence as possible of our client's innocence. The prosecution had to at least appear to be on the side of justice. When the evidence rose to an undeniable level, they dropped their resistance. It was a steeper hill to climb than you'd think.

Then I asked myself honestly, if it was that hard to get someone out of prison with DNA evidence, what did I expect to find out talking with Larry Wilkes that would be as persuasive? In order to get his conviction overturned there would have to be new evidence, evidence that could have changed the outcome of the first trial. Which is exactly what DNA did for a case. Without DNA, he would need a witness to recant, or we'd need to find prosecutorial misconduct, or ineffective council, or some combination of all three. It was a high bar.

Around the prison the desert was sandy and stripped of life. That seemed in harmony with the low, washed-out buildings huddled together against the wind. I got out of the Jeep, locked it, and walked toward the visitor's entrance.

The building was small with glass doors leading to a kind of lobby. That was taken up by a sprawling metal detector. As I walked through it went off. I explained that I had quite a few surgical screws floating around my body. Ignoring me, the guard followed the same routine that had been followed before, a wand was waved over me—it went off repeatedly, then I was frisked in a very intimate way, and finally I was asked to remove my shirt. The guard actually touched the scars on my back. That pissed me off. What did he think? That I'd hidden things in my wound fifteen years ago? 'Wow,' I thought, 'what a useful place to smuggle things into a maximum-security prison.'

When they were done poking at me, I buttoned my shirt and

walked over to the reception desk. I signed in and asked the guard. , "I'm here to see three different inmates, do you know the order they'll be brought out?"

"Do I look like a secretary?"

To be honest, she was behind a reception desk and had just handed me a clipboard, so, yeah, she did. I didn't dare say that, though. I didn't dare say anything. Finally, she nodded at the entrance and buzzed the door so I could open it.

After walking through a second door, I found myself alone in a visiting room about thirty by forty feet. There were about six tables with chairs bolted to the floor. On weekends and holidays, it served for family visitation. During the week it was used for attorney visits. I sat down at one of the tables and waited. The last time I'd seen a clock it was a little after one o'clock. I hoped to be out by three or four and home by eight. I had no intention of taking Lydia up on her offer of a hotel for the night.

Sitting there I noticed something I hadn't during my first visit. The smell. Mostly sweat, body odor, but with it a sickly sweet perfume leftover from Sunday's visitation. And more perspiration. I wondered how often inmates got to shower. I had never been in prison. I'd once spent a little more than twenty-four hours in Cook County Jail. No one offered me a shower.

I waited about twenty minutes and then a door opened and in walked an inmate. Alan Dinkler, who'd been a college student when he was arrested. He was just under six feet and scrawny. I remembered that Selma had described him as very dark-skinned. He wasn't. He skin was more copper than anything else. I shouldn't be surprised he didn't match the description given. He was the wrong guy after all.

I introduced myself and we sat down.

"You're here to tell me about my case?"

"I'm here to ask questions."

"What for? The DNA proved I didn't do it."

"We have to attack the DA's case in as many ways as possible."

"Someone else raped that woman."

"I know." He seemed to be getting angry, so I thought I

should try to establish a little bit of rapport. "You were in college when you were arrested. What were you studying?"

"I was a history major. I was thinking about becoming a lawyer."

"Are you still interested in that?"

"No. I've seen too much."

"Have you been able to take college courses in here?"

"Computers, electronics, machine shop, sheet metal, welding. That's all they have to offer. Doesn't matter though. No one's going to hire you with a felony sex offense on your record even if you do get a jailhouse sheepskin."

"What have you been doing?"

"A lot of reading. Don't ask me my favorite book, though. Ask what you came to ask."

"Tell me about your arrest, questioning and the identification process."

"They just came to my house and took me."

"Why you?"

"They said I fit the description, which is another way of saying I'm Black."

"Were you the only Black student in your class?"

"There were two Black girls. But that's not what you were asking, is it?"

"So they came to your house and arrested you. They questioned you at the station?"

"They did. For about eight hours."

"Let's just do the highlights."

He shrugged. "They asked a lot about why I left class early the night the girl was raped. They tried to get me to say I was getting ready to rape her."

"But her class let out after yours and she stayed late."

"I didn't say it made sense. None of it made sense."

"Why did you leave class early?"

"My mother wasn't well. I hadn't wanted to go to class in the first place, but she made me. My going to college was important. She had dreams for me."

"What else did they ask you about?"

"They told me a lot about what happened to that poor girl. Tried to get me to repeat it. I told them I'd gone home to my mother already, but they just called me a liar."

"Tell me about them taking your picture."

"The mug shot?"

"No, they had another picture. Could they have gotten it from your mother?"

"I don't know what you're talking about."

"The witness, Selma, she said she identified you from a photograph. That it wasn't a mug—"

"No. That's not right. They did a lineup. Just like on TV. Two-way mirror."

Honestly, I wasn't sure if they did that kind of lineup or not. It was on TV all the time, but that didn't mean anything. Selma had talked about a photo lineup. The discrepancy might end up being important.

"During the trial, did Selma identify you?"

"Oh yeah. That's the first thing they did. Had her point at me."

"Did they ask her about the lineup?"

"I don't think so."

"What about Detective Wellesley? Was she asked about the lineup?"

"Yes, I remember that."

"And did she talk about it being a photo lineup? Or an in-person lineup?"

"Well, I remember being in the lineup so she couldn't have talked about photographs, I would have known that was wrong."

"When you were at the lineup, did you see Selma there? In the hallway, or anywhere?"

"No. I didn't really see anything but the room. And the other guys."

"And the other guys were all Black?"

"Yes."

I kicked myself for not asking Selma the same question. For all I knew she was shown six photos with only one Black guy.

And then Wellesley circled back and did another "lineup" to make it appear as though it had been done fairly.

"She writes to me, you know. Selma," he said. "She wants me to know she's forgiven me."

"Yes, she told me that." And then I wondered, "Are you going to be able to forgive her?"

"I was with my mother when the girl was raped. The police called my mother a liar, the lawyers called her a liar, six months after the trial she died of a broken heart. I'm not forgiving anyone."

****

Larry Wilkes was brought in next, after another twenty-minute wait. It was well after lunchtime and I was beginning to get very hungry. The smell of the place made it impossible to think of eating, though. Mostly, I wanted to escape.

Whatever two decades in prison had done to Larry, it didn't show. He was nearly forty, sandy-haired and looked like your typical TV dad. He was a marked contrast to my visit with Danny Osborne, who'd been beaten down and somewhat haunted. But then, Larry had been convicted of killing another man, rather than a teenage girl. Maybe that earned him some respect. Maybe he got left alone.

When he sat down, I said, "I'm Dom Reilly, I work with The Freedom Agenda. I read your letter."

"You're taking my case?" he asked, with obvious excitement.

"No. I'm here to ask questions to see if we'll take your case."

"Oh. Okay." Not as excited.

"In order to reopen a case like yours there needs to be new evidence. Or evidence of misconduct, either by the prosecution or defense. We work with DNA testing a lot because that's clearly new evidence. However, in your case I don't see anything we can test."

"So why are you here?" he asked, now a little grumpy.

"Like I said, I read your letter. I'd like to hear your story directly from you."

He took a long breath and began. "Pete Michaels and I were in a relationship during our last year of high school. I hadn't known I could be in love with a man. I knew what I was, but I'd been told gays were perverts, that we couldn't find happiness. And then I found out that wasn't true... with Pete... he was so... confident, happy, almost carefree. I'd never met anyone like that, never imagined someone could be gay *and* happy."

I was close to ten years older than he was, so what he was saying was familiar. I'm sure I was nodding along sympathetically.

"Anyway, I went away to college in Santa Barbara. It had been in the works for a while. My parents really wanted it, and they were paying for it. Pete had started doing construction work. He had an uncle who worked on the docks in Long Beach who was trying to get him into the long shoreman's union. That's a great union, he would have been set for life." He swallowed hard. "I couldn't take college. Couldn't take being that far away from him."

"You were only there a few weeks."

"That seems like a long time when you're eighteen. I tried to talk to Pete on the phone, but I kept missing him. I don't think his family was giving him my messages. Finally, I got on a bus and went home. My parents weren't happy to see me, but I didn't care. All that mattered was Pete. I kept calling, but he didn't call me back, so I took my mother's car and drove over—"

"Why?"

"Because he wouldn't talk to me on the phone."

"Yes, but why that day? Why did you go over that particular day?"

"We had a signal. Two rings and then hang up. A lot of the time we'd have a plan and I'd know where we were meeting. Sometimes we'd go parking, once we went to a cheap motel. Usually his family would be gone and we'd be in his room."

"So you got the signal that day?

"Yes. I guess that's why I went over."

"Because you thought no one would be home except Pete."

"Yes. That's what I thought."

Some of this sounded a little rote, like he'd talked about it a few too many times. "Did any of this come out at your trial?"

"No. I told my attorney about me and Pete, but he warned me to keep quiet about it because he was sure if the jury knew I was gay I'd get convicted for sure."

I thought about that for a moment. Lydia might be able to use that to make a case for ineffective counsel, but it wouldn't have been considered an unreasonable strategy at the time.

"Are you sure it was Pete who gave you the signal?"

"I've thought about that too. A lot. I don't think he'd have told anyone about us. And I don't know how else anyone would have known the signal."

"You make it sound like he was very comfortable with his sexuality."

"Well, he was. His family wouldn't have been, and he knew that. He didn't want to hurt them."

"In your letter you said the gun was wiped clean of fingerprints. Did they connect you to the gun in some other way?"

"They had a witness who said he sold it to me."

This was new information. "Tell me about that."

"They had this guy we went to school with. Andy Showalter. Everybody thought he was harmless. I mean, he liked drawing Nazis and shit. He got a gun. He said he sold it to me."

"Was it a World War II gun?" I asked, guessing at the Nazi connection.

"No, it was more like a Saturday Night Special. I don't know much about guns. Honestly, I don't even remember seeing it until the trial."

I nodded. "Just to verify, he did *not* sell you a gun."

"No. I don't remember ever speaking to him."

"Was the gun registered to him?"

"No. The gun was stolen. He claimed he bought it on the street."

"Did they provide a motive for the killing?"

He frowned, obviously unhappy. "Yes. They said it was over a girl. Pete's fiancé."

"So you think Pete might have had a fiancé? To please his family? That might be why he wasn't calling you back."

"That's not what happened. I asked my friend to pretend to be Pete's fiancé."

"You did what?" He was telling me he created the motive they used to convict him.

"Her name is Anne Whittemore. We went to high school together. We were all kind of friends. Well, she was my friend mainly. I asked her to lie. Given what my attorney said, given what Pete would have wanted, it seemed the right thing to do."

"Did she know what was going on between the two of you?"

"Yes."

"And she testified that Pete was her boyfriend?"

"Fiancé."

"You didn't fight back, did you?"

He shook his head. "I was too upset. It was all just awful."

"Tell me more about Pete. He has sister, doesn't he?"

"No, he has a brother. Paul, Paulie."

"Was Paulie older or younger?"

"They were Irish twins. Paulie was about eleven months younger."

"So, Paulie was in the grade behind you and Pete?"

"No. We were all in the same grade. Pete was a year older. He missed most of the third grade with some sickness... it might have been asthma."

"You said he was an athlete?"

With a shrug, he said, "Maybe he got over it?"

"So, tell me, who do you think killed Pete?"

"I don't know."

"You've been in here a long time. You don't think about it?"

"I think about it all the time. But everyone liked Pete. He was a great guy."

I wondered about that. Obviously, someone thought he wasn't that great. "What about Andy Showalter? Do you think he had a reason to kill Pete?"

"I can't think of anyone who had a reason to kill Pete."

"Who knew about the two of you?"

"No one. Except Anne."

"Because Pete didn't want anyone to know?"

"Neither of us wanted anyone to know. It was the seventies."

I remembered the seventies very well.

"Could someone have found out?"

"I don't know."

"Were you the only person Pete was involved with?"

"I think so."

"Did he have exes?"

"Not really."

"Not really? What does that mean?"

"He wasn't a virgin. I knew that. But I don't know who he'd been with."

I studied him for a moment. I guess it made sense. Even though Larry was in love, they'd been stealing time to meet, here and there. Most of that time would have been devoted to sex. They probably didn't talk a whole lot. On the other hand, Pete might not have wanted Larry to know who he'd been with.

"Okay, I'm going to have to nose around some. I don't know that I'll be able to get my boss to take you on until I have more. Do I have your permission to talk to some of the people involved?"

"Who are you going to talk to?"

"Andy Showalter. Anne Whittemore."

He nodded.

"You haven't had any contact with them, have you?"

"Anne wrote to me a few times, but she stopped a few months after I was convicted."

"Do you have those letters?"

He shook his head. "We don't get to keep a lot of things."

"All right," I said, about to signal a guard standing on the other side of a door.

But Larry asked, "Would you go and see Brysen?"

"Who's Brysen?"

"I told you about him in my letter. He's the reason I want to get out. I want him to know this is happening."

"Like I said, I'm not sure it is happening. I have to convince my boss."

"Can you go see him anyway?"

"Sure."

He rattled off Brysen's phone number. He knew it by heart.

CHAPTER TEN

April 8, 1996
Monday late afternoon

It was getting late. It had been almost an hour since Larry had gone back to his cell. I'd gone nose-blind to the smell of the place and was now so hungry I was ready to eat the metal chair I was sitting on. Finally, the door popped open and Stu Whatley ambled in. He was a few inches under six-foot, balding on top, still muscular, with cold blue eyes. He sat down across from me, anger wafting off him like too much aftershave.

"Why is this taking so fucking long?"

I ignored that. "I'm Dom Reilly. We haven't met. Lydia asked me to come and ask you a few questions."

"What for? The DNA says I didn't do it. Isn't that enough?"

"Unfortunately, no. District attorneys are doing what they can to slow these cases down and sometimes stop them."

He stared at me like he wanted to chew me up and spit me out. I continued, "I need to talk to you about your arrest and the identification process."

"They arrested me. They broke down my door and treated me like I was the Kansas City Bomber."

It took me a moment, but I figured out what he meant and corrected him. "Oklahoma City Bomber. Timothy McVeigh."

"Yeah, him."

"And they were there because you'd been arrested for felony rape before."

"Arrested, yeah. But the bitch was lying. All I got charged with was assault." He shrugged, and said, "I punched her. She deserved it."

"You like to beat up women?"

"Why do people ask stupid questions like that?"

"It doesn't seem so stupid."

"The only answer you'll believe is yes. That makes it a stupid question."

Yeah, so, he was kind of right about that. I had a strong feeling he liked to beat up anyone he thought might have trouble fighting back. Women, children, fags.

"How badly did you beat her?"

"Who?"

"The woman who accused you of rape."

He just smiled. I decided to move on. "I'm told there was a lineup. You were brought into a room and asked to say a few words in front of the victim."

"Yeah, the *victim*," he scoffed. "It was her and that cunt detective."

"You know, in the event that we need a deposition or have to go to trial, you might want to find better ways to talk about women."

"I know better than telling the truth to lawyers," he said.

Not exactly what I was saying.

"Do you have any reason to believe the victim was influenced by Detective Wellesley?"

"I have every reason. The bi—Detective Wellesley did everything but point at me."

"What about the neighbor who said she saw—"

"Candy Van Dyke," he said snidely. "You don't forget a name like that. Not when she puts you behind bars."

"Was there a lineup where Ms. Van Dyke identified you?"

"No. I didn't see her until she was sitting in court pointing her finger at me. I got the kind of face people remember even when they've never seen me before."

"You didn't recognize her?"

"Never saw her before."

"Were you interviewed by Detective Wellesley?"

"This is bullshit. How soon after I get out do I get paid?"

"That's not what we do at The Freedom Agenda. We will give you a referral to a civil litigator. At that point you can ask him."

"Where does the money come from?"

"What money?"

"When I get paid, who pays it."

"I think it comes from the State of California." I was pretty sure that was right, though maybe it was a particular jurisdiction? I'd have to ask Lydia—

"I want to sue the bitches who put me here. I want every penny they make for the rest of their lives."

****

I found a Mexican restaurant just north of the prison in the city of Corcoran. I had a carnitas plate and a side of guacamole. Really, it was too much food, but having missed lunch I was starving. By the time I cut over to the 5 it was after seven and the sun was setting. I couldn't wait to get home and take a shower.

The prison itself made me feel gross, but talking to Stu Whatley made me feel downright filthy. I'm sure Detective Wellesley felt good putting him away—probably still felt good about it. There was a feeling among some cops, even some prosecutors, that it didn't matter whether a defendant was innocent of the crime on the books, they were guilty of something and therefore should go to prison. I wondered if that was part of what happened here.

Of course, that was bad police work, bad justice. If you worked in law enforcement, you had to hold yourself to a higher bar. And not just a higher bar than the people you policed, that was a bar that could be dangerously low. No, you had to hold yourself to the highest bar. It was a hard thing to do. I can't say I did it well when I was on the job. I wish I had.

I managed to get through most of the Grapevine before I began to fall asleep. Opening the window, the night air wasn't all that cold. I pulled off into a rest area about a half an hour north of Castaic for what I hoped was a short nap.

I dropped into sleep like a stone into a pond. Chin on chest, head hanging, mind abuzz with dreams. I dreamed about Harker. I used to dream about him all the time. My lover from the early eighties. It was the money he'd left to me that I'd given to Ronnie to buy our first house. I owed Harker a lot.

I dreamed we were in my bed; not the bed I shared with Ronnie, but one I'd had in an apartment I'd rented in Hollywood for a while. Harker was sleeping next to me, except he wasn't really. He was floating there just above the mattress. I rolled over to look at him. He smiled at me, then floated upwards, above the bed and then out the window, his body arching over the sill like a pole jumper. He slipped away with the night.

My cellular phone was ringing. That's what woke me. I pushed the buttons until something happened.

"Dom? Dom where are you?"

I cleared my throat. "Still in the Grapevine. I'll be home in about an hour and a half."

"I sold the house in California Heights. My clients accepted the offer."

"Is that the one you showed me?"

"The other one."

Ronnie was good at his job and sellers were beginning to figure that out. That meant I was having more and more trouble keeping up. I spent a lot of time acting like I knew what he was talking about. I could tell he knew I was doing it, but he didn't seem to mind.

"Well, that's great. Good job."

"I miss you. I'm alone here with Junior. He's trying to convince me that things were better when gay sex was illegal."

"It's still illegal in twenty-six states," I pointed out.

"So, can I give him a list of places he could move to?"

"Don't get your hopes up. I don't think he's going anywhere."

"That's too bad. Did you eat?"

"Yeah, I had Mexican."

"I'm taping *Melrose Place*. We can watch it when you get home. I'll make che-che."

Che-che was a Vietnamese dessert soup he liked to make. His mother had made something similar, though his version was decidedly American: bananas, tapioca pudding, coconut milk and peanuts. It was pretty good.

I told him I loved him and said good-bye. I got back onto the freeway. As I drove, I tried to sort through the things I'd learned at the prison. I was even more convinced Larry Wilkes was innocent. I needed to figure out if I could get the transcript to his trial without taking the case. I had no clue how to do that, nor how much it might cost. I could probably put out the money and then ask to be reimbursed if I could get Lydia to take the case.

The first thing I needed to do was find Andy Showalter. I needed him to recant his testimony. Obviously, if he was interested in recanting he'd have come forward before now. I might need the transcript first. If I could catch him in a lie, that might get him to recant.

Anne Whittemore was also someone I needed to talk to. Larry said he'd told her to perjure herself. If I made it clear he now wanted her to tell the truth, she might recant as well. Two recanting witnesses were always better than one.

As I passed Santa Clarita, I turned my thoughts to the rapists. Well, the not-rapists. Alan Dinkman seemed like a decent guy. I'd have to call Selma Martinez and ask if the photo lineup she was shown included only Black men. And I needed to remind Lydia to request that the district attorney find and hand over a copy of the missing photo lineup. We also needed to establish if the photo lineup was handed over to the original defense attorney. That could be enough of a violation to spark a new trial on its own. Combine that with the DNA evidence and the DA should just give up. Didn't mean he would, but he should.

Stu Whatley was another story. He was a real creep. I couldn't be sure whether he was always like that or if he became that in prison. I was leaning toward always.

I was pretty sure Lydia knew exactly who she was dealing with. The trick here would be to not let the prosecution know the kind of person he was. That we could get a new trial seemed certain with the DNA evidence. That didn't mean he wouldn't be retried though. The DA might roll the dice and hope that his vile personality trumped science and a jury would convict him again.

This might be why Lydia was focused on Detective Wellesley. If we had enough evidence that she manipulated the identification process, we would likely stay out of court entirely. That meant I needed to find and talk to Candy Van Dyke.

As I drove, my mind drifting along, picking other subjects until I asked myself why I was so interested in helping Larry Wilkes. I believed him but wasn't sure exactly why. The lack of fingerprints on the gun was certainly a problem. But then people do illogical things when they commit murder. He could have wiped his fingerprints off the gun and then just stayed. It was stupid, but then murder is rarely a crime of the super intelligent.

Love. That was what made me want to help him. Pete had been Larry's first love. I remember what that was like. And I remember how messed up it could get. My first love had been a librarian named Daniel. No one died when we broke up, though it did bring about the end of my time as a Chicago police officer. Our relationship had been full of high highs and low lows. An emotional roller-coaster.

Somewhere along the line, I lost track of him. He was replaced by other loves, intense loves, heartbreaking loves. I was grateful my life was much calmer than it had been in my late twenties and early thirties. I was grateful for Ronnie.

I thought he was remarkable for someone so young. But then he'd grown up in a different time. Things were better. Not great, but better. Despite his mother, Ronnie had been able to find broader acceptance than I had. He'd been in an LGBT group when he was in college. And he'd even pledged a gay fraternity. I don't think he fully understood how lucky he was. How much easier things had gotten in a very short time.

And I didn't care if he understood. In fact, most of the time I didn't want him to understand. Some things in life are hard to understand if you haven't gone through them. I didn't want him to go through any of the things I'd had to face. I wanted his life to be a safe, happy place. Always.

CHAPTER ELEVEN

April 9, 1996
Tuesday morning

Getting Danny Osbourne out of prison had resulted in a substantial amount of publicity, which caused a new wave of letters from prisoners who'd like to be released from prison. Most of them were in California, but a significant amount were from around the United States. Given our budget, Lydia tried to keep things relatively local. Occasionally, she forwarded files to other justice organizations.

My space was at the end of one of the banquet tables. I had a decent chair I'd bought myself at Staples, an inbox, a beige desk phone, and an accordion file folder to keep any loose papers from the cases I was working.

When I got there Tuesday morning, a file was waiting for me. Detective Wellesley. I set it aside. I'd look at it after I wrote up my notes from the meetings I'd had with the victims the prior week and the three meetings I'd had the day before at the prison. That took most of the morning.

Lydia was in her office with the door shut. She did that when she was drafting motions or pulling together question lists for depositions. I didn't really know what she was working on. I did know better than to knock on her door.

I went up front and asked Karen, "Um, did you find out anything about that Hamlet person?"

"Of course I did. Which client did you say that was in reference to?"

"I didn't say. It's personal. I said that, didn't I?"

In a traditional law firm, every move, every question, indeed every thought, would be billed back to a client. Since we worked pro bono we weren't as careful about which case we were working on. That didn't mean personal work wasn't frowned upon—a fact that Karen drove home by raising an eyebrow.

But seriously, what did she think the wine was for?

"I found two private detectives named Hamlet Gilbody. Which seems ridiculous. I suspect they're father and son. Hamlet Senior works out of Chicago, he's nearing sixty. Hamlet Junior is licensed in Michigan. Do you know—"

"Hamlet Senior."

"He's been licensed for ten years. I called the Better Business Bureau. There were a couple of complaints, both about billing. I was also able to establish he's done a lot of work for a law firm called Lackerby, Leone and Cooke."

"Cooke, Babcock and Lackerby," I corrected her.

"Excuse me?"

Immediately, I realized my mistake. Cooke, Babcock and Lackerby was a law firm I'd done business with for years. It appeared that Hamlet Gilbody might have replaced me. They'd apparently lost one of their partners and reshuffled the names. Of course, I should not have corrected Karen. She was far too—

"I thought you were from Detroit."

"I am."

"So how come you think you know law firms in Chicago? In fact, you're a bartender. How do you know law firms at all?"

The way out of that came to me easily. "I've been reading one of Lydia's books, *Operation Tea & Crumpets*. That law firm is mentioned. A lot."

She was still suspicious, but she bought it. Or at least pretended to.

"When are you taking lunch?" I asked.

"Why?"

"I have some notes I need to—"

She held out her hand for the notes I was holding.

"I can do it, it's okay," I said.

"No, you can't. It's my job."

"Well, you're not my secretary."

"Assistant. And it's for Lydia, right?"

I nodded.

"It's not *personal*?"

"No."

"Then it's my job. At least until we get you a computer."

"Oh God, no. Could I maybe have a typewriter, though?"

She opened a desk drawer and pointed at a neat stack of plastic floppies. "I can't backup a typewriter. Besides, the last time I saw a typewriter for sale was at Goodwill."

I frowned. They couldn't be seriously thinking of getting me a computer. That was a disaster in the making.

"Um, also, I have some people I need to find."

She picked up a pen, and said, "Go ahead."

"Andy Showalter from the Downey area, Anne Whittemore also from Downey, and Candy Van Dyke possibly from Silver Lake."

Karen gave me a look, and said, "Sometimes I don't know why Lydia thinks you're a good investigator."

"What's that supposed to mean?"

"Candy Van Dyke? She's a real estate agent. She's got her face on every bus bench in Belmont Shore."

I should have known this. Not because I'm an investigator, but because my boyfriend is a real estate agent. Though to be fair, there were only two or three other real estate agents I could name, and only because Ronnie complained about how bad they were. Plus, Belmont Shore was the happening part of Long Beach for wealthy yuppies. I almost never went there.

I didn't bother trying to explain any of this to Karen. "Thanks. Can you find out where she lives?"

"I'm going to type up the notes for Lydia first."

"Great."

I went back to my area and took a few deep breaths. I'd nearly blown it with Karen—on so many different levels. For one, not knowing who Candy Van Dyke is, and for two, the law firm. Maybe I'd covered that, and maybe I hadn't.

Maybe I had bigger problems than what Karen did or didn't think about me. Hamlet Gilbody, for example. He worked for the law firm Jimmy English used. His granddaughter Deanna Hansen probably used the same firm. I owed Deanna a lot of money—and her investigator was close to finding me.

For the moment, the best thing to do was put it out of my mind. I mean, there wasn't much I could do about it right then, so it was best to not think about it. I decided to make a couple of calls. My first call was to Selma Martinez.

"Hi, this is Dom Reilly. I was out to visit you last week."

"Oh, yeah," she said, sounding disappointed.

"Sorry to bother you. I should have asked this question while I was out—"

"What's the question?"

"You said you were shown photos of men who might have been your attacker. Do you remember if all the men were Black?"

She left a long pause before replying. Then she said, "Only two of them were Black."

"Did Detective Wellesley give you any hints as to which one to choose?"

"Not hints exactly. I mean, she didn't say anything. But I did... I did feel like I knew which one she wanted me to choose."

I nodded, even though she couldn't see me. It wasn't a very useful answer.

"What about the in-person lineup, were all the men Black that time?"

Silence. Then, "That didn't happen. Why did you ask it that way?"

"What do mean?"

"You're asking like I've already said it happened. But I didn't. Do you think I'm lying? Are you trying to trick me?"

"I don't think you're lying." I did try to trick her.

"It was a very bad time. I try not to think about it."

"I'm sorry to bring all of this up."

"I think I remember saying no. I think Brenda wanted me to come to the police station and look at men, the way they do on TV. I said I couldn't. Even from behind a glass. I couldn't—"

"It's all right. You've been very helpful."

"Why do you think there was that kind of lineup?"

"Because Alan Dinkman remembers it."

After a long moment, she said, "Dios mio."

I said good-bye and then sat there for a long time thinking about what this meant or didn't mean. It appeared that Detective Wellesley had wanted Selma to go to an in-person lineup, and when Selma said no, she'd gone ahead and had the lineup anyway. But why? Did she think that by putting Alan through that and then telling him he'd been identified that he'd confess?

Did she show the copied photos to Selma before or after the lineup? Was she trying to make Alan feel like he'd been identified even before it had happened? These were things we'd need to ask Detective Wellesley.

I glanced at the file on Wellesley that Karen had put together and decided to make another call.

"Hi, I'm trying to reach Brysen Yates."

"He's not at this number anymore," a man said.

"Do you have a number where I could reach him?"

"I don't. I think he moved to Mexico. Or he might have gone backpacking in Europe. You never know with Brysen."

"His friend Larry Wilkes gave me this number. If you see Brysen—"

He broke up laughing. "This is Brysen. Sorry, I thought you were a bill collector. Who are you?"

"My name is Dom Reilly. I work for The Freedom Agenda. We are considering—"

"You're going to get Larry out of prison, and then you're going to get him paid, aren't you?"

"We haven't taken his case. I'm looking into it to see if there's anything we can use to get him a new trial. I visited him yesterday and he asked me to call you."

"Oh, isn't he sweet."

"He said you're the reason he wants to get out."

"I'm blushing." He barely took a breath before asking, "He's been in there nearly twenty years, he'll get a ton of money, won't he?"

"I don't know. We don't do civil litigation," I explained.

"But someone will. And he'll get millions of dollars."

"That much is unlikely. Anyway, first we have to take the case. Do you think he's innocent?"

"I was in Corcoran for two and a half years. I don't think I met a guilty man."

That was not reassuring.

"So, you're an innocent man, too?" I asked.

"Absolutely. I had this friend, total airhead. He knew I was in trouble and that my credit was dreadful, so he told me I could take out a card in his name. Then he forgot he said that, and it became this whole thing."

A thing called fraud.

"Oh, I hope Larry gets a lot of money. That would solve so many problems."

"Uh-huh."

"Don't get me wrong, I *love* Larry. I just love money more."

A few minutes later, I hung up. Sitting there I had the queasy feeling I was being taken advantage of. Larry Wilkes was probably as guilty as sin and the only reason he'd written to me was the distant possibility of getting a large pile of money. A lot of guilty inmates wrote to us for help. It was like playing the lottery. The odds were against them, but someone had to win. Why not them?

Lydia tapped me on the shoulder. "You look very serious," she said.

"Just confused. Karen's typing up my notes. I would have—"

"That's fine. Come into my office and tell me about your trip."

I grabbed a cup of coffee, my fourth, and followed Lydia into her office. As we made ourselves comfortable, I thought about where to start.

"Stu Whatley is a piece of work."

"Yes, he is. But he's not a rapist."

"He wants to sue the victim, the witness and the detective. Can he do that?"

"Theoretically, anyone can sue anyone. In order to get the big settlements, you have to show that a person's civil rights have been violated purposely."

"He was purposely put in prison."

"No, he was mistakenly put in prison. Mistakes don't lead to big payouts."

"Malfeasance."

"So, if Detective Wellesley knowingly put innocent men behind bars..."

"Then the settlement will be large."

"But she won't pay it."

"No. When the city reaches a settlement, police officers, witnesses, prosecutors, public defenders, everyone's indemnified. They'll be named in the lawsuit, but nothing will happen to them."

"So, he will be suing those women?"

"Only in theory. Even without the indemnification they don't have enough money to bother with. The big fish is Los Angeles County. What about Alan Dinkman, how was he?"

"Nice. Or at least nicer."

"Not why I wanted you to see him."

"He talked about doing an in-person lineup. But that's a problem because Selma Martinez talked about a photographic lineup, actually a Xerox lineup. I just called her and verified that she didn't do both."

"That's suspicious. Why do you think Wellesley would do that?"

"In the physical lineup, all the participants were Black. In the photo lineup only two of them were. I'm guessing she wanted Alan to think that his identification was more legit than it really was. Maybe she was hoping he'd confess. I don't know."

"What about the victims? Anything you didn't mention on Friday?"

Since I'd just written out the interviews and they were fresh in my mind, I said, "Yes. In the other two cases, the identification process is also fishy. Cammy Wainwright was shown five suspects who didn't fit her description and one who did. Joanne Yardley was put through a somewhat traumatizing lineup, where she was in the room with suspects in order to listen to them say abusive things to her."

"So none of the three had reliable identifications."

"I wouldn't say so."

"Good. I'll read though what you have when Karen's done. Have you read the file on Detective Wellesley?"

"I was about to."

"Look at it closely. I need to know her like a sister. Actually, I need to know her *better* than a sister."

CHAPTER TWELVE

April 9, 1996
Tuesday afternoon

After lunch, I sat down with the file on Detective Brenda Wellesley. It wasn't all that thick.

Brenda Wellesley was thirty-seven years old, divorced, no children. She had a BS in Criminal Justice from San Diego State University. Graduated 1982. She moved to L.A. and went through LAPD police academy in 1985, spending two years on patrol before being bounced up to detective the summer of 1987. That was important to know. Any mistakes she made in these cases were likely to be written off as inexperience, though it was just as likely an effort to prove herself. I doubted the LAPD was a very hospitable place for a woman.

But the next document I read made that seem untrue. It was a performance review from 1988 written by a Captain Bernard Latowski. Alan Dinkman's attorney, a man by the name of Simeon Keystone, had gotten it, though I couldn't see exactly how. It was the kind of document that if it wasn't private, it should be.

The review gave her top marks and said truly complementary things. The only criticism it gave was that she might be a bit too dedicated to the job. Though even as criticism it sounded like a compliment. It also made note that she was very good with victims. That, at least, squared with my interviews. I doubted Keystone used it at trial. In fact, its glowing nature might be the reason he got it.

Wellesley would have testified in each trial as the investigating officer. The prosecution would have used her to create a narrative of the crimes. The crime scene, the condition of the victim, the identification of the perpetrator and his arrest. The victim would testify last, covering some of the same ground but from a more emotional angle.

The transcripts from each of the trials sat in a cardboard box under my work area. I hadn't read them yet. I felt like it was better to get to know everything I could before I read them. It was hard to identify a lie if you didn't know the truth.

Speaking of which, I wondered why Keystone hadn't complained about not having a copy of the pictures Selma Martinez had been shown to identify her rapist. I set Wellesley's file aside and picked up my copy of Alan Dinkman's file. I flipped through it. I verified there were no copies of the pictures. There was also no letter to the DA asking for them. Of course, Alan probably told his attorney about the in-person lineup he'd participated in. So, Keystone wouldn't have asked for anything.

Okay, now it was time for the transcripts. I reached under the table and got my hands on the box. I started to pull it out but then stopped. Selma was probably excluded from the courtroom; most judges made that decision. Wellesley could have said anything about the identification and there would have been no one to contradict her. I pushed the box of transcripts back to where it had been. I'd read it later.

I went back to studying Detective Wellesley. There was a list of addresses that covered the last fifteen years. From 1981 through 1982 she lived on campus at San Diego State in the Maya dorm. From summer 1982 until spring of 1985, she lived at three different locations in the San Diego area. I wasn't familiar with San Diego, so the addresses didn't mean too much to me. What I did notice was the amount of time she spent at each address. She spent two years at the first address, but then six months at the second and only three at the third. I felt like that might mean something, but I didn't know what.

Then she moved up to Los Angeles for the academy. She lived in the Hollywood flats for about nine months. That made sense, she'd have been in the academy for six of that. I knew she worked out of Rampart, so the next address on Lucille in Silverlake made sense. She would have been ten minutes from work. Enviable in Los Angeles.

She stayed at the Lucille address for two years. Then from 1987 to 1991 she bounced around, nine months in one place, six in another. Six addresses in four years. I wondered if this had something to do with her divorce. Had the breakup happened around 1987? Had it taken her some time to get back on her feet? Were there other relationships involved? Ones that also went south? I tucked that away. It might mean nothing; it might mean a lot.

In February of 1994—just after the Northridge quake—she moved to the Fairfax area. I flipped through the file and noted that she'd transferred from Rampart Station to Wilshire around that time. Oakwood Avenue. Pretty nice area if I was thinking of the right place. She must have gotten a promotion and a raise.

At the back of the file, there were some printouts of newspaper articles that mentioned her. I was a little familiar with one of them. In it, she was being given credit for arresting Albert Wanderly, son of an old Hollywood actress who killed three gay men at different times: a costumer, an actor and an antique dealer. The murders happened in a short period and didn't have a sexual component. Some kind of spree killing, maybe? Another article showed her getting a commendation for her work on that case.

There were other articles where she was mentioned. A drive-by, the murder of a prostitute in Echo Park, and a stabbing in Silverlake. That didn't tell me very much.

Around four o'clock, Karen came back and handed me a stack of printouts. "Andy Showalter died in nineteen eight-five."

"How did he—"

"Suicide."

I nodded.

"I got an address for you on Candy Van Dyke. She's in Naples. And Anne Whittemore is now Anne Michaels. She lives in Bellflower. I've got her address—"

"Michaels? Her name is Michaels?"

"That's what I said."

"Okay. This is a possible case I'm checking out. The victim's name is Michaels."

"She's divorced. Her ex-husband's name is Paul Michaels."

"Shit."

****

As soon as I walked into our house, my cellphone chirped. It was Ronnie. "Hey, where are you?"

"I just got home. Where are you?"

"I want to show you something."

He gave me an address on 1st Street.

"What are you up to?"

"See you in a few minutes," he said, mysteriously.

I turned around and walked out to my Jeep. Sadly, I had a decent parking spot which I was unlikely to get again. I would have liked to know what it was I was getting myself into.

Part of me just wanted to stay home and ignore whatever it was Ronnie was up to. Of course, I knew it was a property of some sort attached to a scheme to make us oodles of money. I'd been through this twice with Ronnie, I was afraid I'd be long gone before whatever his plan was came to fruition. Unless the Hamlet Gilbody thing was nothing. Maybe it was nothing.

The building was called El Matador. It was a Spanish-style, courtyard building with terra cotta stucco and deep brown woodwork. There were lots of hand-painted tiles on the stairs and surrounding a fountain. Ronnie rushed over to me as soon as I walked into the courtyard.

"Where did you park? I've been watching for you."

"I'm on the other side of the park."

"But there are spaces down there?" He pointed further down the street.

I shrugged. "I didn't know that."

He gave me an uncomfortable look. He much preferred it when I was predictable.

"So, is this a condo?" I asked, to get him on track.

"Keep an open mind," he said, standing on his toes to kiss me. "It's an amazing deal. It doesn't look that way, but trust me, it is."

I followed him up an outside, private stairway to a unit in the front. He kept talking every step of the way. "This is the largest unit in the building. Two bedrooms, dining room, breakfast room. Large bathroom with both a shower and a bathtub. Cathedral ceiling in the living room, coved ceiling in the dining room... oh, and a tiny little balcony off the breakfast nook. You're going to die."

From experience, I knew it would take a lot more than a cathedral ceiling to kill me. He opened the front door, which was heavy, scarred wood with a tiny wrought iron covered window.

Seeing me look at it, he said, "We'll replace that with stained-glass so no one can look in."

Actually, I was wondering if there was a way to put an alarm on it. Stepping into the living room, which did have the afore-mentioned cathedral ceiling, I immediately saw that it also had two French doors: one in the living room and another in the dining room, both of which opened onto Juliet balconies, and both of which showed severe water damage on the hardwood floor where they'd let the rain in.

"I know it needs work," Ronnie said. "Try to use your imagination.

Wandering through the dining room I found myself in the very, very small kitchen.

"Can I imagine this room bigger?"

Opening the back door, which led onto a wide landing and a stairwell down to the alley, he said, "There's room here for a stackable washer and dryer, and some pantry shelves over there."

I looked at him skeptically. I didn't like that it was open to our neighbors' downstairs and anyone who managed to get in the alley door.

Reading my mind, Ronnie said "No one's going to steal our pasta."

Of course, that wasn't what I was worried about.

Ronnie pointed out the breakfast nook on the other side of the kitchen. It was tiny but charming.

"You're sure you want a condo? You don't want to hold out for a house?"

"It's not a condo, it's a co-op."

He'd explained the difference to me before, probably more than once. I didn't remember it though. Based on the look on my face, he added, "There are only one or two banks in the state that will finance a co-op, that drives the price down. They're only asking sixty-five thousand."

"And you think it's worth that?"

"I think it's worth far more than that... after I get on the board and convince them to convert the building to a condominium. We'll nearly double our money right there."

"How much do you think the renovation will cost?" I asked, looking at the harvest gold appliances and sagging piss-colored Formica counter tops.

"I'm planning to take an immediate second to pay for everything. We'll refinance into one payment down the road."

I noticed he didn't say how much he thought it would all cost.

"Isn't sixty-five thousand low? Even for a co-op?"

"There is one thing."

"Which is?"

"The previous owner died. Right there," he said, pointing at the kitchen sink.

"He died in front of the sink?"

There was an icky brown stain on the linoleum in the exact spot—

"The neighbors found him about a week later. He was still standing there."

That explained the stain.

"Standing?" I asked.

"Slumped? I don't know, they didn't take pictures. His family is in Ohio. They don't want to fly out, so they gave everything to the Salvation Army and now they want to unload this place ASAP. It's not even on the market yet."

"How much do you need?"

"Ten thousand, I think."

"How much do you have?"

"Five. Maybe six."

"Then you can't do it."

"I'm thinking, if we put both our names on the mortgage... We could get an FHA three percent down..."

"You know I don't have credit."

"That's not exactly true."

"Excuse me?"

"You have excellent credit."

"How did that happen?"

"You've got a VISA and a MasterCard in your wallet."

"You gave me those cards. I'm like a guest on your accounts."

"Yeah. I did tell you that."

"You took out credit cards in my name?"

"In both our names. And I make sure we always pay on time."

"That's kind of illegal."

I was about to get really angry, but then I stopped myself. He'd lied to me, tricked me even, possibly even committed fraud —but then I'd done those things to him. Many times. He knew I lied to him and somehow that gave him permission to do the same, didn't it?

I should have known he was lying to me about the credit cards. Or at least it should have occurred to me as a possibility. I mean, if someone hands you a credit card with your name on it, you should ask a few more questions than I had.

"You know I don't want my name on a deed, right?"

"I know you've said that. You've never said why exactly."

"A deed is a public record. Anyone can look up who owns what property."

He glared at me for a long moment. He'd known me long enough to figure out why I didn't want my name on a deed—even my fake name. I didn't want to risk being found. He also knew that whoever was trying to find me was someone I wouldn't talk about.

What he didn't know was that there was literally someone floating around town looking for me. I didn't think he had the name Dominick Reilly, so he wouldn't have searched public records, but he might have the name soon.

Ronnie had stopped glaring at me and was staring at the floor. We'd reached the outer boundary of our relationship, where all the risk resided. We could cross the boundary and who knows what might happen or we could stay where we'd been for years, safe and ignorant.

"When do you want to put in an offer?" I asked.

CHAPTER THIRTEEN

April 10, 1996
Wednesday morning

I was up early the next morning after having not slept well. The entire night my mind had been spinning. Anne Whittemore had married Paulie. That didn't make sense. He married her after she testified that she was his brother's fiancé. What was that courtship like? He couldn't have been *that* grateful she'd testified against Larry, right? And why hadn't Larry told me about this? He had to have known they'd gotten married.

And who was the woman I'd seen coming out of the Michaels' house? Was that Paulie's new woman? Was she the reason he and Anne divorced? An affair resulting in pregnancy is a solid reason to get divorced.

The other name that had my mind spinning was Hamlet Gilbody. Was I being stupid? Should I be long gone by now? I was settled. I'd put down roots. I should never have done that.

I tried to tell myself the fact that someone was in Long Beach asking about bartenders didn't mean much of anything. There were a lot of bartenders in Long Beach. There wasn't any reason to think he'd figure out which one used to be Nick Nowak.

"What's wrong?" Ronnie asked when I fully woke up.

"Nothing."

"You were clingy. All night. You're never clingy."

"I can't hug my boyfriend?"

"Not *that* much."

"Everything's fine," I lied.

I knew I was going to have to do something about Hamlet Gilbody. I also knew I wasn't going to do it that morning. I tried to put the whole thing out of my mind. Best to think about other things. Like Larry Wilkes and getting him out of prison. Around nine, I called The Freedom Agenda and told Karen I'd be working out of the office for most of the day.

"I did some more research on Anne Michaels," she said. "The guy she married, his brother was murdered by a guy named Larry Wilkes. Is that one of our cases?"

"Maybe. I'm talking to Lydia about it."

After a judgmental pause, she asked, "How does Anne Whittemore fits into this?"

"She was Larry's friend."

"Okay. She married Paul Richard Michaels in nineteen seventy-eight, about a year after Larry's trial ended. Their divorce has only been final for six weeks."

This raised a lot of questions. Larry said he'd told Anne to perjure herself and say she was engaged to Pete. How had she gone from a make-believe engagement to one brother to an actual marriage to the other? How much did Paulie know about her fake relationship with his brother?

"Thanks Karen, I appreciate it."

"Nothing says appreciation like V.S.O.P."

"I won't forget that."

A few minutes later, I drove out to Bellflower. It was two cities north of Long Beach. Anne Michaels lived in a sprawling, two-story, apartment complex on Woodruff. The building was a faded orange. I coasted down the 14400 block of Woodruff until I figured out which of the individual buildings she lived in. Then I found a parking space and walked into the building's small courtyard.

Her apartment was on the first floor on the side of the building away from Woodruff Avenue. The sky was cloudy and the temperature down around sixty—California frigid. I knocked on her door, and a few moments later a woman wearing a thick chenille robe answered the door.

I should have known. The woman in front of me was the same heavily pregnant woman I'd seen coming out of the Michaels house in Downey. That raised a lot of questions. If she and her husband divorced during her pregnancy, somebody did something very wrong.

"Hi. I'm Dom Reilly. I work for The Freedom Agenda. We're considering taking on Larry Wilkes as a client. I hoping you'll answer a few questions for me."

"Wait. What? Did Larry do something in prison? Did he hurt someone?"

"No. We represent the wrongly imprisoned."

"Larry wasn't wrongly imprisoned."

That brought things to a halt. "But—" I stopped and then started again. "Larry says he wouldn't have hurt Pete because they were in love."

"He needs to stop saying that. It got back to my in-laws. They don't believe it, of course. But it's a terrible thing to hear about your dead child no matter how untrue it is. I understand Larry wants to get out of prison, but telling a lie like that isn't going to help."

"He said you were his friend, that you knew about him and Pete. He said he told you to lie about their relationship in court."

"None of that's true. Pete was my fiancé. Larry was a friend of mine for a while. I think I'd know if they were fags together."

This was not what I'd been expecting. Obviously, one of them was lying, but was it Anne or Larry? I scrambled for a question that might tell me which one it was.

"Tell me about it. How did you go from being Pete's fiancé to Paulie's wife?"

She glared at me a moment. "My engagement to Pete had been a secret. No one knew about it until the trial."

"Why? Why was it a secret?"

"I was only seventeen and my parents wanted me to go to

college. Well, my mom did. My dad was relieved when I didn't. He didn't want to pay for it."

"Were you popular in high school?"

"You know, I think I've said everything I want to say."

She began to shut the door, but I did the old salesman's trick and shoved my foot in there. A very painful move.

"Move your foot."

"Tell me what happened to your marriage. Why did you and your husband get divorced?"

"None of your business."

"Is that not your husband's baby?"

"Fuck you," she said, as she pulled the door back and slammed it again. This time, I snatched my nearly broken foot back. The door shut. I stood there a moment, then limped to my car.

****

Unfortunately, when someone is in prison they can't receive phone calls, only make them. So I couldn't call Larry Wilkes and ask, "What the fuck?"

I found a McDonald's in Lakewood and had a couple of egg and sausage biscuits in the Jeep. After burning my tongue on their coffee, I tried to figure out what to do next.

The easiest thing to do would be to go see Candy Van Dyke. She lived in Naples, a beachside community with canals similar to Venice. My guess was they were developed by the same developer. It was a wealthy neighborhood, east of Long Beach and about twenty minutes away from Lakewood.

The thing was, I really wanted to talk to Paul Michaels. Though I didn't know where he lived, I did know where his parents lived. Of course, I should do some work for Lydia, which meant Candy Van Dyke. Or...

I pulled out the printouts Karen had given me. I looked up Andy Showalter's last address. It was on Arlington in Downey. I decided that's where I'd be going next. It wasn't that far away. Checking my *Thomas Guide*, I got onto Lakewood Boulevard and stayed on it for about ten minutes. Traffic was relatively light, since there were about four nearby freeways if you fancied sitting in traffic.

The Showalters had lived on Arlington Avenue a few houses down from Dennis the Menace Park, which was shoved up against the 5 freeway. The house was built on a narrow lot, which necessitated building the garage in front of the house rather than on the side. It made the house look ninety percent garage, and it may well have been. I walked up the driveway and found the front door. Over the address it said, THE NORTHS. Obviously, the Showalters didn't live here anymore. I could have turned and walked away but decided it might be worth it to see if the Norths had any idea what happened to the former owners. I rang the bell.

After a long time—I almost left—a woman opened the door and stared at me through the screen door. She was in her late fifties and had dyed her hair a very pale blonde. She wore a lot of makeup, especially for ten in the morning. A cigarette hung from her lower lip.

"You're late," she said.

I decided not to ask who exactly she'd been expecting.

"My name is Dom Reilly. I work for an attorney in Long Beach. We're looking for the family of Andy Showalter. You wouldn't happen—"

"Oh. I thought you were the plumber," she said, her disappointment was as thick as the sludge in her pipes.

"Do you know where the Showalters—"

"Andy was my son."

"Oh, I see. So... um, North? You've remarried?"

"No. We put that name up during Larry Wilkes trial so people would stop coming by the house and bothering us."

"I see. I hope I'm not bothering you."

"You are," she said. She just stood there looking at me, deciding. An ash fell off her cigarette onto her chest. She brushed it off quickly, then looked up and added, "But I suppose it's time."

She walked away from the screen door. I opened it and followed. The house smelled of over-cooked bacon and burnt toast. The living room was to my left. A large, yellow sectional wrapped in plastic filled the room. She'd gone through a swinging door into what I hoped was the kitchen. I had no great desire to squeak my way through a glass of water on that sofa.

Peeking my head through the swinging door, I saw that it was indeed the kitchen. Standing in front of a coffee maker which held a brewed pot of coffee, Mrs. Showalter poured herself a cup. Then she walked over to the table and sat down. Tentatively, as though approaching a wild animal, I walked into the kitchen and sat down across from her.

"It's time for what?"

Ignoring me, she asked, "Why do you want to know about my son?"

"You seem to already know the answer to that."

"My son was twenty-seven when he killed himself. Larry Wilkes' trial was the biggest thing that ever happened to him."

"Do you know why your son killed himself?"

A hard chuckle burst out of her. She took another cigarette out of this kind of purse which held the pack and had a loop on the outside for her butane lighter. I hadn't seen one of those in years.

"You want one?"

Of course I wanted one, but Ronnie would kill me.

"No, thanks."

"Why do people ask that question? Why did your son kill himself? Do you think there's ever a good reason for suicide?"

I wanted to say sometimes. Guilt, shame, a life so ruined it was unlivable. Those seemed like good reasons. I went with, "I suppose there isn't ever a good reason."

"Andy had a problem with depression. He was always a weird kid. Everything we did to make him normal just made him weirder. The older he got, the sicker he got. My husband left right before Andy graduated high school. My daughter doesn't speak to me, she resents the attention Andy got. I've had ten years with a therapist, and I can see that Andy's problems are probably not my fault. It's the probably that's hard to live with."

"I'm sorry this was so hard for you."

"Is. It *is* hard," she said, softly. Then she seemed to rally and shrugged like it didn't really matter.

"Did you know Andy had a gun?"

"No, of course not. As a teenager he was fascinated by Nazis. Cartoon villains. Monsters. He liked to draw. But that was all. We couldn't get him interested in anything else. Certainly not bathing. We'd never have allowed him to have a gun."

That created an interesting picture of Andy as the kid on the outside, the one who'd have been bullied, or at best shunned. For a moment, I wondered if he might be the one who'd killed Pete Michaels and then covered it up by testifying that he'd gotten the gun for Larry Wilkes. But that sounded too organized for the teenager she was describing.

"What was he like during the trial?"

"He didn't do well with stress. By then, we'd gotten him to a psychiatrist. He was taking medication, but it was hard to get him to take it regularly. It would start to work, and he'd stop. My therapist told me that for some people sick is normal. That we're asking them to take medication and not be normal. I think he thought that was helpful. It's not."

"Andy testified to supplying Larry Wilkes with the gun he used to kill Pete Michaels. Do you think that's true?"

"I was at the trial. I know what he said."

"Did you believe it?"

"He said he went to Compton and bought the gun from a drug dealer in a park. The way he talked about it, the way he told the story, it sounded like something he'd made up. His drawings. They were stories. I've never been able to figure out if that makes it more likely or less likely that it was true."

"Did you talk to him about it after the trial?"

"Yes, of course. I tried many times. He became increasingly paranoid, and, in his fantasies, he was always being pursued, threatened. We once had a long conversation about the drug dealers he believed were doing business in our living room while we slept. He was trying to reassure me that they'd promised him we were safe."

"You think that his whole involvement in Larry Wilkes' trial could have been part of a paranoid fantasy?"

"I think so, yes."

"But there's no way to prove it, is there?"

"None that's occurred to me."

"To be clear, you think it's possible Andy made up the whole thing? Do you also think it's possible that someone might have manipulated him?"

"It would have had to be someone who knew Andy well, well enough to understand his fantasies. I don't know who that could be."

"Thank you. You've been very helpful."

"You don't think the Wilkes boy killed his friend, do you?"

"No, I don't."

"Me neither."

****

It was lunchtime when I got to The Freedom Agenda office, but I wasn't hungry. The breakfast biscuits I'd eaten had turned into hockey pucks in my belly. When I walked in, Karen was about to take a bite of what looked like a very yummy turkey sandwich. She stopped before putting the sandwich in her mouth.

"You want something, don't you?"

"How did—I can wait until you have your lunch."

"No, just ask."

"How would I get a transcript for a case we haven't taken yet?"

"California?"

"Yes."

"How old is the trial?"

"About nineteen years."

She shook her head. "Court reporters destroy their records after ten years, that's usually the easiest route. The court itself will have a transcript. They keep their records until the accused is a hundred years old. You'd have to go there and pay whatever they're charging for copying, which is usually around twenty-five cents a page."

Even without knowing how long the trial went on, I knew it would be a lot of pages. It was going to cost hundreds of dollars which I might not ever be reimbursed for.

"Shit."

"Is that Dom?" Lydia called from her office.

"Yes."

"I need to talk to you."

Karen finally took that bite of her sandwich. I walked down the short hallway to Lydia's office. She was reading through a document on her computer screen. It looked dense and very legal. Without taking her eyes off it, she asked, "You read through Brenda Wellesley's file?"

"I did."

"Good. I'm deposing her Friday morning at nine in Edwin's conference room downtown. I'm hoping you can come."

Even if the deposition took three hours, which it wouldn't, I'd be back in time for work at The Hawk. I was also too curious about what Wellesley had to say for herself to refuse the offer.

"Sure, I can do that."

"Good. What are you working on?"

Suddenly, I felt very guilty. I should have been able to tell her about a meeting I'd had with Candy Van Dyke. Except I didn't have that meeting. I had two meetings on a case we hadn't taken yet. I tried avoiding the issue.

"I'm meeting with Candy Van Dyke this afternoon. The witness against Stu Whatley."

Lydia turned around stared me down. "And what did you do this morning?"

"I did a couple of interviews on the Larry Wilkes thing."

"A case we haven't taken yet."

"No. We haven't."

"Anything?"

"I talked to a woman named Anne Whittemore—well, Anne Michaels now. She was Larry's friend in high school. He said he told her to lie and say that the victim was her fiancé. She denies that, says she really was his fiancé. And get this… after the trial she married the victim's brother."

"You think she's lying?"

"I don't know. I also met with a woman named Showalter. Her son testified that he gave the murder weapon to Larry. But his mother doesn't believe that's what happened."

"What does he say?"

"He killed himself in eighty-five."

"So, not much."

"He had a history of mental illness. His testimony may have been part of his fantasy life."

"You do realize that creates a problem. The fact that he was mentally ill doesn't automatically impeach his testimony. And the fact that he's dead doesn't help. There's nothing I can work with."

"I know."

"You want to keep looking, don't you?"

"I do."

"Go ahead. Just be at the deposition on Friday."

"Deal."

CHAPTER FOURTEEN

April 10, 1996
Wednesday evening

Ronnie had appointments until nine, so I decided to go out to Downey again. I wanted to see Paulie Michaels. But I didn't know where he was. I knew a call to information would be useless, there had to be a hundred Paul Michaels in Los Angeles. I decided the best thing to do was to visit his parents first and ask how to get in touch with him. I headed to Downey.

The house on Amorita was still the color of putty and there was still a Big Wheel out front. The only thing new was a ten-year-old Camaro the color of orange soda sitting in the driveway. Unlike the Mercury station wagon, it didn't have any bumper stickers. In fact, it was spotless and looked like it had been recently waxed. It was someone's pride and joy.

I walked up the dried-out lawn to the front door and knocked. A minute or so later, an older woman opened the door. She was in her early seventies and wore a dingy house coat.

"Hi," I said, in my friendliest voice. "I'm trying to find Paulie Michaels. You wouldn't have his address, would you?"

"Who are you?"

"We went to high school together. I'm on the reunion committee and his invitation came back—"

She turned away from me, nearly shutting the door in my face, and called out, "Paulie! Someone to see you." Then she wandered away from the door, which I was happy about. Her son would probably know that we didn't go to high school together. If only because I was about a decade—

And then he was standing in the doorway with a quizzical look on his face. Paulie was losing his white-blond hair, but other than that he still looked like a high school jock. Well, a high school jock who was aging very, very well. He wore a Chevrolet T-shirt—which was very tight and showed off his strong arms and taut belly—a pair of surfer shorts and flip flops.

"What can I do for you?"

His eyes were a mesmerizing blue.

"Are you Paulie Michaels?"

"Just Paul, if you don't mind."

"Sure. Paul. Can you come outside for a minute?"

He stepped outside, anxious and defensive. He tried not to let me see it, but he failed.

"I work for The Freedom Agenda in Long Beach. We've been contacted by Larry Wilkes. He claims he's innocent and I'm just checking that out."

"Why? Are you going to get him out of prison?"

"If we're able to prove he's innocent."

"This doesn't have anything to do with me."

That was interesting. Why hadn't he said that Larry was guilty? Did he think Larry was innocent? And if he did, why hadn't he done anything about it?

"Do you know something about Larry's conviction? Was he wrongly convicted?"

"I don't know anything."

"I met your wife."

"Ex-wife."

"Yeah, you managed to make that happen quickly. Do you mind telling me what happened?"

He glared at me a moment, then said, "It doesn't have anything to do with Pete's murder."

That convinced me it did. I tried to get things on a friendlier basis by asking, "Why don't you like being called Paulie?"

"Makes me feel like a little kid." His arms seemed to get tighter across his chest. "Look, my dad's not well. I shouldn't leave him alone with my mother. It's too much for her."

"Did your wife cheat on you?"

Anger flashed and he shook his head. "She's not like that."

"But she did lie to you, didn't she?"

"I'm going in the house now."

"If you could just give me a few more minutes. Tell me about your brother."

He began walking back to the house.

I said, "I'll just come back."

He stopped, with a heavy sigh he asked, "What do you want to know?"

"Anything. I'd like to get a picture of who he was."

"He was a great older brother. Always took care of me. He was funny, always cracking jokes. Class clown I guess."

"Did he have a lot of girlfriends?"

"Yeah. The girls liked him. I mean, he played the field. And why shouldn't he? He never got past twenty." He was a bit more defiant than he needed to be.

"Was it a surprise when you found out he'd been engaged to Anne?"

"Yes." His throat suddenly seemed to get dry, and he cleared it. It took a few tries.

"But you believed her?"

"There was no reason not to. I mean, there wasn't any other reason for Larry Wilkes to kill my brother."

"What did you think of Larry? Before your brother was killed, I mean."

"I didn't think much of him at all. He was just a kid in my class. I guess he was smart. He wasn't great at sports, so he wasn't part of my gang. I suppose I thought he was a loser."

"Did you think he was gay?"

He bristled. "It was different then. Yeah, we called some kids faggots. We called each other faggots. That doesn't mean we thought anyone was *gay*. That kind of thing happened somewhere else."

A half an hour away in Los Angeles, half an hour in the other direction in Long Beach. These places had long gay histories. He was talking as though Downey was smack in the middle of Kansas. He would have known...

"So, before Anne there was no one specific?"

"I said he played the field, didn't I?"

"You knew girls he had sex with?"

"I knew he had sex with girls, I didn't know which ones."

"You knew that because he'd disappear, and you wouldn't know where he was?"

"He wouldn't talk about the girls he was with. He was a gentleman. That's what he was like."

"You both played tennis."

"Yeah. We played doubles together."

"Why tennis? Why not baseball or football?"

"We played those, just not as well. I mean, Pete was the one who was really good at tennis. I was just okay. He could have had a scholarship to Loyola Marymount, but my parents don't believe in that kind of thing."

"College?"

"They don't trust people who are too smart."

"What about you?"

"I'm going to send my kids to college. Look, I really do need to go back inside."

I was going to lose him in a moment, so I decided to play a hunch. "Your wife lied about being Pete's fiancé, didn't she? You just found out, that's why you divorced her."

His eyes got narrow and mean. He said, "You don't know what the fuck you're talking about."

But I was pretty sure I did.

Driving back to Long Beach I felt like I had more questions than answers. I understood why Anne had told the lie about being

Pete's fiancé in the first place—Larry had told her to. But why keep it up for twenty years? I mean, okay, she'd used the lie to snag herself a husband. So why did she suddenly tell him the truth? And if she had told him the truth, why didn't she tell me the truth?

Did I really believe Pete's parents didn't want him to go to college? There are people in the world who are suspicious of intelligence. That would be why Adlai Stevenson never became president. Egghead is hardly a compliment. But Pete could have gone anyway, he was nineteen, twenty years old. It shouldn't have mattered what his parents thought.

Paulie knew more about everything we talked about. I was sure of it. Clearly, he was close to his brother. So wouldn't he have known, or at least suspected, that Pete was gay? I wasn't sure I believed that he didn't know Larry Wilkes was gay. It's true that straight people can be oblivious, but high school kids, they see things like that and then use those things to destroy you. He would have known.

And if he knew Larry and Pete were spending time together, he could have guessed. But did he *know*? Were Larry and Pete as discreet as Larry thought? Even if Paulie didn't know then, he had to know now. So why not talk about it?

****

The news was full of the Unabomber who'd just been turned in by his brother, Strom Thurmond who'd announced he was going to run for senator again at 93, and Tammy Faye Messner who'd just had cancer surgery in full makeup. Those stories were on the radio as I drove up to Downey.

The courthouse was on Imperial Highway and looked like a four-story, concrete computer punch card. I got there at eight-twenty-five, which had meant I'd gotten up before seven. When I left, Ronnie woke up briefly, mumbled that he loved me, and rolled back over.

The clerk's office was in the back of the first floor of the courthouse. The door was still locked. I waited ten minutes for them to open. That was the first stumbling block. The second was the request form.

I had to fill it out as though we'd already taken the case, putting down Lydia's name as attorney. It asked for her bar membership number, which I did not know. It also wanted to know the date of Larry's trial, which I only knew in the most general sense. It was sometime early in 1977. I didn't know the case number nor the presiding judge. I put down a reason in the broadest of terms "INVESTIGATING THE POSSIBLE INNO-CENCE OF DEFENDANT"

The clerk was a woman of about sixty. A sign next to the window said, MRS. WILLARD. She wore a shirt dress with a small, flowered pattern. Over that, a pink cardigan. Her hair was grey and permed around the edges so that it curled away from her face. I was pretty sure it was a popular style when she was young. She found something she liked and stayed with it.

I could tell she was about to give me trouble over the lacking form, so I launched into a very honest explanation. "I work for The Freedom Agenda, and I went to see Larry Wilkes on Monday. He's interested in our taking his case, and I thought it might be easier for us to decide if we looked at the transcript."

She got a very sour look on her face, and said, "It's public information. What kind of case is it?"

"Murder."

"A case like that could run over a thousand pages. You'll need to pay the copying costs. Twenty-five cents a page. It should be in the range of two hundred and fifty to three hundred dollars."

"Do you take credit cards?"

They did. Then she told me it would take about two hours and suggested I wait at the snack bar. The practiced way she said it made me wonder if she got a kickback for every customer she sent there.

Also on the first floor, I found the snack bar off to the right after you came in. It was a counter with half a dozen tables in front of it. I ordered coffee and a bear claw. The coffee was bitter and the bear claw stale. I ate them anyway.

I asked myself, what I was expecting to find? If the prosecutor was any good, he'd have the first officer on the stand taking the jury through the discovery of the crime and the investigation of the scene. Since they'd only ever considered Larry, it would be interesting to see what exactly led to that, if anything. I wondered what the officer would have to say about Larry's demeanor. The police placed too much emphasis on this. If they didn't think you were upset enough—or too upset—you were instantly moved up the suspect list.

Anne Whittemore. I was interested in reading her testimony. And the Showalter boy. But who else? Who else testified? Was there forensic testimony? Did Larry testify? I doubted that. He would have said so. And it was rarely a good idea. Did he have any character witnesses? Did he put up any defense at all?

I went back after an hour and a half. There were three people in front of me, but when the clerk saw me, she put three boxed reams of paper onto the counter. This was going to be pricey.

When it was my turn, I was presented with a bill for three hundred and twenty-five dollars. I handed over my credit card. I carried the boxes out to my jeep, already planning to take them to The Freedom Agenda, pull out three maybe four giant note-books from the supply closet, a three-hole punch, and get organized.

I put the boxes on the floor on the passenger's side. I couldn't resist opening the top one. I flipped through. I knew exactly what I was looking for and found it on page 215. Andy Showalter's testimony. I skipped through the basic who are you and where do you live questions, and started reading with:

"Can you tell the court how you know the defendant?"

"We go to high school together."

"You've graduated high school."

"Yes, yes, I have. We went to high school together."

"You were friends?"

"No."

"Then why do you think he'd ask you to get him a gun?"

"I don't know. Maybe he thought it wouldn't matter if I got caught."

The defense attorney complained about that and there was

some back and forth, including a conference which was not recorded. The judge said:

"Andy, try not to guess at things. Yes and no are the best answers. Keep your answers brief."

"When did Larry ask you to get him a gun?"

"It was in the morning."

"What was the date?"

"I don't remember. At the beginning of that September. The September when Pete died. I'm sorry, I'm guessing—I don't mean to."

"This is different, Andy," the judge said.

"Is it?"

I reached into the glove compartment and took out a pen. I made a note that Larry was not in Downey at the beginning of September. He was in Santa Barbara. Did his lawyer follow that up?

"What did he say when he asked you?"

"He said he needed a gun because some guys were picking on him. I felt bad for him. I'm sorry, I shouldn't say things like that. But I did feel bad for him."

"Tell us about buying the gun."

"It was forty bucks."

"Where did you buy it?"

"I drove to Compton and bought it in a park."

"And why did you go to Compton?"

"Larry wanted a gun that couldn't be traced."

"And this was how long before the murder?"

"Couple weeks."

There it was, twice. I skipped down to the cross examination to see if Larry's attorney did anything with that. The defense attorney asked:

"You testified that you bought the gun in a park in Compton. Why did you go there?"

"To buy a gun."

"Yes, but how did you know to go to Compton?"

"I guess I heard a rumor."

"The person you bought the gun from, what did he look like?"

"He was, I guess, about twenty, skinny—"

"Black."

"Um, yes, black."

"So, you went to a black neighborhood to buy an illegal gun."

"Yes."

"Do you remember the young man's name?"

"He didn't tell me."

"Not even a first name?"

"No."

"Did the police take you back to the park to look for him?"

"No."

"Can you tell us exactly where the park is?"

"It's in Compton."

"Where in Compton?"

"I don't know the street names."

"Could you take us there?"

"Maybe."

"Maybe? So you're not sure?"

"No. I'm not sure."

"Do you have a car?"

"No."

"How did you get to Compton then? Did your mommy drive you?"

The prosecution objected to that and the judge sustained it. The defense attorney apologized to the court.

"Andy, how did you get to Compton?"

"I borrowed my mother's car."

"Will she confirm that?"

"She didn't know. I waited until she was asleep."

"You waited until your mother was asleep, took her car, drove to Compton, found a black guy in a park, and paid him forty dollars for a stolen gun? And then you gave it to the defendant?"

"Yes. That's what happened."

"Why?"

"What do you mean why? He asked me to."

"Why did you do it?"

"I don't understand the question."

"You said you're not friends with Larry Wilkes. So why did you take your mother's car, drive to Compton, and buy a stolen gun for him?"

"I wanted to be friends."

"You do know this isn't how you make friends."

The prosecutor complained about that not being a question. The judge agreed.

"Why did Larry come to you?"

"I don't know what you're asking me?"

"Did you have a reputation for getting kids illegal guns?"

"No."

"Then why you?"

"I don't know. He just asked."

I skipped ahead, hoping to find the part where the defense attorney asked about when the request was made. I wanted to know what the kid said when confronted with the fact that Larry wasn't even in town when this was supposed to have happened. That what he was testifying to wasn't even possible. But the question was never asked.

I didn't need to skip ahead to the summation to know how the prosecution was going to turn this around. The DA was going to tell the jury that Andy Showalter was an unlikely person to ask to get a gun... and that's why he was asked. The fact that they weren't friends made him the perfect person for this task. That Andy's isolation and desire for the approval of someone popular like Larry made him vulnerable. The fact that Larry wasn't exactly popular himself is something the DA would gloss over.

And the fact that Andy wasn't telling the truth, which was obvious to me, ended up not mattering at all.

CHAPTER FIFTEEN

April 11, 1996
Thursday afternoon

I was familiar with Naples. Ronnie and I went there every Christmas. It was a tradition. For the holiday, the neighborhood went all out so it was worth spending a Thursday night in early December wandering around gaping at the amazing decorations. I wondered if we'd ever gaped at Candy Van Dyke's place. The address was East Naples Lane, but that was little more than an alley. The houses faced the canal, separated from the water by a sidewalk. Many of them had slips with boats moored there, waiting. Rarely used.

The house was a starkly modern box with few windows on the alley and nothing but windows on the canal side. I walked down the sidewalk along the canal until I found the front door. I rang the bell.

A few moments later, Candy opened the door. She was nearly forty, or perhaps just past. She wore a severely cut suit in a large black-and-white herringbone tweed. Her glasses had red frames and covered most of her face. They quickly reacted to the sunshine by turning gray.

"You're Dom Reilly?"

"I am."

"Come in, come in," she said as she walked away from the front door. I stepped into the house, which was elegantly furnished in creams and beiges. Not to my taste—or rather if I had taste it wouldn't be this. I didn't want to live in terror of spilling something.

"I knew who you were the minute you said your name on the phone. I know Ronnie. I'm with Century 21. I do Seal Beach, Sunset Beach, Huntington Beach. I almost never get to work with Ronnie," she frowned dramatically, "but I see him at events and things. You're always working. He's such a little charmer. You're a lucky man."

"I am."

"It's so odd that you're involved with this whole mess about Joanne's rape. Poor thing. I've heard she won't leave her house. Is that true?"

"I don't know. I spoke to her there. She didn't say."

"Brenda came to see me about a month ago. Of course, I feel terrible. I know it's afternoon, but would you like coffee? I have a pot already brewed. I drink it all day long... can you tell?"

"Um, sure, why not?"

"Come into the kitchen. I've been in this house for almost three years. There's so much I'd like to do to it, but I never seem to have the time!"

The house—which was flawless—covered almost every inch of the property, and the kitchen, situated between the living room and a family room, was spacious.

"Have a seat at the bar," she said. There was a breakfast bar on the family room side of the kitchen. I took a seat while she poured coffee into a gigantic mug. "Cream, sugar?"

"Just black."

She set the cup down in front of me.

"So, what exactly can I do for you?"

"I work for the attorney who represents Stu Whatley, the man you identified as Joanne Yardley's attacker."

"Oh, God. Should I send him an apology?"

He didn't seem the sort who'd appreciate that.

"What I'd like to talk about is Det—Brenda. Do you

remember if she influenced your identification of Mr. Whatley in any way?"

"I'm not sure. I remember thinking at the time that she was ambitious. And that was good. We needed more women police officers. We still do. Don't you think?"

I nodded.

"I'm glad you agree. I don't know if a man would have been as empathetic. Don't think I don't like men, I love men. It's just... Men are good at lots of things. I don't know that empathy is one of them."

"The man you saw coming out of Joanne Yardley's house the day she was raped—"

"Well, obviously, he looked a lot *like* Stu Whatley. I described him to Detective Wellesley the day of the rape. A few days later she came by with a photo. A mug shot. She told me he'd been arrested for rape before. She said he was a real bad guy. I don't remember if she said those things before or after I identified him."

"And in court?"

"By that time, I was sure it was him. I mean, they showed me other photos. I became more and more convinced. Oh God this is horrible. That man, he did rape *someone*, didn't he?"

"He was arrested before but pled to a lesser charge."

"So he *might* be a rapist?"

"The only thing we know for certain is that he didn't rape Joanne."

"Oh, God."

I took a sip of my coffee—it was good—and watched her face. She was reconfiguring how she thought about things. How she thought about what she'd done.

"This all means there's someone out there who looks a great deal like Stu Whatley, someone who *is* definitely a rapist."

"I suppose it does. So, you feel like Brenda could have influenced your identification of Stu Whatley?"

"Yes, that's the right way to put it."

****

As I was leaving Candy Van Dyke's, I called Ronnie and asked if he wanted me to pick anything up on my way home.

"There's nothing on television tonight. Can you get a movie?"

"Sure. What are we having for dinner?"

"I went to Ralph's and got some stuff. I'm thinking stir-fry. It has to be fast. I have a client at seven-fifteen."

"Are you sure you want a movie?"

"The house is in Rose Park. They're not going to make an offer, so I'll be home by eight. I promise."

"What movie do you want?"

"*Splash.*"

"We saw that at the movies."

"I know. I want to see it again."

I agreed to look for it, though I had little interest in seeing it again. Then I told him I loved him and said good-bye.

Broadway Video was next to the Park Pantry and across the street from the coffee shop and Star of Siam. Our house was close enough that we could walk to the video store and often did. I parked a half a block north on Junipero and walked back to the video store.

The new releases were next to the door when you walked in, along the window looking out at Broadway. They did not have *Splash*, though there was a poster for it hanging over the checkout counter next to the price chart. They had *The Usual Suspects*; *Showgirls*; *Mary Poppins*; *To Wong Fu, Thanks for Everything Julie Newmar* (we'd seen it twice); *Copycat*; *The Three Caballeros*—I was trying to decide when something drew my eye.

Across the street, standing in front of Star of Siam, was a round, little man of around sixty. What hair he had, which wasn't much, was silver and overgrown. He wore a green Army jacket with a lot of pockets. It suggested he had the mistaken idea he was some kind of action hero. I swear he was staring directly at me, though I wasn't sure he could see me. I went back to looking at the video boxes, except I wasn't looking at them at all. I picked one up and pretended to read the back but held it so I could look out at this man.

Hamlet Gilbody?

Which was ridiculous. There were half a million people in Long Beach, more if you counted the tourists who swarmed the Queen Mary. There was no reason to think this was the private eye from Chicago who was looking for me—other than the fact that he was the right age and dressed like a cartoon detective. And that he was standing there staring at the video store.

I "read" three more video boxes. He didn't budge. Where had he come from? Had he followed me from The Freedom Agenda? Did he know that I worked there? Or had he simply not believed Cindy and decided to hang around in this area until he spotted someone who looked like me?

Blindly, I picked up a video box and took it to the counter. I gave the clerk my video card and then a five. He gave me a buck and some coins in change. Carefully, I did not look out the window to my right.

I was given the video in a small, black plastic bag. I turned and walked to the front door. As I pushed the door open, I allowed myself to glance across the street. He was still there. Watching me.

Turning left, I walked down to Junipero. I turned to cross Broadway. The light was with me, so I stepped into the crosswalk. I looked both ways so that I could see what Hamlet was doing. He'd moved a few feet closer to me, now standing next to a blue Dodge Neon that looked like a rental. I hurried down Junipero and got into my Jeep.

Pretending to adjust the rear-view mirror, I checked to see if he'd come around the corner. He had. He was about twenty feet away. I turned the car on and then pulled out onto Junipero. In the mirror, I watched as he turned and ran back to his car.

I drove down 3rd, wondering what he might do next. Was he really going to try to come after me? There was a lot of traffic on Broadway to deal with, he'd never catch up. I immediately turned onto Lowena, which was L-shaped and fed onto 3rd. He wouldn't know where I'd gone.

I zipped around to 3rd, where I encountered traffic. There were traffic signs at the intersection of Junipero and 3rd, but there was still traffic coming from three directions in a steady flow. I had to wait.

At Junipero, across from the big church, there was a cut-through that connected to 3rd. It required that you yield but not stop. Just as I might have had a chance to pull out, the Neon came through the cut-through and sped down the street toward me. I watched as he drove by me. For a brief moment, we looked at each other.

Deciding I couldn't wait any longer, I pulled out onto 3rd and then took an almost immediate left—dangerously crossing traffic—into Carroll Park. The neighborhood was one of Ronnie's favorites and we walked it frequently. The houses were all about the age of ours, though grander, and I could tell that Ronnie dreamed of owning one someday. The blocks were circular, and on the map you could see that the neighborhood was laid out as a lopsided 88.

I came in at the bottom of an eight, crossed across the middle, and drove along the top of the eight on the right. I was hoping there was an alley I could cut down and get to 4th without going back to Junipero. As I rounded the top of one eight, I realized there were no alleys. Only sidewalks and walkways smaller than a car. I hurried across the top of the second eight and found myself back on Junipero. I looked to my left, hoping the Neon hadn't had time to turn around and look for me. I didn't see it anywhere, so maybe it hadn't.

Hurrying north on Junipero, I turned right when I got to 4th. I wanted to speed down the street as quickly as possible, but there was too much traffic. The neighborhood was primarily residential with a few businesses sprinkled along the way. I passed the Ralph's we sometimes went to. I kept a close eye on my mirrors, waiting for the Neon to appear. My mind was going much faster than the Jeep. Did he know where I worked? Did he know where I lived? How had he found me?

No, he didn't know either. He couldn't. He'd found me by hanging around the intersection of Broadway and Junipero with its four or five popular businesses. And just then, as I waited at the red light at 4th and Redondo, I saw him pull up three cars behind me.

He'd found me. The light went green, and I turned north on Redondo. It was a wider street, two lanes on each side. In my mirror, I saw that he pulled into the left lane and was attempting to get closer.

My first impulse was to floor it and try to get away from him, but I realized I was better off if I didn't seem to be running from him. He'd be easier to lose if he was uncertain whether I'd seen him or not. I continued down 4th, passing Loma, Termino, and finally getting to Ximeno. At that intersection, I turned left.

The blue Neon had gotten closer; not because he wanted to, but the cars between us had peeled off. I could tell he was moving slowly, hoping not to be noticed. The neighborhood we were in was very residential until we got to 7th Street. There I sat at a red light looking over at the high school. To my right a small strip mall. Ronnie and I owned a small house on Bennett just a block from the school.

The light turned and I went through the intersection, then up a slight hill and across Anaheim Street. The neighborhood was not as nice, a bit more industrial with some houses here and there. I passed Bally's; the car wash was on my right. And then I was in the traffic circle. The whole reason I'd driven in this direction.

A Toyota Tercel had gotten between me and the Neon. I got in the innermost lane of the circle. Los Coyotes Diagonal was first, then Lakewood, then PCH going west, then Ximeno where I'd come in. I went around the full circle. The Tercel had veered off onto Lakewood. The Neon was still behind me. An old VW Beetle had gotten in front of it—that's how slow he was going— and a minivan was in the outer lane. He was boxed in. Exactly what I'd been hoping for.

When Los Coyotes Diagonal came around again, I veered across the outer lane in front of the minivan, causing the driver to slam on their brakes and lay on the horn. I floored it. The Jeep sped down Los Coyotes. Never was I so grateful for the 6-

cyclinder engine in what was basically a very small vehicle. When it needed to go, it did.

I hit sixty, getting lucky at the first light. It was green. I changed lanes a few times to get around slower traffic. I was afraid to look in my rearview mirror, though I was fairly certain the Neon had to make another trip around the circle. Just past Polly's Pies, I zipped through a caution light. There wasn't another light for a long way. Quickly, I covered the distance and got to the big intersection with Stearns and Clark. Red light.

The car in front of me had already stopped, so there was no way I could run the light. I waited there. Looking in the rearview mirror, I didn't see the Neon. I doubted that he could move as fast as I could. He'd had to go around the circle again, and then if one of the first two traffic lights had stopped him, he'd be having a hard time catching up to—

The light turned. Still no sign of him. I got through and then was able to zip around the car in front of me. I was flooring it again, up to fifty, sixty, another long stretch without traffic lights. I knew exactly where I wanted to go. I just had to get through one more intersection, which was green. I flew through the intersection and then up the ramp to the 405 going south. There was no sign of the Neon. I'd lost him.

I upped my speed to seventy-five and flew down the 405. Before I knew it, I was at the intersection with the 605. I could have gone north for a while but kept going south. I could have gotten on the 22 and connected to 7th Street to go home, but I stayed on the 405. I'd lost him, but I wanted to really lose him.

I was nearly to Irvine before I felt comfortable turning around. It was almost seven thirty. I'd missed dinner. Ronnie was meeting with his clients in Rose Park.

Forty-minutes later I was back in Long Beach. I pulled up in front of our little house on Bennett. I parked across the street and for the first time in two hours allowed myself to breathe deeply.

The house was just four small rooms and a garage. Ronnie and I had bought it in 1993 for a hundred and forty-five thousand dollars. We'd only been seeing each other a few months, though Ronnie had been clear about what he wanted right from the start. When he asked me to move in with him, he explained the deal like this:

"I can use my commission as part of the down payment, then I have another five thousand I can put in, that brings us to about six percent down. If we can get to ten percent, I don't think the two of us will have any problem getting a mortgage."

"I can put in seventy," I said.

"Seventy dollars? Are you trying to be funny?"

"I mean seventy-thousand."

"You're teasing. That's not very nice."

"I don't want to be on the deed, so I can't be on the mortgage."

"Stop it. You don't *really* have seventy-thousand dollars."

"I do. It was an inheritance. I've never touched it."

"And now you want to give it to me to buy a house your name isn't going to be on? That doesn't make sense."

"I trust you."

"You shouldn't."

"You're not trustworthy?"

"I am. But in general boyfriends aren't."

That made me smile. "Ronnie, I'm already aware of that."

"I think it's time you started telling me about your past."

"That's not a good idea."

"I'm supposed to take seventy-thousand dollars from you and not ask questions?"

"That sounds like a deal to me."

"I'm going to have to think about it."

He thought about it for a few days and then he agreed. Sixteen months later, he took a second on the Bennett house to put fifty thousand down on the 2nd Street house. He rented the little house to a cute, young lesbian couple named Brown and Melissa, who had a three-year-old boy they fostered.

Getting out of the Jeep, I walked up to the front door and knocked. When Melissa answered, I asked if I could rent back the garage for a week or two. I offered her fifty bucks a week in cash. When I asked her not to mention it to Ronnie, the price went up to a hundred. She's nobody's fool. I agreed to her price if she'd throw in a ride home.

I parked the Jeep in the garage, grabbed the video, the box of Larry Wilkes transcripts, and my cellular phone (Ronnie had called twice but I'd ignored the calls.) Melissa drove me home. There wasn't a lot to say on the ride. I asked after Brown and their kid, whose name I couldn't remember, and then we fell into silence. She dropped me off a couple blocks from my house.

I scanned the neighborhood for the blue Neon. I didn't think Hamlet Gilbody knew where I lived, but I couldn't be a hundred percent certain. I didn't see anything suspicious.

When I walked in the house, Ronnie immediately said, "Where've you been?"

"I had to do an interview for Lydia. Last minute. Sorry."

I held out the black video bag. He took it and pulled out the tape.

"*Babe*? You brought home a movie about a pig?"

INTERLUDE

May 1976

The high school was large, fourteen buildings, and taught more than three thousand students in grades nine through twelve. On a campus that large, with that many buildings there were always nooks and crannies, places that were ignored in favor of large, open areas where the popular could congregate. Larry Wilkes avoided the popular places and spent his lunch sitting on the ground behind one of the buildings on Z quad, which was a good distance from the cafeteria. It was against the rules for him to eat there, but he didn't care.

Every night before bed, he made himself a bagged lunch. He made one for his younger sister, too, but she never seemed to appreciate it. She wanted the glamor of buying a cafeteria lunch, and seemed to think if Larry stopped making her lunch she'd be given the money to buy lunch tickets. She was wrong, of course. A bagged lunch was cheaper, so that's what she'd get.

Larry had known he was gay since before there were words for it. When he was young, his father worked at Coca-Cola. He remembered there was a Christmas party his parents went to one year. Larry was left at a babysitter with his sister. After the party, late at night, his parents picked them up and laid them sleeping in the back seat of what was probably a blue 1962 Dodge Polara, though it might have been the maroon 1964 Chrysler New Yorker they had later. He couldn't remember.

What he did remember was his parents talking about the party. His mother had danced with a man who'd been charming and an excellent dancer.

"You know he's light in the loafers, don't you?" Larry's father had said. And Larry knew that meant he was a man like him. That it wasn't another way of saying the man was a good dancer, but instead meant he was an oddity, someone on the outside, someone who'd never have a life like his parents. A life Larry wouldn't have either.

He didn't know how old he was, but he wasn't old. He was still young enough to need a babysitter, young enough to stretch out on the backseat with his sister. It was odd that he knew what they were talking about, but he did.

Later he'd see things on television, news reports about "The Homosexual" and eventually stories about Gay Liberation. While the stories told him there were others like him, they also implied he shouldn't feel too safe. He didn't belong with his family. They wouldn't want him if they truly knew him. The world taught him he'd never have his own family, never have a relationship, never be happy.

And then one afternoon, in the fall of his senior year, Pete Michaels plunked down next to him, and said, "So this is where you go at lunchtime. I've been wondering."

He was speechless. Why would Pete Michaels wonder about where Larry had his lunch? It didn't make sense.

"You don't mind if I sit with you, do you?"

"No. I guess not," Larry said, but he didn't really mean it. He might mind, he wasn't sure. Pete was a popular boy. Popular boys sometimes did awful things. He wasn't sure why Pete was there at all.

"What are you having for lunch?"

"Turkey sandwich and potato chips. And a couple of chocolate chip cookies."

"Today was tuna boats. I can't stand tuna boats. They use too much celery. I couldn't finish them."

And then Larry understood. He held out what was left of his lunch. Surprisingly, Pete seemed offended.

"You think I'm here to steal your lunch?"

Larry pulled his lunch back. If Pete wasn't there to take his lunch, then why was he there?

"Do you need help with your homework?"

"I always need help with my homework. But that's not—you really can't figure out why I wanted to sit with you?"

"Um, no."

Pete leaned in and kissed him. The kiss was sweet, aggressive and then vulnerable by turns. His hand came up and cupped the back of Larry's head. His tongue began to explore, but then he stopped and pulled away—

"I'm sorry if I taste like tuna."

"I don't care."

Pete smiled, the same smile Larry had noticed so many times and never understood his noticing had been noticed.

"Good," Pete said and kissed him again.

CHAPTER SIXTEEN

April 12, 1996
Friday morning

As it turned out, Ronnie loved *Babe* and we had a pleasant night. Except that I was edgy and jumped every time a car drove down our street—which was often.

The next morning, I snuck out of bed at seven, leaving Ronnie snoring softly—probably dreaming of talking pigs—and went down the hall to John's door. Tapping on the door, I felt guilty waking him up. He'd gotten in around two.

"Can I borrow the Lunchbox?" I whispered into the dark room.

He made an affirmative sound and pointed at the dresser. The keys were sitting there in a bowl.

"Where is it?"

"Oh-nan," he said.

I translated that to mean Ocean Boulevard, and said, "Thanks."

The Lunchbox was John's name for his silver 1989 Ford Fiesta with a dove gray vinyl interior. He joked that the car was not much bigger than a lunchbox and about as solid. Well, maybe it was a joke. Honestly, it seemed close to the truth.

I folded myself into the car, my head scrapping the roof. John was only a few inches shorter than me, so it couldn't have been much more comfortable for him. I adjusted the driver's seat so that I was driving in a near reclining position, and then set out for downtown L.A.

Yes, I suppose I could have called Lydia for a ride, but it seemed a better idea to drive separately. I needed to be able to leave if the deposition ran long. I didn't expect it to, but it was always possible there could be some surprising answers that would need to be thoroughly explored.

I wasn't clear on what Lydia's strategy was exactly but had decided not to ask. It seemed to me that it would be wiser to depose the victims first, to expand on the questions I'd asked, and come at Detective Wellesley with all the information. I mean, I had figured out that impeaching Wellesley was key to our case. The only evidence they'd really had at trial had been witness identifications. If they went to trial, they'd have to preserve the identifications and discredit the DNA evidence.

At around eight forty-five, I pulled into the garage below a metallic skyscraper of about forty floors. The offices of Karpinski & Karpinski were on the 32nd floor. After handing the Lunchbox keys over to the valet, I took the elevator up to the lobby. It was disturbingly quiet. I wondered if the building was fully occupied.

I signed in with the security guard and then joined a woman in a blue suit and sneakers in the elevator. That was odd. It was a look from the eighties, and much more Chicago than L.A. In Chicago, women sometimes wore sneakers on the train and then put on dress shoes in the office. Most people in L.A. drove, so if you wore sneakers on the way, you changed in the car. I wondered if she was a transplant.

Getting off at thirty-two, the floor was silent. I remembered my way to Karpinski & Karpinski. When I opened the lobby door, I found an unfamiliar receptionist, though I'd expected that. There was no regular receptionist. The Karpinski brothers hired a temp one or two days a week when they had meetings.

The receptionist was a pretty twenty-something with an under-standably confused look on her face.

"Hi. I'm Dom Reilly, I'm here for the deposition at nine."

"Oh, okay... um, you're early. It's been pushed back to nine-thirty. Can I get you coffee, tea, Perrier, Evian?"

"Evian would be great, thanks."

"Have a seat," she suggested.

She turned and walked away. A short way down the hallway, she opened a door, realized it wasn't the breakroom, and shut the door. Then she continued looking. I wondered if I'd ever get my bottle of water.

Brenda Wellesley walked into the lobby a moment later. She had drab brown hair pulled tight into a knot at the back of her head. I knew it was her because she was wearing an LAPD uniform: long-sleeved navy shirt, matching navy tie, stars at the collar, stripes on the sleeves, badge over her heart. There was a hat on her head, and she wore a pair of white gloves. Even from across the room I could smell the dry-cleaning chemicals wafting off the uniform.

She wouldn't have worn it much. Detectives worked in plain-clothes. Dress uniforms were reserved for publicity shots and funerals. No, she was making a point. She was asserting her authority and attempting to intimidate anyone who challenged it. I doubted that would work on Lydia.

The receptionist came back with my water. She handed it to me, and before she could say anything to the detective, Wellesley said, "Let's get this over with."

"Oh, I'm sorry, the deposition has been pushed back to nine-thirty," the girl said apologetically. "Can I get you something? Coffee, tea, Evian, Perrier?"

Glaring at the girl, Wellesley sat down. I studied her profile. There was a tiny bit of sag in her jowls, and she was wearing much more makeup than I'd thought at first. A tiny, healed scar ran along her hair line down to her jaw.

I tried to stop staring at her by looking at the magazines on the coffee-table in front of us. Two copies of *Time* magazine. One with the headline "The Truth About Whitewater" and another that offered "The Search for Jesus." Both sounded more like fantasies than reality and neither interested me. There was also a copy of *George* with Howard Stern on the cover—I couldn't tell whether this was before or after the one Karen had been reading —*McCall's*, featuring comedienne-turned-actress, Brett Butler; and *Vanity Fair*, displaying a bunch of half-naked Olympians. I went with *Vanity Fair*. I barely had time to get to the Olympians' spread, when Lydia walked in. She wore a navy power suit with a pink blouse and a gold crucifix at her neck. I couldn't remember her saying anything about religion. Maybe she was religious or maybe it was a ploy. She glanced at the receptionist and smiled, then she looked at Brenda Wellesley.

"Hi, I'm Lydia Gonzalez."

Wellesley remained silent.

"Have you been offered something to drink?

More silence.

"Well, if you change your mind just ask... I'm sorry what is your name?"

The receptionist said, "Jeanine."

"Jeanine will get it for you."

The conference room was windowless and claustrophobic, with a table and eight chairs taking up most of the available floor-space. In one corner, was a rail-thin woman in her mid-thirties. She had badly dyed blonde hair and sunken eyes. When she saw us, she smiled, showing us a very expensive mouthful of bright white caps.

"Hi! I'm Elaine Joy from Eyes on Justice. I'll be videotaping this morning's deposition."

"Excellent," Lydia said. "The woman we'll be deposing is Detective Brenda Wellesley. We just saw her in reception, she's wearing her dress uniform."

Lydia put her briefcase in a chair and opened it to take out a yellow legal pad with questions written in tiny block print.

"So I'll be panning from the detective to you as you ask questions?" Elaine Joy asked, uncomfortably.

"No panning. Just choose an angle on the detective and stay there."

Elaine seemed to pout. Her job seemed frightfully easy. "Will she be alone?"

"No, she'll have a union rep with her and Assistant District Attorney Ramon Gutierrez." Lydia placed two pens next to the pad.

"So, I should have all three in frame?"

"No, God no, just Detective Wellesley. Her answers are the only important thing this morning. And I doubt anyone will ever look at the video."

"Oh." The disappointment in Elaine's voice was palpable. She seemed to have confused the deposition with a major motion picture.

Just then, Ramon Gutierrez walked into the room. He was a short, rumpled man with black, darting eyes. He had a thick briefcase that rivaled the one Lydia had brought.

Detective Wellesley followed him. With her was a man I didn't know; a white guy nearing sixty. He seemed almost as annoyed by the whole thing as Elaine Joy.

"Hello Ramon," Lydia said. "Nice to see you. This is my investigator, Dom Reilly."

Gutierrez nodded but basically ignored me. "Detective Wellesley has brought her union rep, Joseph Colson."

"Yes, I see that."

Colson stuck out a hand to shake, Lydia shook it but didn't say anything to him directly.

"Well, we made it on time after all," she said. "We should go ahead and get started. Do you have everything you need? Were you offered water? Coffee?"

"We were, thank you," Ramon said.

"All right then," Lydia said, then turned to Elaine. "I think we're ready."

Elaine pressed record.

Lydia sat down and positioned her pad directly in front of her. She picked up a pen and looked ready to start checking off the questions she'd written. I looked closer at the pad and saw that the questions were gibberish. It was all nothing more than a prop. Lydia introduced herself and me, again, then everyone else in the room.

Then, she spent almost ten minutes establishing Detective Wellesley's credentials, her education, marital status, family history. It was information we already had, so not useful to anyone in the room except perhaps Elaine Joy.

Wellesley began to shift uncomfortably in her seat. She wanted to get on with it, which I think was what Lydia was hoping for. She segued immediately to, "Detective Wellesley, as you should be aware, you're here to discuss three of your cases: the rapes of Cammy Wainright, Selma Martinez and Joanne Yardley. You recall those cases?"

"Yes."

"And you've had time to consult your reports and notes to refresh your memory?"

"Yes."

"You're aware that my clients Peter Linder, Alan Dinkler and Stu Whatley have all recently been proven innocent by DNA evidence?"

Wellesley sat there stone-faced for a moment, then, "I'm aware of the DNA evidence."

Lydia paused for a moment. Then she asked, "You don't believe DNA evidence is accurate?"

The detective inhaled as though to answer, but her union rep touched the back of her hand. She looked at him for a moment, and then said, "No."

"You personally informed each of the victims of the DNA results?"

"Yes."

"Did you attempt to convince them that DNA evidence is unreliable?"

"Detective Wellesley is entitled to her own opinions," said ADA Gutierrez.

"And in the event of a new trial, sharing those opinions with these victims could be considered witness tampering."

I could see Guitierrez' jaw tighten. "I'm not sure a judge would see it that way."

"And I'm not sure a judge wouldn't," Lydia said, her tongue

razor sharp. "Detective Wellesley, did you direct the witnesses to any scientific journals so that they could form their own opinions?"

"No."

"Did you suggest that they go the library? Or contact a science professor?"

Wellesley fumed silently. Gutierrez stepped in. "You've made your point, Lydia. Please move on."

She gave him a big, friendly smile, glanced at her notepad, and asked another question. "Now, Detective Wellesley, you went through an identification process with each of these victims. Was it the same each time?"

"I followed procedure."

"That isn't what I asked."

"Procedurally, we're given leeway. Depending on the situation."

"Meaning, it's procedure to use photo arrays or physical lineups?"

"We're allowed to use either."

"And show-ups? You're allowed to do those?"

"Yes."

"Thank you." She glanced at the notepad in front of her. "Let's start with Candy Van Dyke, the witness in the Yardley rape. She remembers being shown just one photograph, a mugshot of Stu Whatley. Is that correct?"

"I don't recall."

"You just said the identifications followed procedure. Is it procedure to show a witness just one photo for identification purposes?"

"It's acceptable. It's similar to a show-up."

"Tell me again, what is a show-up?"

"You walk a victim or witness by the suspect to see if they recognize them."

"It's meant to seem like a coincidence?"

"I suppose."

"But holding a single photo out to a witness would not be a

coincidence. So it would not actually fit the definition of a show-up, would it?”

Wellesley sat quietly. She glanced at her union rep, waiting for him to say something. Finally, the ADA said, “Ms. Gonzalez, that’s more of a statement than a question.”

“We can move on,” Lydia took a bottle of water out of the tote she carried along with the briefcase. She unscrewed the top and took a sip. “Regarding the Wainwright rape, the victim was shown an array of six photographs. The suspect, Peter Linder, and five others. However, the five fillers looked nothing like the description given.”

“That’s your opinion,” ADA said.

“The hair color is significantly different.”

“She said ‘blond’,” Detective Wellesley said. “Blond covers a wide range. We don’t always know what a witness means by blond.”

Lydia left a long pause. Then, “Selma Martinez says that she made her identification from a photo array. There’s none in the case file we received.”

“We’ll have that checked,” ADA Gutierrez said immediately. “At most it’s a photocopying error.”

“Our client recalls being part of an in-person lineup. Can you account for that discrepancy, Detective Wellesley?”

The detective sat there closed mouthed.

Lydia tried again, “I’ve heard that the LAPD will occasionally put a suspect into a lineup to encourage a confession. Is that what you did?”

No response.

“Did you put Alan Dinkman in a lineup and tell him he’d been identified?”

It seemed as though she wasn’t going to reply to that either, but then she said, “I don’t recall.”

“You don’t recall putting him in a lineup? Or don’t recall telling him he’d been identified?”

“I don’t recall.”

“If you don’t recall that suggests there could have been incidents where you did tell suspects they'd been identified even though they had not been. Was this a common practice?"

"We're allowed to say whatever we need to in order to get a confession."

"Which includes lying."

"Yes."

"But after you lied to my client, he did not confess. Is that correct?"

"Your client did not confess. You already know that."

"Selma Martinez told my investigator you showed her copies of photos rather than actual photos. Do you recall how many times the photos were copied?"

"I would not have shown her copies. I would have shown her photos. I don't know why she would say that."

"And since there's nothing in the file, we can't confirm that."

"I would not have shown her Xerox copies."

"Then why would she say you did?"

"You don't understand. Rape victims are traumatized. They've been through a terrible ordeal, they can't be expected to remember everything in detail. They need—" Wellesley stopped, her face flushing red at what she'd just said. "I didn't—that's not —years have gone by, that's what I meant."

Lydia smiled. "You admit that a rape victim might not remember their rape accurately."

"I... no, I don't admit that."

"Meaning that you don't take that fact into account when you're investigating a case?"

"Stop twisting my fucking words!" Wellesley raised her voice. "You think you're some kind of avenging angel getting innocent people out of prison. Well, you're not. What you're doing is tearing the whole thing down, putting bad people back on the street. And that means people will get hurt!"

This was a disaster. Gutierrez stood up, and asked, "Lydia, could we step out for a moment?" The two lawyers stood and left the room.

Wellesley turned to her union rep, and said, "Couldn't you

have done something? She's going to twist my words and three criminals are going to go free."

"I'm here to protect *you*. Not your convictions."

"It's the same thing. Rapists, she's getting rapists released."

"What if they're not rapists, though?" I asked.

She looked at me as though I'd just appeared in a puff of smoke. Then she leaned forward, drew back her lips into a snarl, and said, "These are rapists. You can't just let them go. Don't act like you don't understand. You get it. You used to be police."

That sent a bolt through me. How much did she know about me? We'd researched her, had she returned the favor?

"I've never been on the job."

"I don't believe you. Police can always tell police."

"Just like police can always tell a bad guy?"

She smiled, hard and mean. "Yeah, just like that."

I was about to explain that policework should be about facts, not hunches, when Lydia and Ramon came back into the room. "We're finished," Lydia said. "I want to thank everyone for coming. Elaine, you can stop the video now."

Wellesley looked stunned as she and Colson stood. "What do you mean we're finished?" she said to Ramon. "Aren't you going to ask me questions?"

"We've reached an agreement," he said.

"No! You can't do that. We have to fight this. We have to stop this."

"Brenda, calm down," Colson said. "We'll make sure whatever agreement they made protects you."

"I'm not talking about me!"

Gutierrez tried to guide her by the elbow, but she snatched her arm away. "Don't touch me." She gave Lydia and me a final dirty look and stormed out of the room.

When they were gone, Lydia smiled at me, and said, "Our clients are getting out of prison."

"Just like that?"

"They couldn't possibly go to trial. And not just because of the DNA evidence. The identifications no longer have any credibility."

"Do you think there are others? Do you think Wellesley convicted other innocent men?"

"I would say it's likely."

"Are we going to find them?"

"I just promised the ADA I wouldn't do that."

That was horrible. That meant there could be more, possibly many more, innocent men in prison because of Wellesley and we couldn't help them.

"Was that a good idea?"

"I have to represent my clients' best interests. That's what I did."

"But—"

"Don't worry. I promised not to pursue any more cases involving Detective Wellesley. I didn't promise not to tip off other attorneys. I'll be flipping through my Rolodex when I get back to the office."

That made me feel better about it all. "When will they be out?"

"Hopefully by the end of next week."

CHAPTER SEVENTEEN

April 13-14, 1996
The weekend

I can't say what Ronnie saw in me. I was getting closer to fifty than I ever thought I'd get, my hair going gray at record speed, my skin crinkling up like used wax paper. My face looked like I've been punched too many times—probably because I had been—and I was thin to the point of scrawny. And yet there were times when he looked at me that I was sure I was the sexiest beast on the planet. I had no idea how I'd be able to leave him. But I was going to have to. Hamlet Gilbody was getting close.

I got back to Long Beach around noon. I circled the neighborhood a few times looking for a blue Neon. When I didn't see one, I parked a couple blocks away, then walked home. Once inside, I made myself a grilled ham and cheese sandwich. I ate it quickly with some potato chips and a root beer. Then I went upstairs and woke John up—again.

"Can you take me to the airport? I need to rent a car."

John sat up in bed and stared at me. "Why?"

"Personal reasons."

"Fine. It's time for me to get up anyway."

He dressed quickly and we were on our way to the airport

about twenty minutes later. He drove, leaning forward into the steering wheel, basically opposite of the way I drove the Lunchbox, though probably just as uncomfortable.

"Could you not mention this to Ronnie?"

I could have told Ronnie I'd had a fender bender and my car was in the shop, but then he might try to take over and call our insurance agent. He was like that; always taking care of me. No, the less he knew, the better.

"Is your car having an affair?" John asked.

"No. I'm just not using it right now."

"Did the two of you have an argument?"

"You mean me and my Jeep?"

"Of course, I mean you and your Jeep. If you had an argument with Ronnie, I'd know all about it. Junior would tell me."

"Good to know you're well informed."

"Always."

John dropped me off at the small Long Beach Airport. I told him not to wait. If I had trouble renting a car, I'd grab a cab. The airport was one of the few places in Southern California where you could get a cab without having to call first. It was not a city like Chicago or New York where you could simply step off the curb and hail a taxi. In most cases, you had to call and wait, like you would for a pizza.

Since I'd spent part of the day in the Lunchbox, I popped for a midsize car and rented a green Ford Taurus, a car that looked something like an aerodynamic frog. It had plenty of headroom though, so I was much happier.

I drove home planning to get ready and go to work at The Hawk. On the way, I realized I couldn't go in. In fact, I couldn't ever go in again. Hamlet Gilbody assumed I was a bartender, just as Richland Keswick had. Sooner or later, he was going to walk into The Hawk. I didn't want to be behind the bar when he did.

After circling the neighborhood a few times, I went into my house, called the owner of The Hawk, and told her I had a stomach flu. Then I went downstairs and got a bucket from the kitchen, a book from the living room—*K Is for Killer*—and a bottle of Pepto Bismol from the upstairs shared bathroom. Then

I set up in our bedroom to pretend to be sick for the next three days.

Ronnie got home around nine. When I told him I'd thrown up twice, he took my temperature (suspiciously normal), and ran to Ralph's to get me ginger ale and crackers. When he got back, he asked, "Are you nauseous?"

"It comes and goes."

"It's strange you don't have a fever."

"I have a headache," I lied, hoping that distract from my lack of a fever. "And chills."

"Do you think you could hold down some Tylenol?"

I shook my head.

"How about an ice pack for your head?"

"I'll be fine. Ginger ale and crackers are all I need."

"I made an offer on the co-op. They have until end of day Monday to respond."

"You think they'll take it?"

"It's not a bad offer. And they want to get rid of it."

"So, they'll take it?"

"Hmmmm. I think so."

"You're nervous though."

"People are unpredictable."

"What about the money? Do you have what you need?"

"No. I'll figure it out. It's all contingent on my getting financing, so worst case the deal falls apart."

Without another word, he went downstairs to make himself some dinner. I nibbled on crackers and ginger ale. I didn't want the deal to fall apart. Ronnie wanted this, so I wanted it for him. I just needed to figure out how to help.

After a few minutes, I settled in to reading my book. Kinsey Millhone always made me feel a little bad about myself. She spent an inordinate amount of time jogging and still managed to figure things out faster than I ever did. I was asleep by ten with the book open on my chest.

I woke up around three and started worrying about what I was going to do. Ronnie slept next to me. I didn't have much to pack. Some clothes, a few books, a picture of Ronnie, maybe two…

In the basement, I'd hidden a travel bag filled with a gun, ten thousand in cash, and some necessary documents to get me started again. I'd take the Jeep; it was paid for. I could "sell" it to my new self or trade it in on something else.

Which way would I go? Obviously, not west. That was nothing but water for a very long way. My real choices were north and east or some combination of north and east. I'd have to pick up a job soon. Real soon. It was easy to get bartending jobs, but I'd been found that way twice. Of course, I could avoid gay bars. And cities with gay ghettoes. Maybe that was the right idea. I shouldn't be involved with anyone after Ronnie. I'd been foolish to try and build a life with him. I might have to pick up and run again. I shouldn't involve anyone else. Shouldn't have a boyfriend. Shouldn't even have friends.

I could leave in the morning, after Ronnie went to work. It was a good time for Lydia since we'd just finished three cases. It wasn't a good time for Larry Wilkes. There wasn't much I could do about that, though. Was there?

I finally fell asleep around four. In the morning, I woke around eight-thirty. Ronnie was already up, showered and dressed. He gave me a big smile, and said, "Hey, you made it through the night without puking."

"Not exactly."

"You threw up?"

"Once."

"Why didn't I hear you?"

"I was very quiet."

He glared at me suspiciously. He threw a couple times a year when he drank too much. When that happened, it sounded like he was being drawn and quartered. I knew he thought it was impossible to vomit quietly.

"Come on," I said. "Bulimics puke quietly all the time."

"Are you bulimic?"

"Of course not."

He was still suspicious but had clients waiting. As soon as he left the bedroom my mind was spinning again. I didn't feel right about leaving without at least getting Lydia to take Larry Wilkes' case—I didn't feel right about leaving Ronnie either, but I knew he'd be better off without me. Larry Wilkes would not be.

I waited almost an hour and then snuck downstairs, wearing just a pair of boxer briefs. I hurried into the living room and picked up the three boxes of Larry Wilkes transcripts from where I'd left them. I turned around to find Junior watching me.

"Are you better? I heard you were on death's door."

"I had the stomach flu," I said, hoping he'd want to keep his distance.

"And you thought a little exercise might help?"

"I'm a little bored."

"Well, let me carry those for you." He reached out and started to take all three boxes but got a feel for their heft, and said, "Maybe just one." He took the top box.

I led us upstairs, attempting to walk gingerly, trying to keep slightly bent over. At my bedroom door, I said, "Well, thanks. Put your box on top of the other two."

As he did, he said, "If there's anything else I can do..."

He'd barely done that. I backed into my room and let the door fall shut. Putting the boxes on the bed, I opened one and started flipping through trying to find Anne Whittemore's testimony. I skipped the basic information and started reading more closely with the assistant district attorney's question:

"What was your relationship to the victim, Pete Michaels?"

"He was my fiancé."

"When did you become engaged?"

"It was around prom."

"Did you and Pete go to prom together?"

"No. We had our own event. Just the two of us. It was very romantic."

"Why is that?"

"Our engagement was a secret. My parents wanted me to go to college. They didn't even know he was my boyfriend. They're very strict."

"You're not in college now though, are you?"

"When I turned eighteen, I realized I could say no. So that's what I did. I told my parents 'No, I don't want to go to college.'"

"Is that when you told them about you and Pete?"

"No, I didn't tell them about Pete until after he die—was murdered."

"Why did you wait?"

"I didn't want it to seem like I wasn't going to college so I could be with Pete."

I wondered if her parents knew she was lying? Were they sitting in the courtroom listening to this? Did it have any connection to reality? Honestly, her parents sounded like Pete's parents.

"Tell us about your relationship with the defendant, Larry Wilkes."

"Well, we went through all of school together. I've always known him."

"So you were friends?"

"I guess. For a while."

"Did something happen?"

"I told him about being engaged to Pete and he got all weird about it. Like I should have known not to do that because Larry liked me too. I mean, it was weird and kind of scary."

"Did you tell your fiancé about it?"

"Yes."

"And what did he say?"

"That I shouldn't worry. That he'd make sure Larry never bothered me again."

"And did he?"

"He told me he beat Larry up and that Larry would leave me alone."

"Did he?"

"No. Pete had to beat him up two more times."

"Then what happened?"

"I guess Larry got tired of getting beat-up because that's when he killed Pete."

The defense objected to her saying that, since she had no direct knowledge of the murder. The judge agreed, but the defense didn't want to let it go. When he began his cross, the defense attorney asked:

"*You were not present when Pete Michaels was killed, were you?*"

"*No.*"

"*So you have no idea who killed him.*"

"*Pete beat Larry up a few times. Larry was there when Pete died. I don't think that's hard to—*"

"*That's guessing.*"

"*It doesn't seem—*"

"*A fact is something you know to be true. Do you know that Larry killed Pete?*"

"*No, I don't know that.*"

"*And you don't know why Pete was killed.*"

"*Well, yeah—I mean, I guess—okay, I don't know.*"

"*Are you popular Anne?*"

"*Popular enough.*"

"*So if I brought your classmates in and asked them if you were popular, they'd say you were?*"

"*Can he do that?*"

She must have looked at the judge and asked that question because he answered.

"*Yes, he can do that. Though, I'd like to know why he'd do something like that.*"

"*Anne, let's try again. Are you popular?*"

"*Not really.*"

"*Was Pete popular?*"

"*Yeah. Everyone liked Pete.*"

"*So how did a popular boy like Pete and an unpopular girl like you get together?*"

"*That's why Pete was special. Things like being popular didn't matter to him.*"

This is where I would have expected him to ask if she was making the whole thing up. But for some reason—possibly Larry himself—he stopped there. He didn't ask the question.

I skipped forward. When the prosecution finished, Larry's attorney asked the court to dismiss the case based on lack of evidence. The judge agreed to consider the motion and adjourned for the day. That must have been suspenseful at the time. It wasn't for me. There was almost an entire ream of paper continuing the trial. Plus, I'd seen Larry in prison.

Basically, as nearly as I could tell, if you believed Andy Showalter and Anne Whittemore then there was plenty of evidence. If you didn't, well, then there was almost none. Of course, Larry's presence at the crime scene was persuasive. There was no one providing an explanation for that, and I was fairly certain Larry never took the stand.

At that point, I scanned back to the beginning of the prosecution's case. The DA put the lead homicide detective on the stand. A man named Harper.

"When you arrived at the scene you found Larry Wilkes there."

"Yes."

"What was he doing?"

"He was holding onto the victim, crying."

"Would you say he was remorseful?"

The defense attorney objected to that, and the judge agreed.

"How would you characterize the defendant's demeanor?"

"Remorseful—"

"Your honor!" the defense objected.

The prosecution had made the point though. But it didn't make much sense given the later testimony. Someone who convinced someone else to get them a gun, then went and killed someone in a very premeditated way might feel remorse. Eventually. But immediately? I didn't think so. However, it was the only logical explanation for Larry's tears—if you were unwilling to entertain the possibility they were in love.

CHAPTER EIGHTEEN

April 14-15, 1996
Sunday evening/Monday morning

By Sunday night, I'd made a couple of decisions. First, I'd try to stick around until I could get Lydia to take Larry's case. Second, I wanted to help Ronnie get the co-op he wanted.

That afternoon, I snuck down to the basement. It was surprisingly small, about the size of one room. Ronnie and I had many conversations about this. Our working theory was that the house was built with a simple crawl space and the full basement was dug and "poured" later. It was somewhat rough-hewn, which fit with our theory.

We didn't use it for much, other than some storage, and the washer and dryer. With a loud scrape, I pulled the washer out a little bit away from the wall. The back of it was a thin metal sheet. Right after we moved in, I'd unscrewed the bottom bolt and bent the sheet back. Inside, I kept my getaway bag: a vinyl travel bag that was about four inches by ten inches and another three inches thick. Inside it, I kept the key to a P.O. Box I rented in North Hollywood at a Mailboxes Etc.; Nick Nowak's birth certificate and social security card (Dom Reilly's were upstairs with Ronnie's important papers—if I left I wouldn't need them); the ten thousand dollars in cash, a Beretta 92S; and Nick Nowak's Nevada driver's license, which I got in '86 when I spent six weeks shacked up with a lounge singer named Bucky Diamond. The license was valid for eight years and renewable by mail. Even years later Bucky was kind enough to forward it to my Mailboxes Etc. address.

The seventy thousand I had when I left Chicago had been too much to show up at a teller's window and withdraw, so eventually, in 1988, I contacted Owen Lovejoy, Esquire, and asked him to help me move the money to an account belonging to Dom Reilly—though I never gave the name to Owen. After I signed the necessary paperwork and overnighted it back to him, he moved the money into an escrow account at his law firm. Then, using a company called DigiCash, he anonymously transferred the money to an account in California. I promptly got a cashier's check in the full amount, then opened a new account at a different bank. Eventually, that was the money I gave to Ronnie as a down payment for our first house.

I suppose I could have siphoned off some of it for a rainy day, but I didn't need to. I was already bartending at that point, so I began saving cash every week. That's where the ten grand came from. It was my getaway money. It was easy to grab, and it meant I'd never have to circle back and ask Ronnie for money.

Ten thousand was just a nice, easy number. I didn't need or not need that much cash. I counted out twenty-five hundred in fifties and hundreds. Maybe I was being stupid, maybe I'd need every penny. I had no way of knowing. What I did know was that I wanted to leave Ronnie with something toward his condo. Leaving and never seeing him again was terrible. Knowing he was one step closer to his dream of being a real estate mogul made it a bit better.

I went back upstairs and put the money under his pillow, planning to talk to him about it later. I hunted through the covers and found *K Is for Killer*. I read, for a couple of hours I think, and then fell asleep. I slept fitfully; my head full of weird dreams of dead people. Owen was there, as were Harker and Ross. I kept thinking they were in pain and only I could stop the pain, but I didn't know how. I had to figure it out. I abruptly woke a little after eight in the morning. Ronnie wasn't next to me.

When I got downstairs, I found him in the kitchen making breakfast and watching the *Today* show on a small portable TV. Katie Couric was telling us that the one-year anniversary of the Oklahoma City bombing was coming up and that we should tune in for their weeklong special coverage. It sounded depressing. The money I'd left under Ronnie's pillow sat on the marble countertop.

"Oh, you found the money. Good."

"It made a big lump in my pillow."

"I was going to talk to you about it last night, but I fell asleep."

"Mmmm-hmmm. Dom, where did it come from?"

"I saved it."

"Twenty-five hundred dollars?"

"Yeah, I work for tips. I put twenty, twenty-five dollars away every week." Sometimes more.

"You've been saving this for two years?"

"I guess. You're better with numbers than I am."

He didn't say anything, just started plating scrambled eggs for both of us. I consoled myself with the idea that he probably wouldn't be making me breakfast if things were all that bad.

"The money is to help you buy the co-op."

"Yes, darling, I figured that out. You do realize, I have to provide three months of bank statements to get a mortgage. Believe it or not, mysterious cash deposits are a bad thing. It makes lenders nervous."

"I didn't think about that."

I reached to take the money back.

"Not so fast. I'll buy groceries, gas, use some money orders to pay bills. That way the money in our account stays in our account. No one will ask what we've been living on."

"Okay then," I said with a shrug. He was still obviously angry, even as he set my breakfast in front of me. I was too on edge to sip my coffee, though I needed it badly.

"You've been saving money and hiding it from me."

"I didn't—"

"It's probably best if you don't talk." He collected his thoughts. "I know you keep things from me. We've talked about that. But that's about the past. You're not supposed to keep things from me now, in the present. You promised."

"I did."

I took a moment to think this through. He was right, of course. He usually was, but that didn't mean I could tell him anything. The more he knew the more danger he was in. I couldn't tell him I might be disappearing without notice. I couldn't tell him that I might—that I *would* be leaving soon. Very soon.

"Some things about the past... well, they're in the present as well. They're not as easy to separate as you'd like them to be."

"Dom, that sounds like a riddle."

"Look, I wanted you to have the money because I want you to have everything you dream of. I suppose I shouldn't have done that."

His eyes narrowed. "In other words, you're an asshole because you love me so much?"

"Something like that."

He looked at his breakfast as though he wasn't sure what to do with it. I still hadn't touched mine.

"Is there more you're not telling me?"

"No, that's all there is."

Said the man who wished he could stop lying.

****

It was Tax Day. I keep things as simple as possible, doing the EZ form. I don't want to draw any more attention to myself than necessary. Ronnie on the other hand goes all out. I swear, he deducts everything right down to his cologne.

"I have to smell nice for clients, don't I?"

Immediately after breakfast he left for a last-minute meeting with his tax accountant. I had another cup of coffee, turned off the *Today* show, then went back upstairs for a shower. It was almost nine. Given my hours at the bar, Lydia didn't mind my starting late on Mondays.

Once I was dressed, I walked around the block twice. I didn't see any blue Neons or any other possible rentals—other than the green Taurus I was driving. After the second spin around the block, I climbed into it, keeping a sharp eye on the rearview mirror.

When I got to The Freedom Agenda, no one was there. There was a note on Karen's desk saying she was downtown researching a few things and that Lydia wouldn't be in until afternoon. I turned around and left. Then I headed out to Downey.

After driving around the high school twice, I parked on Brookshire, across from the school's swimming pool. A logical guess since the gym was nearby. As I stepped onto campus, I saw that there were two rows of tennis courts. Eight, in all. South of them were two terra cotta buildings with red tile roofs. Boys & Girls locker rooms?

A few steps later and I discovered I was right. I walked into the Boys building. I found myself in a large lobby. To one side, a hallway led to a series of offices for coaches and teaching staff. On the other side, the locker room and showers. The only furniture in the lobby were several glass cases. I scanned their contents until I found the two long shelves devoted to the tennis team.

There were trophies and team photos for the years the team did well in their division. I scanned the shelves to find 1976, the year they'd placed second in the state. They'd received a small trophy—a bronzed tennis racket—which sat next to the photo. I found Paulie and next to him his brother, Pete. They bore a striking resemblance. Pete had more freckles and darker blond hair, but other than that they looked very similar. They'd placed third in both 1974 and 1975. The brothers played both years. The team did not win a trophy in 1973, so I couldn't be sure they weren't on the team.

Also in the photos were the nine other players and, of course, the coach. The coach was in his mid-fifties, rugged, handsome, with a well-maintained body and salt-and-pepper hair. He reminded me of someone, but I couldn't think who.

I looked at the other photos and found him in 1966, 1964 and 1959. Then I moved in the other direction and found the coach in 1977and 1978. After that he was gone. The team did well in the eighties. Second once and third twice. But they had a new coach by then.

I wrote down the coach's name, Bernie Carrier, in a little flip notebook I carried in a back pocket. For good measure, I wrote down the seven tennis players in 1975 and 1976. It probably wouldn't be useful, but since I was there, why not?

Coach Carrier would be in his seventies. I wondered how to find out more about him. Where did he live? How could I find him? It was almost lunch time. A bell went off and I could hear movement outside. Then, almost immediately, boys began to scurry into the locker room. I peeked around the corner to see if there were any teachers in their offices. There weren't.

On my way out, I stopped an extremely tall teenager.

"Can you point me to the administration building?"

The boy literally pointed. South and east, I think. I got lost anyway. When I finally found the administration building about forty-five minutes later, I ended up face-to-face with an assistant principal named Gloria Whigham. She was nearly sixty and wore a very stern look that made me worry I might get detention for the questions I was there to ask.

"I'm doing a piece for the *Downey Daily News* looking at the growth of tennis as a high school sport. Would you be able to put me in touch with Bernie Carrier?"

She flinched when I said his name. I had a hunch she might. "We don't give out faculty information. Past or present."

"Okay, what about alumni?" I pulled out my little pad and began reading names.

She stopped me after three. "We don't give out information on students either. Past or present."

"I know this is a big ask, but could you maybe give my number to them? I'm looking to talk to either a coach or players from a winning team from the seventies. Bernie Carrier would be perfect."

Again she flinched, and looked away this time.

"If you could maybe give him my number? And maybe a few of the players. That way you haven't broken any rules."

She stayed silent.

"How about I write my number down for you. I flipped to a new page in my notebook and wrote out my name, *Downey Daily News* and my phone number. The way she held it between two fingers made me wonder if she thought it was radioactive.

CHAPTER NINETEEN

April 15, 1996
Monday afternoon

I was pretty sure Karen wouldn't be in at all, which meant I could go back to the office but there wouldn't be anyone there to help me search Lexis/Nexis. I knew better than to attempt it on my own. Karen kept the password taped to the bottom of her center desk drawer, but I was too afraid of turning her PC into a smoldering, molten pile of junk. People—mostly Ronnie—assure me that's not possible. That you can't just hit a few wrong keys and destroy a computer. I didn't believe them.

I decided I'd go old school and went to the library. The Long Beach Main Library was a concrete structure sunk into the ground with lawns running up its sides and onto the roof. If you're the kind of person who just loves a good bomb shelter, this is the library for you. To find the reference area, you have to go even deeper into the ground. Tucked in the back, I asked the reference librarian if they had *The Press-Telegram* on fiche.

"We do but we only have from nineteen fifty-two until nineteen eighty-eight."

"All right. You have an index?"

She showed me to a low table with a dozen thick books, black and well-used. I sat down and pulled over the volume labeled C-

D. I looked up Bernie Carrier's name and found that there were dozens upon dozens of dates listed. They covered several years, tending to focus on the months of May and June. There were no listings after 1978.

I pulled a sampling of dates in 1974, then went back to the reference desk and asked for the appropriate fiche. It took a few minutes, but the reference librarian eventually came back with about twenty brilliant blue fiche sheets in a tray. She nodded toward a room behind me. I walked over and let myself in. There were three projection machines on a long table. I sat down at the furthest one. There was an instruction sheet taped to the table. I'd done this before, but it had been a long time. I slipped the fiche sheet between two plates of glass. I pushed it into place and the glass clamped down on the sheet.

I scanned through the newspaper projected onto the screen. I had to adjust to moving in the opposite direction from the one I wanted to go in. It was obvious this was done with enlarging mirrors. After spinning around for a minute or two, I figured out that one fiche sheet covered one day's edition of the paper, given that there was enough space on the four by five sheet to put 80-100 tiny pages. That made it easier, all I had to do was find the sports section.

I read through thirteen or fourteen articles about the Downey Boys' Tennis Team without finding anything of interest. At first, the articles were small, including the final scores, the names of the coaches and where the games were played. As the season progressed, individual players were mentioned—the Michaels brothers several times—and projections about the possible season outcome. There was a time when it looked like the Downey team could win statewide. The final three articles included team photos. None of the photos were the same as the one I'd seen at the high school; these were taken by the newspaper.

I was able to blow up the article to get a better look at the photos, but they still weren't that great. For a quarter I could get a copy of whatever was on the machine's screen. I took copies of the articles with photographs, then went back to the reference desk. I returned the fiche I'd borrowed, then asked for the dates in 1975. I also requested five dollars in quarters.

Back at the fiche machine, I skimmed through another season of tennis. This time there were only two team photos. I made copies. There were a few other dates I could have checked out, but I decided to find an empty table and look over the photographs I now had. I knew what I was looking for. Larry had said that Pete wasn't a virgin. It made sense to look at his teammates as potential boyfriends.

Spreading out the photos, I looked for relationships between the boys. In each of the photos, Pete and Paulie Michaels were posed next to each other. Mostly the other boys looked at the camera and smiled. Except in two the photos, one of the other boys, the same boy was looking at Coach Carrier.

Skimming the captions, I saw that the boy's name was John Hazeltine. There were a lot of reasons why John might be looking at his coach in two of the photos. Coach Carrier might have said something that bothered him. No, that wasn't it. The look on John's face wasn't annoyance. It was intense, positive... reverence maybe? Or—

Then I wondered if John was looking at the coach at all. In each of the photos with John looking that way, the coach was standing there with his hand on Pete's shoulder. Was he actually looking at Pete? Or was he looking at Pete because Coach Carrier was touching him?

Was I looking at jealousy? Or was it reverence? It might have been lust. The copies I was looking at were larger than the photos in the newspaper. I could see the pattern of the dots used to make up the images. That meant the quality wasn't good enough to come to a real decision about what I was looking at.

It was about then that I realized who Coach Carrier reminded me of... John Gavin. A younger John Gavin, I guess. I wasn't entirely sure how old the real John Gavin was in the nineteen seventies. Coach Carrier was in his early fifties then. Were they the same age?

Gavin was good-looking enough that Hitchcock didn't really have to explain why Janet Leigh would steal a bag full of money in hopes of living happily ever after with him. I remembered the first time I saw *Psycho*. I would have stolen the money too.

It wasn't hard to imagine that a gay teenager might have a crush on Coach Carrier. That raised a lot of possibilities about Pete's murder. John Hazeltine could have imagined something going on between Pete and the coach, and killed him because of it. Maybe something *was* going on between John and the coach, or maybe not. It almost made sense that nothing was going on. Murder was delusional, it didn't have to be based on much.

On the other hand, there could have been something going on between the coach and one, or both, of the boys. It was the seventies. Things were different. Gay sex was illegal in most places and frowned upon where it wasn't. That meant guys didn't stop to wonder if it was okay to have sex with a sixteen- or seventeen-year-old kid. There wasn't much difference between having sex with them or a twenty-one-year-old. Either way it could land you in jail and ruin your life. And teenagers certainly didn't think about things like that.

I'd known a couple of guys who lost their virginity early with guys in their twenties and thirties. I remember one of them said, "I wanted him and there was no way I was taking no for an answer." He was fourteen when he made that decision.

Of course, this was all before the McMartin trial, and before people began accusing Michael Jackson of having sex with preteens on a regular basis. Gay guys thought of things differently after that. Or at least most of us did.

So maybe there was something going on between Coach Carrier and John Haseltine. Or even Coach Carrier and Pete Michaels. Something that eventually got Pete killed. Something I was going to find out about.

Before I left the main library the day before, I used their rack of phonebooks to find all the John Hazeltines in the Los Angeles and South Bay areas. There was one in Inglewood, one in Compton and two in Downey, one of which was a Jr. I had a strong feeling John Haseltine Jr. was the man I was looking for. I wrote down his number and address—along with the others just in case.

I drove out to Downey, for the second time in one day, and found Hazeltine's apartment building on the corner of Dinwiddie and Old River Road. The two-story building was flesh-colored with cheap metal windows that looked crooked. The intersection was busy and parking tricky. I found a spot about two blocks away and walked down. When I reached the building, I found that the security door was broken and standing open.

Haseltine lived in 2E. As it was around five-thirty, I wasn't expecting to find him home. The majority of people in Los Angeles County did not live near their work. He was probably still fighting traffic to make it home. Of course, I had no idea what he did for a living, if he indeed did anything.

Reaching 2E, I knocked. Looking around the courtyard, I thought, Ronnie would be appalled. While the co-op he wanted was hardly perfect, this place was shabby and had none of what he called 'good bones.' Its only real hope was to be torn down and built again.

Surprisingly, the door opened. A man in his late thirties stood behind a screen door. He was pale, freckled, had at least two cowlicks in his thick brown hair, and looked like he could use a good meal or two. He squinted at me, and said, "Yeah?"

"Are you John Haseltine?"

"I am."

"And you were on the tennis team at Downey High in seventy-four?"

He eyed me suspiciously, and asked, "Who are you?"

Not having had time to prepare a cover story, I went with the truth. Well, sort of the truth. "I work for the attorney representing Larry Wilkes. I'd like to talk to you about Pete Michaels' murder."

He didn't respond.

"Could I come in for a few minutes?"

He thought about it, then stepped out of my way. Once inside the dark apartment, my eyes adjusted and I saw that the small living room was lined with shelves, shelves that were crowded with toys. Many of the toys were still in their original boxes. A quick glance told me that he was especially interested in movie tie-ins, particularly sci-fi: *Star Wars, Star Trek, Krull*.

"You like toys," I said unnecessarily.

"It's how I make my living. I used to go to a swap meet every weekend. Now I sell on the computer. AuctionWeb."

He didn't offer me a place to sit, there were very few, or a glass of water. So standing there in the center of his living room, I asked my questions. Haseltine lit himself a cigarette and sat down in front of his computer.

"Did you like Pete Michaels?"

"No."

"Why not?"

He shrugged. "I just didn't."

"I heard he was a popular guy."

"He was. I just didn't like him."

"Did that cause problems on the team?"

"No. I wasn't very good. I lost most of my matches. No one paid much attention to me."

"If you lost your matches, then you were the reason the team came in third."

"I guess you could look at it like that."

"Did anyone on the team look at it that way?"

He shrugged.

"What can you tell me about Pete Michaels?"

"He was coach's favorite."

Without knowing exactly what that meant, I played a hunch. "And you wanted to be coach's favorite?"

"My therapist says it's because of my dad. I was his favorite until I was eleven. She says I keep trying to recreate that relationship. I never make it happen though."

I stood there awkwardly in the center of his living room. This was exactly what I'd feared it was. Except it wasn't. Haseltine wanted to be with the coach, but Pete Michaels stood in the way. Or at least that's what Haseltine thought.

"Did you kill Pete Michaels?"

"What? No! I mean, why would I? School was over. The

team was over. My chance to be Coach Carrier's favorite was gone."

"I want to be clear about something. Do you know for a fact that the coach and Pete Michaels were having... a relationship?"

"I think everyone knew. They pretended they didn't, but they did. We went places, you know. We were that good. We competed all over the state. When we stayed in hotels. Pete didn't sleep in the room with his brother. He slept with Coach. No one talked about that. Ever."

CHAPTER TWENTY

April 16, 1996
Tuesday morning

On the way to the office, I stopped at a coffee shop in what was called the East Village. It was a strange name, I thought, since it was west of most of Long Beach. Of course, Ronnie had let me in on the fact that it was real estate agents who named most neighborhoods these days, and the East Village sounded like the kind of place most city dwellers might want to live. The fact that it only had a nice block or two and the rest of it was crap didn't deter anyone, least of all real estate agents.

I don't remember the name of the shop, but I picked up three fancy coffee drinks: a whole milk latte for me, a vanilla soy milk latte for Karen and a double mocha for Lydia—her regular was a nonfat cappuccino, but I knew that she preferred a double mocha. I always made a 'mistake' with her order. I would have gone to Hot Times, my neighborhood gay coffee shop, but it was across from the Park Pantry and the video store. I couldn't shake the idea that Hamlet Gilbody was camped out on that corner waiting for me to return.

I walked into The Freedom Agenda office with a cardboard tray of coffee drinks. Karen was on the phone, frowning at whoever was at the other end. I handed her a coffee and she took it without a thank-you.

"No, that's not how we're doing this—" her tone was one I'd heard before and never wanted to be on the receiving end of, so I hurried down to Lydia's office. She, too, was on the phone.

"We're attempting to arrange for all three men to be released Friday morning and then we'll have a press conference in front of the prison. Are you able to be there—yes, Peter Linder is being transferred down from Solano on Wednesday. Do you have anything Friday? It would be good for you to be there."

I was sure she was talking to Edwin Karpinski. I handed Lydia a coffee. She took it, mouthing a thank-you. When she took a sip, she made a blissful face and then rolled her eyes.

"I'll be in the back," I said softly.

She held up a finger to keep me there.

"I'll call you back as soon as things solidify. Thank you, Edwin." Then she hung up.

"Looks like everything will be happening on Friday, in Corcoran. Sorry about that."

"No problem."

"You deserve to be there though."

"I'm fine."

She gave me a dubious look, then said, "Tell me what's going on with your pet project."

"I think I'm starting to find people who had motives to kill Pete Michaels."

She frowned. It wasn't evidence and I knew that.

"It seems that Pete Michaels was having a relationship with his tennis coach."

"How old was Pete?"

"Seventeen the first year, eighteen the second."

"What year was it?"

"Seventy-four, seventy-five."

"Sodomy laws got taken off the books in seventy-six."

"Pete was killed in seventy-six."

"I'm thinking about legal exposure for the coach, as motive."

"I don't know exactly when they became involved. Or what

the age of consent was then. It's possible it was all legal. Or at least legalish."

"There would still be an ethical problem," Lydia pointed out. "Teachers aren't supposed to sleep with their students regardless of the age of consent."

Which reminded me of something. Coach Carrier wasn't just a coach. He taught something, as well. I never asked what that was. I tucked that away for later, then said, "So if Pete threatened the coach with exposure, he'd have lost his job. That's a motive."

"Did Larry Wilkes know about this relationship?"

"I don't think so. He didn't tell me about it."

"That's a problem. If Larry knew about it and told his lawyer and then his lawyer decided not to bring it out in the trial... that would be ineffective counsel."

"I could ask Larry, maybe he did know."

"I think you're right that he would have told you. Is that all you have?"

"Well... I think there's more to it. According to one of the teammates, the whole team knew about Pete's relationship with the coach, which means his brother knew about it. When I spoke to him, he didn't say anything about it."

"You think the brother had a problem with him being gay?"

"It's possible."

"It's still not enough. At the very least, we need a witness to recant. And even that won't fly with a lot of judges."

"I'll go back and talk to the brother again."

"We need something physical. There's nothing we can test for DNA? Could this kid have struggled with his attacker? If there were fingernail scrapings we could test those."

"I don't know if they were taken. We'd have to take the case to find that out."

Lydia frowned. "I don't want to get this guy's hopes up if there's nothing to work with. Do you know what his sentence is?"

"Twenty-five to life."

"And he's been in for twenty years?"

"Yes."

"Has he got credits for good behavior?"

"I don't know."

"They keep changing that system. He could have several years accrued."

"You think he should wait for parole?"

"I think he may have to. I need you to finish up by the end of the week. We'll be looking at new cases starting next week. I'm going to need all your attention."

****

Right after lunch, I drove up to Downey and sat outside the Michaels' family house. As I'd suspected, Paulie's orange Camaro was in the driveway. Once I'd collected my thoughts, I got out of the frog car and crossed the street. Paulie must have been peeking out a window, because he came out of the house and walked down the driveway. When he got close, he said, "Don't come around my parents' house anymore."

"Are you inviting me to your place? You'll need to give me the address."

"I told you, this doesn't have anything to do with me."

"Yeah, but I think it does."

"You think I killed my brother?"

"No. But I think you know Larry Wilkes didn't."

"I don't *know* anything."

"Did you know your brother was having sex with your tennis coach?"

"No."

"Where did you think he was sleeping when you were on the road?"

"Sometimes I'd have girls visit me, so I didn't really care where he slept. Other times I thought he was with a girl somewhere..."

"You don't seem very surprised by my question, though."

"I'm just starting to figure these things out. I know how dumb that sounds."

"So, you do think there was something between the coach and your brother?"

"You can't go around asking questions like that. My parents aren't okay. My dad's not that healthy. Something like what you're saying gets back to them and I don't know what'll happen—"

"Do you think Larry Wilkes and your brother were in a relationship?"

"You didn't hear a word I just said, did you?"

"Come on, give me something. Your wife perjured herself at the trial, didn't she? She was never engaged to your brother."

"No. No, there wasn't. Okay? Are you happy?"

"How did you find out?"

"Anne had some dental work before she found out she was pregnant. She asked for the gas they use, so I had to drive her. On the way home she confessed that she wasn't Pete's fiancé, that she wasn't involved with him at all. That she'd lied to the court, to everyone, to me."

"She's still lying," I said.

"I know. She's tried to tell me that what she said wasn't true, that she was drugged and delusional. And she was, she was drugged. And that made her tell the truth."

"And that's why you left her?"

He nodded. "I asked her not to have the baby. She refused. Even when we found out the laughing gas at the dentist might have hurt the fetus. She wants to use the baby to get me back. But... I don't want to be with someone who's been lying to me for twenty years."

"When did you start thinking Larry Wilkes might not have killed your brother?"

"A few months back. Around the time I started thinking Pete was gay."

"Who do you think killed your brother?"

"My wife."

I was not expecting that. "Why do you think your wife killed him?"

"Because she's lying. Because she's always been lying. And because she sent an innocent man to prison."

"Larry asked her to lie at the trial."

"He did?"

"His attorney didn't think he'd have a chance if the jury knew he was gay."

"She used that lie to get close to my family, to get close to me."

"That may be so, but it doesn't mean she killed your brother."

He seemed unhappy that I'd said that. I decided to leave motive alone—I didn't think she had one—and move on to opportunity. "Did she have a connection to Andy Showalter?"

"Well, we were all at school together."

"You went to school with hundreds of other kids too."

"Yeah. He kind of stuck out though."

"Do you have any reason to think he'd have gotten the gun for her and then lied about it? Any reason to believe she had that kind of influence over him?"

"No."

"Larry and Pete had a signal to let each other know it was safe to come over. That's why Larry went over that day. Do you think she might have known what the signal was?"

"What are you talking about?"

"If it was safe to come over, they'd call the other one and let the phone ring twice. To let them know."

"Oh. Yeah, that happened a couple of times. I teased Pete that it was some girl too afraid to talk to him."

I nodded, then said, "Whoever killed Pete signaled Larry to come over. Probably so he'd get caught and take the blame for your brother's death. Do you think Anne knew everything she needed to know in order to do that?"

"I don't know."

"I don't think she killed your brother."

He looked disappointed again. Then his mother was at the front door calling his name. "Paulie. I need help with your father."

He said one more thing to me. "Please stop asking questions. Please just go away." And then he went inside.

Well, I wasn't going to just go away. I was going to go talk to his ex-wife. She and I had a whole lot of things to talk about. She lied at Larry's trial. A lot. If I could get her to recant her testimony that would be one thing in his corner.

Climbing back into the frog car, I drove directly to Anne Whittemore's apartment in Bellflower. When I got to her front door it was open, so I knocked on the screen door. Inside, the TV was blaring. Music videos. It might have been Hootie and the Blowfish, but I'm not an expert. Not my kind of music. I knocked again and the teenage girl I'd first seen with Anne came into focus. She glared at me like I'd ruined her day.

"Is your mother home?"

"No. She went for a walk."

"She went for a walk?" I asked, probably sounding a little dubious.

"That's what I said, isn't it?"

"I know it's just... she's a little pregnant."

"Dude, she's a lot pregnant." Then she couldn't help but smirk. The little comedienne cracked herself up. "She thinks it's going to make the baby come. It won't. She's been walking all week."

"I'm going to go look for her. If she comes back, tell her I'm looking for her."

"Sure. Some creepy old guy is stalking you. Like that?"

"My name is Dom Reilly."

"I won't remember it."

"Then I guess you'll have to go with creepy old guy."

That cracked her up.

"Do you have a younger brother or sister?"

"You mean beside the one in my mommy's belly? No."

"Why is there a Big Wheel in front of your grandparents' house?"

"That's mine. My grandfather's not all there. He thinks I'm seven."

"Sorry about that."

She shrugged and walked away. I walked out of the building onto Woodruff. It wasn't what you'd call hot, barely into the seventies, but the sun was strong when it broke through the clouds. Which it seemed to be doing more and more. I looked one way down Woodruff, then the other. I didn't see any pregnant women chugging along.

With the occasional backward glance, I walked down to the next intersection, Rosecrans Avenue. About five hundred feet down, there was a taco place. Anne Whittemore was just passing it. I started walking toward her and soon I could see that she was red-faced and sweating, pumping her arms as she power-walked.

When she got close to me, she said, "I don't want to talk to you."

Honestly, I was surprised she *could* talk.

"Your ex-husband thinks you killed his brother."

"What?!" She stopped walking and immediately bent over, hands on knees, inhaling deeply.

"I told him I didn't think you did."

"Oh, well, thanks for that."

I was beginning to see where her daughter got her diffident attitude.

"He told me you admitted that you weren't Pete's fiancé."

"I was drugged. I didn't know what I was saying."

"You want your husband back, right?"

"Yeah. He's the father of my kids."

"Then you're going to have to start telling the truth."

She looked up and down the street, and said, "Why are there never any benches?"

"You know Larry Wilkes didn't kill Pete Michaels, don't you?"

"I don't know that. I wasn't there. I know he told me to pretend to be Pete's fiancé. That's all I know for sure."

"Are you willing to recant your testimony?" She was right. It didn't exactly prove much of anything. It might not help Larry at all.

"Why do you think I'll get my husband back if I do that?"

"Because he's mad about being lied to for twenty years."

She looked out at the traffic, her face full of doubt. I had her talking though. I wondered if I could find out anything useful.

"You and Larry were friends. You hung out a lot in high school?"

"Yeah, I guess. We smoked cigarettes, weed, got drunk when we could."

"Did you know he was gay?"

"Sort of. I mean, you didn't talk about things like that. Not then. Not like now."

"Were you around when he started seeing Pete Michaels?"

"I think they kept a lot of that secret. Larry wasn't around as much. Then there were a couple of times when Pete was there. Larry said he was buying pot. Looking back, maybe that's not what was going on."

"Can you think of anyone who might have killed Pete?"

"Sure, my husband."

"Really?" My first thought was that she was playing tit for tat. He'd accused her of murder, so she accused him.

"He didn't exactly like faggots when we were kids."

"And you think he likes them better now?"

She smiled for a moment, then she huffed away.

I walked back to the green Taurus and drove to Long Beach. Lydia and Karen were both still rushing around coordinating the release of the three not-rapists. I slipped a note in front of Karen asking her to get information on Coach Carrier when she had time. That earned me a death stare and the words, "Tomorrow. Late."

Into the phone she hurriedly said, "No, not you. Lydia needs to speak to the ADA this afternoon. No later than five."

I went into the back and spent the rest of the day reading through the letters we get, occasionally stopping to think through what I knew about Pete Michaels' murder.

It was possible, even likely, that Anne Michaels would recant her testimony. But I didn't know if that meant anything at all. Her testimony established motive. But her withdrawing it might simply provide another motive. She could tell the court that Larry wanted her to lie—which was the truth. If a judge knew that Larry and Pete were involved, he or she might assume that was the motive. Larry killed his lover.

Many judges, possibly most judges, would simply decide that Larry felt deep shame about the relationship and killed his lover. The lack of motive then would not be a problem since a judge would supply one in a moment. It was certainly prejudicial and unfair, but it was also reality. I was going to have to find something else. But what?

Around four that afternoon, I got an idea. I dialed a number and waited while it rang.

"Mrs. Showalter?"

"Yes?"

"This is Dom Reilly. I stopped by to see you—"

"Yes, I remember."

"I just have a quick question. Did Andy have anything to do with the tennis team?"

"Oh God no. The social aspects of sports were beyond his abilities."

"I see. So he wouldn't have had any contact with the boys on the team or Coach Carrier."

"Well, Mr. Carrier was Andy's health teacher. He gave Andy the only A he ever got in all of high school."

"Thank you," I said. "I think I needed to know that."

CHAPTER TWENTY-ONE

April 16, 1996
Tuesday evening

When I got home, I circled the block three times and then parked four blocks away on Ocean. Walking home, I kept my senses heightened while I thought about what to do.

At first glance, my leaving would make it a terrible time for Ronnie to buy a condo, I mean, co-op, but then when I thought about it, it was the perfect time. If he couldn't handle the mortgages alone, he could get a roommate. Or he could upgrade the co-op, wait until it went condo, and then sell it for a big profit. Financially, Ronnie would be fine. There was always some trick he could pull out of his hat to make things work.

On the way up my front steps, my cellular phone chirped. I assumed it was Ronnie, telling me he was on his way home and asking if I wanted him to pick up some dinner—I did. I was thinking Mexican. When I said hello, there was a woman on the other end.

"Yes, hello. I got a strange call from Downey High School this afternoon. I'm told you want to talk to someone about Bernie Carrier."

"I do yes. Do you know him?"

"I'm his wife. This has something to do with high school tennis?"

"Uh-yes. I'm writing a story."

"Are you?"

I could tell she didn't believe me. The only thing I had going for me was her curiosity. I knew better than to satisfy that over the phone. "I'd like to meet you, and maybe your husband, tell you more about the story I want to write."

"I'm sure you would."

She left a long silence. I suspect she hoped I'd provide more information, that I'd pitch myself, that I'd beg. I kept my mouth shut.

Finally, she asked, "Where are you?"

"Long Beach."

"I live in Signal Hill. Can you come over now?"

She gave me the address and I promised to be there in twenty minutes. I turned around and walked back to the rental car.

Signal Hill is a small city surrounded by Long Beach. There's not much to it, you drive north on Cherry Avenue and up a condominium covered hill. At the top of that is a small observation park with fabulous views. Then, the road descends the other side of the hill and before you know it, you've left Signal Hill.

Mrs. Carrier's condo was on the cleverly named Hill Street and climbed upwards in steps. Her step was near the top. I parked and found the entrance to the topmost part of the condo. The name on the door was Blanchard, something I planned to ask her to explain.

I have to say, I was completely shocked when she opened the door. She was young, in her mid-thirties. Very young to be Coach Carrier's wife. She wore her hair in a boyish pixie cut and no makeup.

Not believing my eyes, I asked, "Is Mrs. Carrier in?"

She laughed. "I'm Sammy Blanchard. AKA Mrs. Carrier. Well, Mrs. Carrier number two. Bernie's first wife lives out in Norwalk."

"You don't use his name?"

"I don't. I prefer my maiden name."

"I take it you're no longer married to Coach Carrier?"

"Coach Carrier... I haven't heard that in a long time. Um, no, we're still married. Why don't you come in and tell me why you're here?"

Sammy turned and walked away. She was wearing capri pants and a sleeveless top, both of which emphasized the fact that she was a girl without a lot of curves. Her figure was straight up and down. Not that I cared one way or the other.

"So, I'm writing a story about high school tennis—"

She gave me a disappointed look. "Yeah, why don't you go out onto the deck and think up a better story than that one. I'll bring some iced tea, unless you'd like something stronger."

"Iced tea is fine."

I walked through her comfortable living room out onto the very large deck. The view was stunning. We could see all of Long Beach—well, the part that was to the south. Below us was Cherry Avenue, thick with traffic. That had to be annoying. A million-dollar view and a soundtrack that was akin to a demolition derby. Looking at the horizon, I tried to pick out where my house was but couldn't quite find it.

Sammy came out with a tray of iced tea and glasses. She poured a glass and handed it to me. After she poured herself one, we sat down on iron chairs, which were not especially comfortable. She took a pack of Merits out of her Capri pants and lit one.

"I only smoke on the patio. I can't stand the smell inside. Weird, I know. So," she said, looking me over. "If you were one of Bernie's students it was a very long time ago. No offense."

"None taken."

"Oh God, you're not the father of—"

"I don't have any kids."

"That's a relief. It happened once. Horrible. I don't like to think about it."

"If you didn't believe me, why did you call?"

"There's never anything good on television. Did you notice that?"

"I mostly rent videos. So... I work for The Freedom Agenda."

"Oh, really. Well that's interesting."

"You've heard of us?"

"Yes. You got that Danny kid out of prison. A few months ago, wasn't it?"

"Yes, we did."

"How is he?"

"Danny? Free."

She smiled and asked, "This has something to do with the Michaels boy, doesn't it?"

"I believe Larry Wilkes is innocent."

"He probably is."

"Where is your husband? Will he be home soon?"

"He doesn't live here."

"You're separated?"

"No. Not exactly," she inhaled deeply, taking extreme pleasure in it. "Do you mind very much if I just tell you my story from the beginning? I don't get to tell it very often."

I doubted I had much say in the matter, so I nodded agreement.

"Bernie was my high school health teacher," she began. "I was fifteen the first time I saw him. He was fifty-six. A forty-one-year age difference. Scandalous, don't you think?"

I shrugged wanting to remain noncommittal.

"Anyway, I was in love, instantly. It was dramatic, the kind of dramatic that appeals to a teenager. I set my sights on him, began staying after class, pretending I didn't understand things I understood perfectly well. Soon I was teacher's pet. Then I was more. Much more."

She put her cigarette out and lit another.

"I can't begin to describe how thrilling it was to have a man like that love me, not to mention I was a mere child stealing a grown woman's husband. The power. My parents were very social—alcoholics in case you can't read between the lines—so they were gone a lot. Bernie and I had a signal. When they left, I'd call his house and let it ring twice then hang up. He'd make an excuse and come to me. Eventually I convinced him to marry me, or vice versa. That part's a little fuzzy. He divorced his wife and we were married when I was seventeen."

She enjoyed her cigarette.

"Bernie lost his job, of course. But he found another one in Fullerton. He had a friend there who got him on as a shop teacher. I think they felt as long as he wasn't near young girls... It was years before I fully understood. I've always been something of a tomboy, and then the thing with Pete Michaels—which happened right before he met me. I think Bernie thought if he could be with me then everything would be all right. It wasn't though. He was back to boys soon enough. About ten years ago there was another boy, Ricky Tamayo. Spoiled little brat. His parents found out what was going on. Ricky's father beat Bernie nearly to death. Brain damage. Pretty severe. He's in a home. I go to visit once a month. The staff thinks I'm his granddaughter. So does Bernie."

She stubbed out her cigarette.

"Things were hushed up. It was called an accident. Since it happened on school grounds there was a settlement, and they've generously maintained his teacher's insurance. In the end, I've done well for a skinny little tomboy with daddy issues."

"Why do you think Larry Wilkes is innocent?"

"Pete Michaels asked Bernie for money to move to Santa Barbara. And by asked, I mean, threatened to expose him if he didn't give him ten thousand dollars."

"He told you that?"

"He did. I think he told me to keep me in line. I was certainly afraid of him for a while. And then someone let the Tamayos know what was going on with their son."

I had a strong feeling I knew who tipped them off. Of course, I was sure she was telling me the truth. I recognized the signal with the telephone, something Pete picked up and used with Larry. What I wasn't sure about was whether any of this was evidence that could be used at trial.

"Your husband is brain damaged?"

"He'll never stand trial, if that's what you're asking."

"Would you be willing to testify if we can get another trial for Larry Wilkes?"

"No. Absolutely not," she said. "My lawyer would never allow it."

I sat for a moment trying to figure out if there was another way to this information. Sammy was very likely the only one who knew about the attempted blackmail. Larry didn't know since he hadn't mentioned it. And... he was hardly a credible witness. Maybe Pete mentioned wanting to move to Santa Barbara, but it's doubtful he added that he was trying to pull the money together through blackmail.

"Do you know anything about how your husband convinced Andy Showalter to get him a gun? Or even why he chose Showalter for that task?"

"No. I didn't ask a lot of questions about the murder. It seemed like the more I knew the more danger I was in. To be completely honest, I tried hard to *not* know things."

And that was it. I'd reached a dead end. I'd proven that Larry Wilkes was innocent—to myself at least. But I still didn't have anything that would get him out of prison.

CHAPTER TWENTY-TWO

April 17, 1996
Wednesday morning

The next morning before I left the house, I nudged Ronnie and asked, "Hey, what's going on with the co-op? Did they accept your offer?"

"They countered. So I countered the counter."

"Is that good?"

"Yeah, we'll make a deal. We just haven't yet."

I got to The Freedom Agenda late—again. I tried to convince myself it didn't matter. All I had planned was a short conversation with Lydia and then a phone call to Corcoran Prison to schedule a meeting with Larry Wilkes. I could write him a letter saying that we declined to take his case and save myself the drive, but that felt cowardly. I'd raised his hopes, I could at least be the one to dash them.

The phone was ringing off the hook. When she saw me, Karen put the latest call on hold, set the receiver down, and frowned at me.

"What's going on?" I asked.

"Edwin planted a story in the *L.A. Times* about the three alleged rapists getting out of prison.

"Ah." I nodded sympathetically. It came out this morning?"

She nodded. Then she hit the hold button, and said, "I'm sorry, Lydia's not available at the moment. I suggest you call Edwin Karpinski's office."

Then she clicked off.

To me she said, "I have something on Bernard Carrier. He's in a home called Cardinal Convalescent. He's been there for more than a decade. I haven't been able to establish what happened to him, but he's in a 'post-traumatic confusional state'."

"How did you find that out?"

"I called and pretended to be with Medicare. I said I needed more information for billing purposes." She picked up the ringing phone, and said, "Hold please."

"Good job."

"Mr. Carrier is barely able to speak and has trouble identifying people. Even people he's known a long time."

"Yes, his wife said he thought she was his granddaughter."

With a frown she asked, "You've met his wife?"

"Last night. She called me."

"She called you?"

"I left my number at the high school."

She raised an eyebrow, and asked, "Downey High where Bernard Carrier worked until nineteen seventy-eight when he married Samantha Blanchard age seventeen?"

"Yup. That high school."

"I feel like I wasted my time."

"Oh, no. You're confirming everything Sammy said to me."

"Is this your pet project?" Lydia asked coming around the corner.

"It is."

"Any progress?"

I nodded. "Pete Michaels attempted to blackmail his tennis coach and was killed because of it."

"So we're certain Larry Wilkes is innocent," she said, sounding unhappy about it.

"We are. *I* am."

"Did you get a confession?"

"Bernie Carrier has a traumatic brain injury."

"Post-traumatic confusional state," Karen added.

"So that's a no."

"His wife says her husband confessed to killing Pete Michaels prior to his injury."

Lydia stood a little straighter. "That would be new information. And it's an admissible hearsay exception."

"She won't testify though. She said her lawyer wouldn't let her."

Lydia raised an eyebrow. "That's a provocative statement."

"Her husband was nearly beaten to death ten years ago. It's possible she encouraged his assailant."

"Incitement to commit assault, possibly. But it's way beyond the statute of limitations. She would not be putting herself at risk."

"Some lawyers are overly cautious."

"Is that a dig?"

"No." Well, maybe it was. I asked, "Could we subpoena her if we took the case?"

"We could compel her to give a deposition, and if she says that her husband confessed to murdering Pete Michaels, that will likely get us a new trial. But it's also likely she won't say that, isn't it? And since the conversation we want her to testify to was between her and her now mentally incompetent husband, she can lie with impunity. *And* she could rely on spousal privilege and say nothing if she wants to. Unless she comes forward voluntarily, we can't use her."

We stood there awkwardly for a moment.

"There must be something else," Karen said.

"I think Anne Michaels will recant her testimony."

"That just speaks to motive," Lydia said. "You can change the reason and all the same things happen. That's what a judge would say." I'd already figured that out, but it was good to have confirmation.

"I'm sure I could find something in discovery," I said, though it was unlikely I'd be around that long. Lydia gave me a look that said I was incorrigible.

"The problem with our taking a case like this one is that it could drag on for years. There's no smoking gun, nothing to threaten the DA with. They could easily dig in and make this drag out for six, seven, eight years. When did you say this guy is up for parole?"

"Five years."

"If we do anything, we should help with that. It's fifty-fifty whether he'll get out on his first try at parole, but if we get the right mix of people speaking for him, if he's contrite and remorseful given that he was so young when he was convicted, it might improve those odds."

"That's the best we can do?"

"Unless you find something concrete. But I need you to let this go, Dom. We can't get so caught up saving one guy that we fail a dozen others."

When Lydia went back to her office, I asked Karen to help me make arrangements to see Larry Wilkes the next day.

CHAPTER TWENTY-THREE

April 18, 1996
Thursday morning

On the drive up to Corcoran, I listened to KCRW until the signal broke up. They'd begun their one-year anniversary coverage of the Oklahoma City bombing. The story they decided to air—which would likely never hit the big networks—had to do with the media's rush to judgement. In the first twenty-four hours after the bombing, the reports indicated that the terrorist was likely from the Middle East. There were even suggestions that we bomb whichever Arab country was most likely to have supplied the terrorist and worry about whether we were right later. The press was left thoroughly confused when they learned a nice-looking, white Christian boy had committed the worst ever terrorist attack on American soil. How would we ever process that?

When I finally lost the signal, I put in a CD. Jane Olivor's *Best Side of Goodbye*. Not my normal fare. I'd mentioned her once to Ronnie and he'd gotten me the CD. She reminded me... well, she reminded me of so much.

While I listened, I tried to focus. I needed to be thinking about Pete Michaels' murder. I was on my way to the prison to tell Larry Wilkes we would not be taking his case. I desperately wanted not to be doing that, so I ran through the murder mentally, hoping to find some tiny bit of possible evidence I might have overlooked.

Pete Michaels met with his killer, Coach Bernie Carrier, on September 18, 1976. A Saturday. Sometime in the afternoon. His parents and his brother were out. But not together. Pete must have set up the meeting himself, he was the one who'd have known his family's plans. So Coach Carrier would have known what the meeting was about: blackmail. He'd likely agreed to Pete's terms and had come to hand over the money. Except he had no intention of doing that. He'd obtained a gun, so he went with the intent to kill Pete.

There were no fingerprints on the gun. That meant it was wiped. Or the coach wore gloves. But was that before the murder or after? If it was before, it implies a great deal of planning—including the gloves. After, suggests Bernie went hoping not to have to kill Pete. I decided to go with before.

So, no fingerprints on the gun—Coach Carrier was wearing gloves. And what about the bullets? Were there fingerprints on them? Could you even get fingerprints off a bullet casing? I had no idea.

Then I began to wonder about gunshot residue. Had Larry been tested for it? What were the results? I'd skimmed through the transcripts a couple of times and I didn't remember anything about that. I made a mental note to ask Larry about it. I knew that he had not fired a gun, so would that test tell us that? And if so, why hadn't it been done?

Then I wondered if phone records had been pulled. Coach Carrier and Pete had been in contact. They had to have set up the meeting that Saturday afternoon. Of course, if the information wasn't collected during the trial, it's likely gone. I couldn't imagine the phone company keeping call records for twenty years. That was another question for Larry.

If Coach Carrier wore gloves of some kind, he must have entered and kept his hands in his pockets. Certainly, if Pete had seen the gloves—that brought up an interesting question: Were there any signs of a struggle? Was it possible Pete scratched the coach? That would result in DNA under his fingertips and we could test that. If it was there and if it was collected. Something else to ask about.

Winding my way through the Grapevine, I paid nearly as much attention to the murder I was re-enacting in my mind as I did to the freeway in front of me. After shooting Pete, Coach Carrier called Larry using the signal he'd had with Pete. I wondered how he knew they used the same telephone code? Had it been part of the conversation when Pete was working his way up to blackmailing him?

Had Coach Carrier known Pete's parents would be home soon? Did he know they'd walk in on Larry? Or did he simply expect Larry to come over, see that Pete was dead, and call the police? It wasn't unheard of for murderers to call the police and pretend they didn't do it. Did he know the police would automatically suspect Larry?

When I arrived at the prison it was nearly one in the afternoon, and I felt like I'd explored every detail of Pete Michaels' murder ad nauseam. There really wasn't much we could do, and I felt like a man on his way to the gallows—not an inappropriate feeling given where I was.

I dragged myself through the complex and mind-numbing process of entering the prison. I found myself in the same visitors' room I'd visited twice. After an unsurprising half-an-hour wait, Larry Wilkes was brought in. He gave me a hopeful smile.

"It's nice to see you again. I hope you've brought good news."

"Mostly I have questions," I said. That wasn't exactly true, but I wanted to let him down easily, if possible.

"What kind of questions?"

"Well... first, did you know that your friend, Anne Whittemore, married Paulie?"

"She what? Really?"

"You didn't know?"

"I had no idea."

"How is that possible? They were married nearly twenty years ago. No one ever mentioned it to you?"

Jutting out his jaw, he said, "I'm in prison. No one in my family speaks to me. They don't write to me. They don't visit. I told them what really happened. That I loved Pete and couldn't have killed him. My father said he liked me better when I was a murderer."

"That must have been a terrible thing to hear."

"Anne was my best friend in high school. I guess I know now why she stopped writing."

"You never get any mail?"

"I've gotten a few letters. Women who want to marry a prisoner. I don't know how they find me."

I wasn't sure whether to believe him a hundred percent. It didn't make a lot of sense that he wouldn't know Anne married Paul Michaels. But then, maybe it was strange enough to be true.

"Let's talk about what happened when you were arrested. Were you tested for gunshot residue?"

"No."

"Why didn't your attorney bring that up at trial?"

"He didn't think it was a good idea."

"He didn't think it was a good idea?" A bell went off in my head. We were back to ineffective—

"I was covered in Pete's blood. I'd been holding him. Sobbing. The blood would have gotten in the way of the testing. My lawyer thought that it was a good thing the test wasn't done since my holding Pete would have transferred residue from him to me. He was sure the test would have been positive, so he didn't make a big deal about it not being done."

"Did they get phone records?"

"Mine."

"Not Pete's?"

"No."

That was evidence the police had focused on Larry and only Larry. Of course, that was not enough for a new trial. I realized I was frowning when he said, "You look unhappy."

"Just a few more questions. Do remember if there was evidence of a struggle. Did Pete fight back?"

"I don't remember anything like that."

"He was dead when you got there?"

Larry couldn't answer. He just nodded his head.

"You used a phone signal to say the coast was clear. Who else knew about that?"

"No one."

"Tell me what you know about Coach Carrier."

"The health teacher?"

"Yes. He was also Pete and Paulie's tennis coach."

"What does he have to do—"

"You told me Pete had had previous sexual relationships. I've learned he was involved with Coach Carrier."

I could see that he was struggling with that.

"He was old," he said, softly.

"Yes, he was quite a bit older than Pete."

"There are men in here, that's what they did. That's why they're here. They had sex with kids Pete's age."

I nodded agreement.

"I spoke with Coach Carrier's wife. She says he told her that Pete was attempting to blackmail. Pete wanted money to move to Santa Barbara."

"He wanted to—he never told me that." He became very quiet. "He wanted to be with me? And it got him killed?"

"That's not your fault."

"If we hadn't been in love..."

"The only person responsible for Pete's death is Coach Carrier."

"Have they arrested him?"

"No. His wife is refusing to testify. And there's a bigger problem. He continued his behavior with teenage boys. He was beaten by the father of one of them that left him with severe brain damage. It's unlikely he can be prosecuted."

"This is a lot to take in."

"I know."

We sat quietly for a long time. He cleared his throat before he could speak again. "You're not going to be able to get me out of here, are you?"

"It would be very difficult and could take a very long time. You're up for parole in less than five years."

He nodded.

"I think we'll be able to get Pete's brother to speak on your behalf."

"Will he tell them I'm innocent?"

"No. You'll need to tell the parole board you're remorseful. That you're sorry you killed Pete."

"I can't tell them I didn't do it?"

"They won't believe you."

He looked like he was actively trying not to think about that. He said, "I called Brysen. He said you called him. Thank you."

I nodded.

"He's very excited about the money. But there won't be any, will there?"

"No, there won't be."

"Don't tell him that, okay?"

"I don't expect to talk to him again."

"This is really over, isn't it?"

"I'm sorry. I'm afraid it is."

****

I made it home by seven-thirty. Ronnie and I met at Osteria De Medici, a family-style Italian restaurant in a strip of storefronts a few blocks from our house on Broadway. I was standing out front, scanning the street in both directions, making sure Hamlet Gilbody was nowhere to be seen.

"Looking for me?" Ronnie asked when he walked up. He wore a very dark pair of blue jeans, ironed and creased, a lavender dress shirt and a white linen jacket. It was about as professional as he liked to get. He didn't care for ties and thought a full-on suit would intimidate his clients.

After we were shown to a table in the back, Ronnie sighed heavily, and said, "You don't know how happy I am to be here.

Right before I left the office one of my mother's friends called me. Immediately, I thought 'oh my God, she's dead,' which left my head spinning in all sorts of directions. But no, she called to tell me I'm a bad son."

"I don't remember your mother having friends."

"Well, employee. Chin Li. She runs one of my mother's dry cleaners."

"So your mother paid to have you insulted."

"Basically."

That meant the situation was getting to her but not in a way that offered any hope.

Our waiter arrived. He squealed when he saw Ronnie and bent over to kiss him on the cheek. His name was Rod. He was fiftyish, tall, with a receding hairline and the complexion of a life-long alcoholic. He looked down his nose at me, and said, "Hmmm, it's you."

He was not a fan of mine. I'd cut him off several times at The Hawk. I knew he'd eventually drink himself to death, I just didn't want to be the one who served him his last drink.

Ronnie ordered for us. The lemon orzo soup, Caesar salad, prosciutto and penne for me, and carbonara for him. A glass of Napa Valley chardonnay for him and an iced tea for me.

Once Rod walked away, I said, "You know, I can order for myself."

"Isn't that what you wanted?"

"Well, yes." I hated that I was so predictable.

"Let me know if you want something different and I'll shut up."

I decided to let it drop. I'd figured out long ago that, since there was much about my past I didn't share with Ronnie—well, any of my past—he compensated by 'knowing' me very, very well in the present.

"We're going to have to go on a budget," he said.

"Said the man who just ordered a nine-dollar glass of wine."

"It's rude of you to point that out."

We were quiet for a bit. Well, longer than a bit; long enough for me to wonder if something was wrong. Then

Ronnie said, "They accepted my offer on the co-op by the way."

"That's great. Isn't it?"

"Do *you* want the co-op?"

"I gave you money for it, didn't I?"

He gave me a look that made it clear he noticed I'd avoided answering the question. I tried changing the subject.

"I drove up to Corcoran today. I've been looking into a twenty-year-old murder. The guy who's in prison for the murder is innocent. But I can't prove it. I had to tell him we couldn't take his case."

"That must have been depressing."

"It was."

Rod returned with Ronnie's wine and my iced tea. The wine he set down carefully for Ronnie; my iced tea nearly ended up in my lap. When Rod was gone, Ronnie said, "I have a mortgage guy at Chase. He thinks he can get us into a decent mortgage with twenty percent down, and then we can put an immediate second on it with a hundred and ten percent cap. That would give us close to twenty thousand to begins renovation."

"Begin?"

"I don't think twenty thousand is enough. But if I can convince everyone in the building to go condo..."

"There's a cost related to that as well, though, isn't there?"

"It's not awful. We'll deal with it when we get there."

"Twenty percent down is about twelve thousand dollars. Where is that coming from?"

"My commission is almost two thousand, that gets applied. John is paying two months' rent in advance. That's another thousand. If I can manage to launder two thousand of what you gave me, that's five of it. I have another five coming in commissions over the next six weeks. That leaves me only two thousand short."

He sipped his wine, then asked, "You don't have any more money stashed away, do you?"

"No." I lied. I was tempted to give him more, but I knew better than to short myself. If I was going to run away, I needed to stay away.

"You know I'm still upset with you."

"Because I gave you twenty-five hundred dollars?"

"Don't try to sound like a hero. You keep too many secrets."

I had to admit that was true. Not that it got us anywhere.

Ronnie took a sip of his wine, and said, "It may be a nine-dollar glass of wine, but it tastes like twelve."

CHAPTER TWENTY-FOUR

April 19, 1996
Friday dead of night

I dreamed there was a chipmunk chirping in the bedroom. First, he was scurrying around the floorboards. Then he burrowed his way into my pants. And then I woke up enough to realize it wasn't a chipmunk chirping. It was the damn cellular phone Ronnie bought me. I crawled off the bed, found my jeans on a chair, pulled the phone out of my pocket, and answered—well, croaked into it.

"'Lo?"

"Dom? Is this Dom?" a woman asked.

"Uh-huh."

My eyes had opened enough to figure out it was still dark. Very dark. It was the middle of the night.

"Could you come please?"

"Come where? Who is this?"

"I tried to call Brenda, but she said they wouldn't let her come. I don't want to call the police."

Brenda was obviously Detective Wellesley. And she was police, so what she was saying was a bit contradictory. This had to have something to do with—

"Candy? Is this Candy Van Dyke?"

"I said that didn't I?"

"Has something happened?"

She broke into wrenching, hiccupping sobs.

"I can be there in about ten minutes. Are you safe?"

She sobbed something that sounded something like a yes.

"Are you alone?"

She was.

"Do you need medical attention?"

"I don't think so."

Still holding the phone, I pulled on my jeans and found a shirt. I had a pair of sneakers downstairs by the back door. I slipped out of the bedroom before Ronnie could wake up. The clock on our nightstand said 3:14AM.

Once I was in the hall, I asked, "Someone hurt you?"

"Yes."

"Do you know who?"

"Stu Whatley."

I was at Candy's door thirteen minutes later. The house was brightly lit. We'd stayed on the line right up until the time I parked. She became calmer, but I still didn't get a whole lot of information about what had happened. Several times, she said, "He thinks he can get away with it. He doesn't think anyone will believe me. I think he's right. No one *will* believe me."

When she opened the door, she wore a two-pieced zebra-striped lounging outfit. Disconcerting. She could have been about to entertain. In fact, everything about her and her house said, 'We're about to have a party.'

I asked, "That's not what you were wearing?"

She shook her head.

"Where are the clothes you were wearing?"

"In my bedroom hamper."

"Do you have a paper bag?"

"Somewhere."

"We should put your clothes into a paper bag."

"I'm not reporting this."

"That's fine. You might change your mind. We should put

the clothes in a bag and then you can throw them away in a few weeks, when you're sure."

"I'm sure."

"Humor me."

She looked at me uncomfortably for a moment, then walked down a short hallway to the kitchen. I followed her. Walking through the swinging door, I noticed immediately that the kitchen was perfect. Everything was white oak, including the appliances. In the center of the room sat a giant island—bigger than the queen-sized bed Ronnie and I slept in. Candy walked across the room, opened a double-doored pantry, and pulled out a brown paper bag.

"Will this work?"

"Yes, that's exactly what we need." We stood awkwardly for a moment. I took the bag from her. "Where are the clothes?"

"This way."

She led me up a flight of stairs to the second floor and into the master bedroom. It was as spacious and as white as the kitchen. Not a thing was out of place.

"Is this where it happened?" I asked.

"Yes."

"You straightened everything up."

"I did."

"The sheets are in the hamper with your clothes?"

"Yes, they are."

"We'll need another bag."

Without a word, she left the room. The room was on the canal side of the house. One wall was drapes over glass. The drapes were half open and I could see out to the balcony, which ran the length of the house. Unlike the pristine bedroom, one of the chairs had been knocked over.

I debated whether to call Lydia. On the one hand, I worked for her and should be telling her everything. On the other, our client was the accused rapist. She should be as far away from this as possible. I shouldn't even be there. I could, eventually, possibly, be accused of attempting to influence Candy into not reporting the rape. The fact that it wasn't true didn't mean it wouldn't happen.

When she came back, I asked, "Is there someone we should call? A friend? A family member?"

"I called you. I don't have the kind of friends you call in a crisis. And as for my family, well, most of the time they are the crisis."

It sounded like something she'd said before, before she was raped. The look on her face made it obvious she was having the same thought. Anything normal in the middle of a crisis felt wrong.

"It's okay to feel whatever you're feeling. There isn't a right way to do this," I said.

I was trying to be kind, but all I really wanted to do was grill her on what happened. There had to be a way to get Whatley, whether Candy reported the rape or not.

We put the sheets into the second bag. Gently, I asked, "Is there a reason that chair is knocked over?"

She looked out onto the balcony, quickly slid the glass door open, and went out to right the chair. When she came back in, she said, "I got away from him. Briefly. The chair fell over when he pulled me back inside."

"Did you have a chance to yell?"

"I screamed. Quite loudly, I think."

"But no one..."

"I've had complaints that I play my television too loud. If anyone heard, I'm sure they thought it was some program."

"When did this happen?" I wondered. Did people think she was watching TV at two in the—

"It started around midnight. That's when he got here."

That was almost four hours ago. That put things into a horrible perspective.

"I'd like to take you to the emergency room."

"No, I don't think so."

"You may be injured in ways you don't recognize," I said, probably too vaguely.

I knew that HIV could be easily contracted in prison where

Stu Whatley had been for most of the last ten years. This had been all over the news, not to mention John and I having talked about it. Candy needed to go onto AZT for her own protection. It was the last thing in the world I wanted to tell her. That's what doctors were for.

"Ways I don't recognize?" she asked, looking offended. "I was there. I think I know exactly how I was injured."

"You could have been given a social disease."

She stared at me a moment, absorbing that.

"I'll see my doctor this week."

"I have a friend who's an ER nurse at Long Beach Memorial. We could go and see him."

She got quiet again. I felt like I might have made some progress. 'Friend' had a safe ring to it. And it might be embarrassing to talk with her regular doctor.

"You know, I almost didn't come forward. After Joanne's rape," she said.

At first, I had no idea what to say to that. Then, "He was the wrong man, but he was a rapist. You probably saved a lot of women."

"And got myself raped in the bargain."

"I am sorry…"

"If I go and see your friend, he'll have to call the police. I'm not an idiot."

"I'm not trying to trick you. I'm trying to help. You called me to help you. And this is the best help I can offer you."

In a small voice, she said, "Fine. We'll go see your friend." With that, she left the room. As she turned and walked away, I noticed there was a small blood stain on the back of her outfit. We were doing the right thing.

I picked up the paper bags and left the bedroom.

Candy found her purse and we left the house. The Taurus was parked in the alley in front of her garage. I got her settled in the passenger seat and walked around to the driver's side. Before I got in, I called Ronnie.

"Is John working?" I had no idea what I'd say to Candy if he wasn't.

"It's almost four in the morning, why aren't you in bed next to me? Are you okay?"

"I'm fine. It's a friend."

"What friend?"

"I can't tell you, it's confidential."

"Is it something to do with work?"

"Is John working?"

"I think so, yeah. I don't hear him snoring."

"Thank you. I have to go. I'm not sure when I'll be home." I added an "I love you," to soften the stonewalling he was getting. Then I clicked off.

It took about fifteen minutes to get to the hospital. I illegally parked in a handicapped space. Candy and I hadn't said much on the ride. I was afraid she'd change her mind if I asked too many questions.

"This car," she said.

"What about it?" I thought she might tell me Stu Whatley was driving something like it. I was wrong.

"How does Ronnie tolerate it?"

"I usually drive a Jeep Wrangler that he helped pick out."

"That makes more sense. So why are we in this heap?"

"If we could maybe not mention it to Ronnie."

She thought about that a second, then said, "And people wonder why I never married."

Inside the hospital, I walked up to the reception desk and told the older woman sitting there, "I'd like to see John Gallagher."

"I'm sorry, the staff can't stop what they're doing to see friends."

"No, I'm with someone who needs medical attention."

"That's still not how this works. You need to have your friend add their name to the list. They'll be seen in triage, prioritized, and then called into the ER when space is available."

I leaned over the counter and got uncomfortably close to her. "She's been sexually attacked. She's in a fragile state and likely to bolt at any moment."

The woman looked at me deciding if I was a liar, and said,

"Just a moment." She picked up a phone, hit an intercom button and, though I couldn't hear her, presumably asked for John. A minute or so later, he came out in bright blue scrubs with a smear of blood at the hip.

"What's going on?"

"John, this Candy Van Dyke. She was attacked shortly after midnight." I noticed her flinch when I said this.

"Come with me," John said. He brought us to a room with the word TRIAGE on the door. We stood there, waiting. Obviously, someone was inside. John turned to Candy, and asked, "Are you in any pain at the moment?"

"Yes, of course. It's mild though."

"Have you spoken to the police yet?"

"No. I don't really want to."

"All right," John said. "I will need to call them. I can put it off a bit, but it's the law. When they get here just tell them you don't want to make a statement. They may try to persuade you. Hold your ground. After a few tries they'll give you their contact information, and if you decide to you can go into the station and give a statement at a later date. As we treat any injuries, we will be collecting evidence. That's hospital policy. After an attack, a patient can be in shock—"

"Yes, I know. I may change my mind. That point has been made."

The door to the triage room opened and an elderly Mexican woman came out with three younger family members. The nurse, a girl in her late twenties, came out after them.

"Shar, I'm going to need the triage room for a bit."

She looked like she might object for a moment but then glanced at Candy, taking in the situation. She sighed heavily.

"Fine."

"Could you bring me a gown and a kit. And then take a break or something."

Shar rolled her eyes, and said, "Yes, sir."

"Thank you."

I didn't get the feeling he was actually in charge of her—given the rolling of the eyes and the snark in her voice. But I imagine certain things take precedent. Once we were in the room, John said, "I'm sorry, I should have said this before. I've been trained to take care of victims of sexual assault. If you'd rather have a woman take care of you, I can make that happen. Or if you'd like a woman present while I conduct the examination, I can ask Shar—"

"Are you gay?"

"Very."

"It's fine."

"Are you comfortable taking a seat?"

"Yes, I'm okay."

We sat down. John behind a small desk, Candy and I on spindly plastic and metal chairs. He took a clipboard and pen out of a desk drawer.

"Candy, this is what will be happening. I'm going to take a history, which will include basic information about you and your health. When Shar comes back with a kit and a gown, you'll take off your clothes and stand on a large piece of paper. I'll examine you for—"

"No."

"You're not comfortable with that?"

"I've showered. I've changed my clothes. I don't see the point."

"Well, you may not have washed away all the evidence. And... you're bleeding. Conceivably, your attacker's semen could be mixed with your blood. I need to collect a sample."

Candy blushed.

"There's nothing to be embarrassed about. You've had a terrible experience. There's no shame in that."

"What will I wear home?"

"I think I have a raincoat in my car," John said.

"I'll look like a flasher."

John smiled and then continued his spiel. As soon as there's a bed available, we'll go into the ER for a more detailed pelvic examination. I'll take photographs of any bruises or contusions. Since the attack happened a few hours ago, you should plan on taking more photos in a day or two. Once we're in the ER, I'll probably take a moment and call the police. Before you go, I'll do a blood test and give you a prescription for antibiotics. If you'd like I can give you a prescription for AZT. Unfortunately, we won't be able to test for HIV tonight. It takes HIV antibodies four to six weeks to show up in your system."

There was silence. I doubt it had occurred to Candy she might have been infected with HIV. This was a whole new kind of violence being done to her.

"She'll take the AZT prescription," I said for her.

John nodded and then asked, "Are you ready to start, Candy?"

"Yes, yes I am," she said, more firmly than I expected.

CHAPTER TWENTY-FIVE

April 19, 1996
Friday early morning

It took almost half an hour to get a bed in the ER. Meanwhile, we created quite the bottleneck. New patients arrived but were not triaged. When Shar returned with the gown and kit, she mentioned that someone, I didn't catch the name, was upset and unlikely to forget this.

"She'll be fine," John said calmly. I suspected he was right, since not giving a rape victim immediate attention would be a PR nightmare. Particularly someone as prominent as Candy. I mean, her face was on bus benches.

John had just finished the pelvic exam when Ronnie burst into the curtained space.

"Oh my God," I said. "How did you get in here?"

"You can get in anywhere if you look like you know where you're going."

I have to admit I sort of knew that. Back in the day, I'd used a manila envelope to get into office buildings in Chicago. Apparently, my boyfriend could do the same thing without props.

Seeing who was in the bed, he said, "Candy, darling, what happened?"

For the first time since she called me, she crumbled and began to sob.

"I didn't tell him any—" I began.

"No, he didn't," Ronnie said. "I married a secretive bastard."

That comment had layers to it.

"Can you talk about it?" he asked.

Candy pulled herself together, took a few long breaths, and then said, "When I lived up in L.A., my neighbor was raped. I thought I saw the man leaving her house. I was wrong, I guess. That man was just released from prison."

"One of the men you got out," Ronnie said to me, giving me a look like I was personally responsible. Which was not that far from what I was feeling in that moment.

"Anyway, he showed up at my door. Stu Whatley, that's his name. He showed up at my door earlier this evening. I thought he was there for an apology, which seemed very reasonable. I let him in. I realized he was very angry right before... he grabbed me and pushed up the stairs. He talked a lot. Telling me things. What he wanted to do to me. He wanted to do it in my bedroom. On my bed. He wanted me to hate my own room. To hate my bed. He wanted me to know what it was like to live somewhere I didn't want to be."

Ronnie had pulled a chair up next to the bed, taken her hand in his and was petting it. "You're so brave," he said.

"I got away from him. Just for a minute. I was out on the balcony, screaming. No one heard though. He threatened to kill me if I tried anything else like that. I gave up. I stopped struggling."

"That was very smart of you," Ronnie said.

"He said no one would believe me if I reported him. I think he's right. I made a mistake when my neighbor was raped. They'll think I'm making another mistake."

"Did he actually say his name?" I asked. A defense attorney would try to discredit her I.D.

"Yes, he did. When I opened the door he told me who he was. I knew though. I'd seen pictures of him before his trial. I'd seen him in the courtroom. Wearing a cheap gray suit. I'm not wrong. Not this time."

It was beginning to seem like she might make a very credible witness. I was about to say so when a very young police officer pushed back the curtain and stepped into the space. His hair was blond and clipped close to his head, his eyes blue, his uniform tight enough to show off his muscles. He looked like the kind of kid who'd grown up on the beach with a surfboard tucked under one arm and then gone right into the marines. He wore a navy blue uniform with two chevrons on his sleeve and introduced himself as Corporal Todd Lance.

I guessed that the conviction rate fell with each step away from the crime scene. Had Candy called from her house the minute Stu left they might have sent an actual sex crimes detective.

Corporal Lance confirmed that Candy was the victim and then asked the rest of us to leave. I knew that was probably a mistake on his part, but I wasn't going to pipe up and say so.

John went back to work, while Ronnie and I walked out to the waiting room. We stood near a wall since there were no chairs available.

"You shouldn't have come," I said.

"Don't be like that. Candy wasn't upset to see me."

"You were very good with her, and you still shouldn't have come."

"You wouldn't tell me what was happening. I thought it might have something to do with Lydia."

"Lydia's just your client."

"My clients become my friends. I thought that awful husband of hers might have done something."

"Duncan is a dick, but he's harmless."

"That's what they say about serial killers before they catch them. So have you called Lydia?"

"No. I feel like there's a conflict of interest here. Stu Whatley is her client."

"Is he?" Ronnie asked. "I mean if they arrest him, she won't represent him. Will she?"

"Probably not."

"Then there's no conflict. You should call her. She'd want to know about this."

I felt like I was about to betray Candy Van Dyke. Like I was not on her side. But I was on her side. I wanted to see Stu Whatley pay for what he'd done. I was a little concerned that Lydia might not be concerned about that.

As I took my cellular phone out of my pocket, my boyfriend said, "Uh-huh. There's a bank of payphones just as you come into the ER. Night rates are better, but they're still crazy. There's no reason to spend money if you don't have to."

I said okay and walked away. I tried not to be pissed. I hated being told what to do. More than that, I hated being told what to do and how to do it. Ronnie did that a lot. I ignored it. Given who his mother was I was lucky he was not a whole lot more messed up.

"Lydia?" I said into the gray receiver which was probably an inch thick with germs. "It's Dom."

"It's so early. Something going on?"

"Just after midnight, Candy Van Dyke was raped by Stu Whatley."

There was an ominous silence on the other end of the line.

"He seems to be under the impression no one will prosecute him because of the previous misidentification."

"Is he going to be arrested?"

"I don't know. Candy is with a policeman right now, but I don't think she wants to pursue this. She's concerned she won't be believed."

"I can't talk about this. Not until I get to Stu and make it clear that I only represent him for his wrongful conviction and that our relationship goes no further than that. How did you get involved in this?"

"Candy called me."

"Why did she call you?"

"I don't know. Maybe I have kind eyes."

"You don't. She must have thought you'd believe her though."'

"I do believe her."

"All right. We'll talk about it at the office."

I went back into the ER, no one tried to stop me. Corporal Todd stood outside the curtain with John and Ronnie. When he saw me coming, he said, "You're Dom Reilly?"

"I am."

"She's not willing to make a statement. I gave her my card. She said you brought her here."

"I did."

After a long look in which he took the measure of me, he held out his card to me. "I'd appreciate if you'd take this. In the event she changes her mind. I've had victims so sure they don't want to report that they destroyed the card. A week later they don't know where to call."

"Sure. I'll hold onto it."

"She didn't say much, but what she did say makes me think this guy will do it again."

That's what I was afraid of.

***

The day had already begun when Ronnie and I got home. After Candy was released, we took her (in Ronnie's black Mercedes 190E) to the twenty-four hour pharmacy at the CVC on the traffic circle. She walked out with a large bag of antibiotics, AZT and half a dozen pregnancy tests. The pharmacist had obviously done this before because I overheard her say, "You'll need several tests. You can take the first one in about a week, then test once a week until you have a period. Test once after your period just to be certain."

Candy said, "Thank you."

Of course, when we dropped her off, we offered to stay with her and make breakfast.

"That's kind of you, but I don't think so," she said. "He got what he wanted. I don't think he'll be back."

"You're sure?" I asked.

"Yes, I am. Thank you both for everything you've done. I

need to get some sleep. I can cancel my appointments today, but I have a full day tomorrow."

She looked at Ronnie knowing he'd understand. He said, "I've got a couple of open slots. I could help out if you need... and I promise not to steal your clients."

"I'll be fine, thank you."

Ronnie pulled away and drove us home. We putzed around making breakfast—well, he made breakfast. I made coffee. Junior came down and had a bowl of cereal: Count Chocula, which couldn't have been good for his health. That meant Ronnie and I couldn't talk much about Candy. I think John had gotten home from his shift while we were with Candy at the pharmacy. I was going to have to do something nice for him. I appreciated what he'd done for Candy.

"I should drive you to your car," Ronnie said, before leaving for work.

"That's okay, I'll pick it up later."

"I have time."

"I think I'm going back to bed," I lied.

"Okay."

As soon as he left, I snuck into John's room, got the keys for The Lunchbox, and drove down to The Freedom Agenda. It was close to ten. Karen was on the phone but looked calmer. I slipped around the corner into Lydia's office, shutting the door behind me.

"How is Candy?" she asked.

"Probably better than she should be. In a few days this is going to hit her. Hard."

She nodded. She wore a powder blue suit with a red bow around her neck. She must have noticed me looking at it, because she said, "The DA is holding a press conference on the steps of City Hall—"

"I thought you were doing that in Corcoran?"

"The whole thing turned into a pissing contest. Now the DA and Edwin will be duking it out for credit."

"You might want to tell Edwin to let the DA win."

"That crossed my mind."

"Are you going to tell Stu Whatley you can't represent him?"

"I already have. I called him about an hour ago and made it clear that I only represent him for his wrongful conviction."

"You didn't mention the rape."

"Of course not."

"How did he take it?"

"Perfectly. He wasn't suspicious at all. I made it seem like I was asking him for a donation when the time comes. Several times, I said that the only legal work we do is getting wrongly convicted prisoners out of prison. That all of our income is donations, and that we don't do any other defense work that would provide more income."

"He bought that?"

"Well, it *is* true, Dom."

"Okay."

"He did make it clear we weren't getting a donation from him."

"Ungrateful son of a bitch."

She smiled, a little meanly. "He doesn't know it yet, but he won't be getting any money. I'm going to tell Edwin about the rape. He'll be dropping Stu."

"Doesn't that violate attorney client privilege?"

"Stu didn't tell me anything, you did."

I nodded. "Okay. Can't he just get another lawyer?"

"He can try. Anyone he hires will have to call me for the files. I'll mention what happened to Candy and that it was reported to the police. It was reported, wasn't it?"

"We went to the ER, so yes. I don't think she gave the police Whatley's name. At this point, she doesn't want to pursue it."

"Doesn't matter. Just the possibility a judge might allow her to testify during a civil trial is enough to prevent Stu from getting representation."

"So he made a big mistake."

She nodded. "He did. I do need you to go and check on Joanne Yardley today."

"Why is that?"

"While I was on the phone with Stu, he asked a couple of

questions about double jeopardy. He said he took a few creative writing classes in prison. He thinks he might write about someone who's wrongly convicted, then gets out of prison and commits the same crime. He thinks that person can't be tried."

"He thinks if he rapes Joanne Yardley, they wouldn't be able to try him?"

"Apparently it's a common belief among prisoners. I explained that wasn't true. That double jeopardy meant one crime at one *time*. Being convicted of shoplifting at Target doesn't give you carte blanche to shoplift there whenever you feel like it."

"Did he understand that?"

"He told me I was wrong. That I didn't understand the law."

"In other words, he's an idiot."

"Unfortunately, idiots are always dangerous."

"Okay, I'll go see Joanne."

****

I drove back to the hospital and picked up my green frog. Then I called John and left a message that he needed to take a cab to the hospital and told him where The Lunchbox was. I'd pay him back for the taxi ride later.

Then, without calling ahead, I drove to Joanne Yardley's house in Elysian Heights. When I got there, I parked the Taurus and walked back to her intercom and pressed it.

"Hello."

"It's Dom Reilly. I need to talk to you."

After a long moment, the intercom buzzed and the gate began to slide to one side. The dogs had started to bark, which I thought was a good thing. Or at least I hoped it was. The neighbors might be so used to the dogs yapping away that if someone did break in they wouldn't pay a bit of attention.

Before I reached the house, Joanne was out on the porch asking, "Why are you here? You got your guy out of prison. I saw it on TV. Can't you leave me alone?"

I got to the porch and standing at the bottom of the two

steps that led up to the porch, I said, "Candy Van Dyke was raped last night."

"By Stu Whatley," she supplied. "You wouldn't be here otherwise."

"Yes, by Stu Whatley."

"You think he's coming for me next."

"He thinks he can't be tried if he rapes you. He thinks it's double jeopardy."

"How do you know what he thinks?"

"He was asking my boss hypothetical questions."

"It isn't double jeopardy, is it?"

"No, that's not how it works."

"Good. Thanks for warning me."

She turned and started back into the house.

"Hold on," I said. "I'm not going to abandon you. I can take you to a hotel or a friend's house... I can take you home to my house if you have nowhere else to go."

She looked at me for a moment, then said, "Come in for a minute."

I followed her into the small house, the dogs barking as I walked in. Annoying, but I could see how they made her feel safer. She went directly to the kitchen, opened a drawer, and pulled out a small pistol. I couldn't see what kind. She set it on the counter.

"There's another one in the nightstand next to my bed."

"Thank you for not pointing it at me," I said.

"I've had training. A lot of training. Before I was raped, I believed in strict gun control. Actually, I still do. I wasn't going to have guns in the house without understanding proper safety protocols."

"You don't ever get depressed?"

"I'm not going to all this trouble protecting myself only to turn around and commit suicide."

I nodded.

"Let me show you the perimeter." She turned and walked to the back door. I followed. Once outside, we were in a lovely, terraced backyard, which was carefully landscaped and well taken care of. There was a six-foot, cedar privacy fence around the yard. Standing there on the patio off the backdoor, I noticed that the planting didn't begin for nearly two feet from the fence.

Joanne led me up the next two terraces. We were about twenty feet from the back fence.

"My neighbors behind me, the Smiths, have chickens. They make a tremendous amount of noise when anyone is in the yard."

"And your neighbors on either side?"

"No chickens, but fences and lights with motion detectors." She studied me a moment. She obviously knew this wasn't as much security as I would have liked. She nodded her head toward the fence saying, "And then there's this."

We walked over near the fence on the south side of her property. She pointed to the top of the fence. About an inch below the top there were three lines of barbed wire. They were placed so that there was a barb every inch or so. I leaned in and looked down the side of the property. The fence went all the way to the street where it met the retaining wall, the one where I'd noticed the broken glass painted into the top.

"Be careful," she said, looking down at the foot of the fence. There was a tripwire that ran the length of the fence.

I wondered for a moment if it would open up a giant pit under my feet with spikes sticking upward. "What happens if it's tripped?"

"All my security lights pop on, alarms go off, the security company is called, and an armed guard is here in five minutes or less. I'd let you trip it just to see, but false alarms are a hundred and twenty-five dollars. I had a possum for a while; cost me a fortune."

"You've got a pretty good system," I said, to reassure her.

Of course, if Stu Whatley had walked by the house in daylight, and stood on his tippy toes to see the broken glass, he'd know to bring something—a thick rug, a large piece of cardboard —to put over the retaining wall in the front. Once he was over that, he'd be on the porch in thirty-seconds. I doubt that it was easy to get through Joanne's front door or window, but I also didn't think it was impossible. I'd already decided I'd be sitting in my rental all night in front of her house.

"Well, I just wanted to make sure you were prepared. It seems that you are."

"Thank you. I appreciate the heads up."

CHAPTER TWENTY-SIX

April 19, 1996
Friday afternoon

It was lunchtime, so I drove to Taco Maria's on Hyperion. I picked up three carnitas tacos with a side of guacamole and chips. I ate one in the Taurus, making a mess, and then drove across town to Wilshire Community Police Station on Venice Boulevard. It took a good forty-minutes. Not a big deal, I knew Whatley would be at a press conference downtown most of the afternoon.

On the way, I called the owner of The Hawk, a straight woman named Marley who owned several properties on the stroll.

"I'm not going to be in this weekend."

"This is a long stomach flu."

"Yeah, um, I don't think I'm coming back."

"Thanks for the two weeks' notice. Robbie's gonna be pissed. He doesn't like working a whole shift."

"Couldn't be helped."

"He said some private eye keeps showing up. Straight. Older. He's looking for someone who sounds a lot like you. Is that what's going on?"

I decided to turn that into a joke. "Yeah, my ex-wife is trying to get back child support. Fifteen grand."

Marley laughed. "You're lying. You're as queer as a three-dollar bill."

"Thanks, I'll take that as a compliment."

After a moment she said, "Feel free to come back when you straighten out your problems. I always appreciated that you didn't rob me blind."

Sometimes it doesn't take a lot to please people.

Wilshire Station was in the Miracle Mile area right below La Brea. Unlike other police stations of my experience, it was clean and quiet. A one story, brick and concrete building, it looked to have been built in the sixties or seventies. I was there to see Detective Wellesley, though I had no idea what hours she kept. I was just taking a chance that she'd be there.

Actually, it was more than a chance. Given the recent collapse of at least three of her cases, it was likely she was on desk duty, which meant she'd be working a regular 9-5 work week.

I asked for her at the front desk, gave my name, and was told to take a seat. I wasn't sure she'd remember who I was. If she did, I could end up sitting there a very long time. If she didn't, she'd at least meet me out of curiosity—come to think of it, curiosity worked in my favor either way.

After about ten minutes, she came out to the bench I was sitting on. She had on a white shirt, a bolo tie and a pair of navy pants. If there was a jacket that went with this ensemble, she'd left it elsewhere. I was sure she didn't own an iron.

She gave me a wry smile, and said, "I thought I recognized that name. Come on back."

I followed her down a short hallway into a communal office space with about ten desks spread around a large room. She led me to a desk and the pointed at the chair next to it.

"Have a seat. Can I get you some coffee?"

"I won't be long. But thank you. It was kind of you to offer."

"Not really. No one's cleaned the coffee maker since the eighties. Our coffee is disgusting." She sat down and took a sip from a cup of Starbucks. "So what do you want?"

"Stu Whatley raped Candy Van Dyke last night."

She had the decency to scowl when I said that but remained silent.

I continued, "I'm worried about Joanne Yardley. Whatley was asking his attorney hypothetical questions about double jeopardy."

She raised an eyebrow. "But you work for his attorney."

"I do."

"You just broke attorney client confidentiality."

Rather than explain Lydia's reasoning, I stared Wellesley straight in the eye, and said, "Ooopsy."

"What is it you want me to do?"

"At the very least there should be a police presence around Joanne Yardley's house."

"Well, first, that's no longer my district. I have no jurisdiction there. I could call over to Rampart, but I'd have to explain the situation and you probably don't want me doing that."

"So you're going to do nothing?"

"I assume you've warned Joanne."

"Of course."

"That's all I could do, and you've already done it."

She was unpleasantly calm about the whole thing. Between grit teeth, I said, "A woman is in danger of being raped."

"No, Mr. Reilly. *Fifteen* women are in danger of being raped today. Just as they are every day. And you're worried about one."

This was pointless. I stood up and walked away. I almost got to the hallway but instead turned around and went back.

"You know you can do what we did. You have samples in those old cases. You have Whatley's DNA profile."

"Those are no longer my cases."

"You could find out whose cases they are, couldn't you?"

"Do you know the term 'cleared by exceptional means?'"

"No. That's a new one on me."

"It's what happens when you put criminologists in charge, you get new lingo. It's sounds good, doesn't it? Cleared by exceptional means... Sounds like we did a good job. Like we tried really hard. In reality, it sucks. We want to clear cases with arrests. But with some kinds of crime, it's not always possible. Rape is one of those crimes. Most rape cases we clear are cleared by exceptional means. It means we know who did it. We've gathered all the evidence we can. And we don't have enough to charge. There's not enough science. Or the victim's memory is bad. Or they refuse to testify altogether. So an exception is made and the case is cleared."

"All right, thanks for the education."

"Stu Whatley was the prime suspect in five rapes we couldn't charge. All cleared by exceptional means. I put him in prison. I did my job. I don't know what the fuck you're doing."

****

I should l have brought more snacks. I'd found a parking spot two houses down from Joanne's place on the other side of the street. I adjusted my mirrors so I could watch her house, and then experimented with scrunching down in the seat. I thought it unlikely anyone trying to get into her place would notice me. It was late afternoon. I figured I'd be staying until the sun came up the following morning. Yes, I definitely should have brought more snacks.

Vengeance. Stu didn't just see opportunity. It wasn't just that he could get away with raping Candy, that he might get away with raping Joanne. He wanted vengeance on these women. The fact that he was guilty of other rapes, that he had deserved to be in prison even if he was there for the wrong reason, that didn't seem to bother him. He'd been wronged and he wanted payback.

For a while, I actively tried not to think about Stu Whatley. He wasn't worth my time. Instead, I thought about leaving California. Where would I go? Should I go someplace big, like New York City? Or should I find some tiny little place in the middle of nowhere? Maybe I should split the difference and move to the suburbs. What kind of job would I get? Bartender was not a good idea. I'd already decided that, so maybe it was time for something new. I liked what I was doing for Lydia. Yeah, it didn't work out with Stu Whatley, he was definitely someone we should have left in prison. But most of the work we did was for the innocent. The truly innocent. I wouldn't mind doing it again. How much was I going to miss Ronnie? A lot. More than I could think about.

I should go soon though. Monday? Tuesday? I had to feel like this Stu Whatley mess was handled. I couldn't leave while he was running around raping women I'd interviewed. Women we'd made unsafe by getting him out of prison. Was Tuesday soon enough, though? Gilbody was nosing around The Hawk. What if he decided Dom Reilly might be his guy? What if he started asking questions like where did I live? Did I have another job?

I didn't think Robbie would say anything. Robbie kept to himself. I'd worked there a year before I learned he had a boyfriend. He told me in a slip of the tongue and then made me promise not to let any of the regulars know. He liked flirting with them—and often fucking them. He just didn't want them knowing much about him. Of course, one of the regulars might —my flip phone chirped. It was Ronnie.

"Where are you?" he asked, a chill in his voice. I wasn't used to that. "And don't tell me you're at The Hawk because I'm sitting at the end of the bar."

"Elysian Heights. In front of a witness's house. I think Stu Whatley might try to attack her."

"Mmmm-hmmm."

"What does that mean?"

"It means mmmm-hmmm."

"No, it means more than that."

"That isn't your job, Dom."

"It kind of is. I'm the one who put this woman in danger."

"No, Lydia did that. Is she sitting next to you?"

I was silent. He knew she wasn't sitting next to me.

"You should call the police. Isn't that what they're there for?"

"They're not going to do anything."

"Well, can she just go to a hotel? Can't you take her to a hotel and come home?"

"I tried that, but I think she's a little agoraphobic."

"Also not your problem."

"I'm getting the sense you're angry at me."

"This would be a bad time for you to lose your bartending job."

"I won't lose my job," I said. I couldn't lose it, I'd already quit.

"You're risking everything for someone you don't know."

"I'll be home in the morning. We can talk about it then."

He left a very chilly silence.

I said, "I love you."

He hung up.

He was right, of course. If the situation were reversed, I'd never allow him to do something like this. Not that I was doing much. I was sitting in a car outside someone's house. If Stu Whatley did show up, I'd call the police. Which reminded me to check the charge on the mobile phone. The little battery was half full. That should be fine. I hadn't planned to take any other calls, so I wouldn't be using a whole lot of my remaining charge.

Anyway, there really wasn't a lot of risk here. I doubted Stu would be able to get onto Joanne's property via the back. His only real option was over the retaining wall in front. I tried to remember how tall he was. I'd only met him once. He'd walked across the visiting room and sat down.

He was shorter than I am. I'm six-three, though, and that means most people are shorter than I am. Was he six foot? He needed to be to see the glass on the wall, which was five something. Five-two, five-three, maybe five-four. I remembered Stu sitting across from me. I was looking down a tiny bit. He was five-eight, five-nine.

By nine o'clock the sky was black as pitch. There were no stars, they never seemed to come out in L.A. I never saw them much in Chicago either. In fact, I'd only seen stars a few times in my life. Mostly when I was floating around the country after I left Chicago. Seemed like I'd be seeing stars again soon.

The sunsets in L.A. were pretty, though. I'd missed a lot of the one earlier. West was to my right and the sunset was blocked by houses. It was what remained of a working-class neighborhood. There were some working-class people still around. They left their garage doors open and worked on their cars in the driveway. They were disappearing though.

Spread around were houses with signs in front that told you who was rehabbing their kitchen. A few houses down a second floor was being added, along with white columns in the front. The old families would hold on for a while longer, until some minor finance guy came along and offered them a crazy amount of money—basically for the location and the view—and they wouldn't be able to resist selling. Maybe this time the house would come down, and up would go a modernist box from one edge of the prop—

"Fuck."

I woke up. I hadn't even realized I was asleep. I was out of the Taurus in a flash, leaving the door hanging open behind me. I could see a man standing at Joanne's retaining wall staring at his hands. There was a streetlight three houses down and he was defined in profile. It was Stu Whatley.

I moved quickly but didn't run. Didn't want to make any more noise than necessary. He took off the jacket he was wearing, folded it over, and threw it over the wall. He was going to try again. He reached up and got a hold of the wall and then began pulling himself over.

I got there in time to grab him by the waistband and pull him onto the sidewalk. He ended up sitting awkwardly on the ground, hitting the concrete with a little bounce. I wondered if he'd broken his tailbone.

"What the—" he started, then focused on me. "You. What are you doing here?"

"Stopping you from hurting someone."

"You work for my lawyer. You have to keep your mouth shut."

"Lawyers have to report crimes if they think they're about to be committed."

He didn't like that but kept his mouth shut. Rolling over, he pushed himself off the ground. Yeah, I was right. The way he was moving made it obvious he'd hurt—

Then he punched me. Right below the belly button. That

wasn't fun. I thought for a moment I might puke on his head. He was barely standing when I pushed him back down onto his butt.

"Fuck," he said. Yeah, that time he hit his tailbone hard. I took a moment to puke on the back of a black Ford Explorer. When I stood up again, Stu was half running, half hobbling down the street. I was about to turn and head back to the rental when the door to Joanne's house opened. Standing on the edge of her porch she said, "You need to go."

"Whatley was just here," I said, dumbly.

"Yes, I know. I was going to shoot him, but you kept getting in the way." She sounded very annoyed by that.

"I was just trying to keep you safe."

"You did that when you warned me. Now go home."

She walked back into her house and slammed the door. Maybe Ronnie was right. I was risking a lot for someone I didn't know. Someone who didn't even appreciate it.

Bent over a bit, I walked back to the ugly green Taurus. Before I turned the car on, I called Lydia.

"Stu Whately attempted to break into Joanne's house a few minutes ago. Her security measures stopped him, then he and I had a little altercation."

"Are you okay?"

"I'm going to have a bad bruise."

"And Stu?"

"He was limping last time I saw him."

She was silent, so I asked, "How was the dog and pony show?" meaning the press conference.

"Edwin and the DA competed for sainthood."

"Did you tell Edwin about Candy Van Dyke?"

"Briefly. He's got a meeting with Stu first thing Monday morning. Stu insisted. I'll fill Edwin in on all the details over the weekend."

"What do you think will happen?"

"He's going to fire Stu as a client."

"Are you sure he'll do it?" Edwin had always struck me as the kind of lawyer who was all about the money. This would guarantee there'd be no referral fee.

"If he doesn't, I'll rip off his balls and wear them as earrings."

"Ouch," I said, trying hard not to visualize that.

"He knows I'll do it, too."

"Okay. I believe you," I said, then asked, "What do you think Stu will do?"

"I suspect he'll keep raping women until he gets caught."

We were both quiet for a bit. Finally, I said, "I wish there was something we could do about that."

"There isn't anything we can do. I don't want to live in a world where people are punished for what they might do. That would be a very dangerous place."

"I hate to break it to you, but this world is already a very dangerous place."

There wasn't much to say after that.

CHAPTER TWENTY-SEVEN

April 20, 1996
Saturday

Saturday, after pretending to sleep half the day, I pretended to go to work. I left at the normal time, even though Ronnie wasn't there to see it. He was off somewhere working, but still... I didn't want to take the chance that Junior might mention I left late. Of course, there was no guarantee he wouldn't show up at The Hawk, but he'd tried that the night before. I doubted he'd do it two nights in a row.

And... I had no place to go. I thought up a couple of useful things to do. Stopping by the Bennett house and paying my rent for the use of the garage. Going out to the airport and paying my rental car bill in cash so it wouldn't show up on Ronnie's credit card—well, my credit card, I guess. Either way, I didn't want to leave him stuck with the bill.

Since I was out that far, I went to an Italian restaurant at the Lakewood Mall. The mall was in the center of a giant parking lot with a few buildings at the edges. One of them was Manfredi's. I sat at the bar and had chicken penne in pesto. The gimmick at Manfredi's was that you order one pasta dish, you get two. Both are big enough to feed an army.

That meant I had a fettuccini alfredo I didn't know what to do with. I couldn't bring it home without an explanation. So what did I do with it? I was paying the check, when I remembered there was a tiny refrigerator at The Freedom Agenda. The kind of thing you bought a teenager when you wanted them to go to their room on a semipermanent basis. Also, it was only seven-thirty. I could do some work. Take a nap. Drink some lousy coffee. Kill time until I could go home at 2 a.m.

When I got there, I parked the rental a couple streets away and walked down the alley to let myself into the back. I could have gone in the front but there were streetlights, and I couldn't be sure Hamlet Gilbody wasn't lurking about somewhere.

I turned on as few lights as possible and put the fettuccini alfredo into the refrigerator; I'd have it for lunch on Monday. Before I sat down, I did some stretching. My stomach was stiff and I was tempted to do everything bent over. That meant I had to do the opposite. I arched my back to stretch my stomach and groin muscles.

The bruise was coming in strong and was tender when I poked at it. I might have been poking at it too much. Also, I didn't know exactly what I was looking for, so the fact that I kept poking it was kind of dumb. I had hoped John would be home so I could ask him to take a look, but I'd managed to miss him.

I could have just started reading letters but decided to organize Larry Wilkes file and then put it away. The file was not especially thick, which made me feel like I hadn't done a lot. There were the news stories about the murder, addresses Karen had gotten me, notes from all my meetings, including those with Larry himself—well, the first meeting. I did need to take a few minutes and write up notes on our final meeting. There were the copies of photos that had appeared in the sports section of the paper. Photos that showed Coach Carrier and Pete.

I flipped back to the very first things in the file. The newspaper articles about the murder. I read through them again. I couldn't help it. I knew what was there but, hey, I didn't have much else to do. I turned them over and was about to skim through all the addresses Karen had given me, when I realized something was wrong. I went back to the articles. One of them contained this line:

"No motive has been given for the murder, though a source suggests that the victim had recently become engaged."

There was something wrong with the timing. The article was dated September 20, 1976. Pete was killed on the eighteenth. Larry had been arrested immediately. Anne would not have been able to visit him in jail until after the article came out. There literally wasn't time for her to have visited Larry so he could tell her to pretend to be Pete's fiancé before the article came out. So who was the source the article referred to?

I decided I ought to verify this with Anne. She might know something I wasn't seeing. I picked up the phone and called her —her number was also in the file.

"You need to leave me alone," she said, after I identified myself.

"Just a quick question. When did Larry tell you to pretend you were Pete's fiancé?"

"I don't remember. Why does it matter?"

"One of the first stories about Pete's death mentions an engagement. It was published two days after his death."

"Okay, well, I don't know anything about that. I don't think I went to see Larry until about a week or so after he was arrested. He called and begged me to come and see him. We were still friends, so I did."

"So, you have no idea why the article would say something like this?"

"No, I don't."

"Do you think Larry got the idea from the article?"

"Maybe. I don't know—Oh shit!"

I thought for a moment she was remembering something. "What?"

"Baby just kicked my liver. I have to go."

And then she hung up.

I considered tracking down the reporter who'd written the

article mentioning the love triangle but decided that would be pointless. Most journalists were a bit more ethical than Richland Keswick and actually protected their sources.

No, I was going to have to go about this in another way. Who would benefit by making an anonymous call to the police—or the newspaper—and telling them there was a love triangle? Coach Carrier maybe, but—

Oh. Wait a minute. Sammy Blanchard called the parents of her husband's final victim and told them what was going on. Would she have made the call? I skipped forward in the file until I got to the notes I'd made about our conversation. I needed to check the dates. Unfortunately, there weren't really any dates in my notes. I remembered that she'd taken control of the interview, that she wanted to tell the story her way. I kind of remembered that she met Coach Carrier when she was fifteen and married him two years later. After the interview notes, there was a page of information Karen had gotten me on the coach. He married Sammy in March 1978. The murder took place in September 1976. That meant Sammy met the coach in the spring of 1976. They overlapped. Oh my God, they overlapped! I closed the folder, turned off the few lights I'd turn on, and rushed out of The Freedom Agenda.

When I walked into Sammy Blanchard's condo, I smelled that she'd been smoking inside. So, she lied to me when she said she only smoked on the deck. I had a strong suspicion it wasn't the only lie she'd told.

She hadn't wanted to let me in. Claimed she was expecting a friend. I lied and said my questions would only take a minute. She wasn't the only one who could lie.

Once I was inside, I noted that she was wearing a T-shirt with a food stain on it and really needed to wash her hair. I didn't think she was expecting a friend. Right away, she pulled the "I only smoke on the balcony routine" and we went outside. The sounds of Saturday night traffic were loud, and that told me why she was so insistent on talking to me outside.

"You know we could stay inside," I said. "I'm not wearing a wire."

"You watch too much TV," she said.

"I'd say the same about you."

"Why don't you ask your questions. I'd like to get this over with."

"You said someone let Ricky Tamayo's parents know what Coach Carrier was up to with their son. That was you, wasn't it?"

"Wouldn't you say they had a right to know?"

"Actually, I'd say you were angry at your husband and wanted to punish him."

"I didn't know what would happen. I'm not clairvoyant."

"It's not the first time you made an anonymous call, is it?"

"You got me. When I was a teenager, we used to call people and ask if their refrigerator was running. When they said yes, we'd tell them to go catch it. That's what you mean, isn't it?"

"There's a newspaper report that refers to a source saying Pete Michaels was murdered because he was engaged. You're that source, aren't you?"

"You think because years later I called the Tamayos and told them Bernie was fucking their son that it was me? That's kind of a stretch don't you think?"

It was a stretch, but that's why you ask questions, to see how people react. My next question was going to tell me a lot.

"Actually, the reason I think you made that call is that you're the one who killed Pete Michaels."

She tried to laugh but ended up sounding like a deflating tire.

"When you told me your story, you made it sound like you got involved with Coach Carrier after the murder, but that's not true, is it? You and Pete were involved with him at the same time, and you didn't like that. So you convinced the Showalter kid to get you a gun. Then you went over and shot your rival. You called Larry Wilkes and gave him the signal to come over. The same signal Coach Carrier used with you. Then you left."

"You make me sound like the worst kind of girl."

I waited. Crossing my fingers that she'd tell me what I'd gotten right and what I gotten wrong. She just stared at me. Cold as ice.

"Are you waiting for me to confess?"

"Don't you want to get it off your chest?"

"No. I don't. You have nothing. You can't connect me to the crime scene. Or murder weapon. Or even the victim."

"I have motive."

"What motive?"

"You were jealous, so you killed Pete."

"You can't prove that. You can't even prove Bernie was having a thing with Pete. And if you can, you can't prove that I knew about it. You can't prove I was jealous, so you don't have a motive, do you?"

She was right. I didn't have anything. What I did have, she was the source of. All she had to do was deny she'd told me anything. So it was nothing. I couldn't connect her to Pete's murder at all.

"I think it's time for you to leave," she said. I decided she was right. If I stayed there much longer, I might push her off the balcony.

I drove back to The Freedom Agenda, let myself in, turned on the light, and sat down at my makeshift desk. I tried to read one of the many letters waiting to be considered, but I couldn't focus. There had to be some way to tie Sammy to the murder. I mean, when she planned it, when she killed Pete Michaels, she was sixteen at most. I didn't believe a sixteen-year-old could plan the perfect murder. In fact, I didn't believe anyone could.

Except it was the perfect murder. No one involved knew anything about her. Even Pete—especially Pete—didn't know anything about her relationship with the coach. His brother didn't know. Anne Whittemore didn't know. No one—

Wait. Andy Showalter knew she was involved. He'd gotten her the gun. I picked up the receiver on the desk phone I'd been given and dialed Mrs. Showalter's number.

"This is Dom Reilly. I'm sorry to call you so late." It was nearly eleven.

"It's all right," she said. "I don't sleep much."

"Do you remember a girl named Sammy Blanchard? She was about two years younger than your son, Andy."

"Sammy Blanchard? Are you telling me she's real? She's an actual person?"

"Yes, I met with her tonight."

"I think you should come over."

CHAPTER TWENTY-EIGHT

April 21, 1996
Sunday in the wee hours

Twenty minutes later, I was in Downey. It was just after midnight but all the lights in the Showalter house were on. When she opened the door, Mrs. Showalter wore a pink shell and a tight pair of black pants. Somehow, she wore more makeup then she had the first time I met her. She'd just lit a cigarette, a very long one, and waved it around like a wand.

"Come on in. Would you like a drink? I decided to have one."

I had the feeling that decision had happened much earlier in the evening.

"No, thank you. I think I'll just hear what you have to say and go." Not that I had any place to be.

"Well, have a seat then," she said, leading me over to the living room with its plastic-covered yellow sectional. I sat down, with a big squeak. In front of me was a Mediterranean-style coffee table, very dark wood. Except when you looked closely, it was wood printed paper over pressboard.

Mrs. Showalter brought over a large drawing pad that had been leaning against the wall. Twenty-four by thirty-six. Awkwardly, she spread it onto the coffee table and sat down next to me.

"I haven't looked at this in years. It's a little bit heartbreaking," she said, flipping the pad open to the first page. The image covered every inch of the page. It was dense and chaotic, there were words and images mixed together. The first thing that struck me—and this was probably the part she found heartbreaking— was that it was good. There was a lot of talent on the page. A lot.

"It's hard to know what you're looking at, at first," she said. "This pad starts in seventy-five. See, a lot of this page is devoted to Germany's invasion of Poland in thirty-nine."

I could pick out tanks, the date September 1939, Hitler speaking to a crowd, Nazi soldiers lining up Poles to shoot them. The drawing was in pencil and smudged around the edges where it had been touched.

Mrs. Showalter carefully flipped forward a few pages.

"I would put this page around January of seventy-six."

In the center of this sheet, there was a portrait of Sammy over her name. It was a good likeness. I could see that it was her right away. Surrounding the portrait were little sketches of Sammy. Candids almost. She was carrying her schoolbooks close to her chest, raising her hand in class, eating her lunch. He was stalking her in an odd way.

"Honestly, I thought he made her up until you said her name. You can see that none of this seems very real," she said as she flipped a few pages. Now we were looking at images that did tell a story. A young man, presumably Andy, lurking next to a tree in a park. Then he's following a boy in a hoodie, reaching out to touch the boy's shoulder, turning him around. The boy seems to have no face, it's hidden, deep in the hoodie. Then there's a close-up drawing of the gun in someone's hand. Money in another hand. Then the boy is holding the gun. The images float around the page nearly in order. It's almost like a cartoon strip, except there are no speech bubbles. Just the occasional word drawn into the background. On this page, it was the word FAVOR. Next to which, he'd put a heart.

"He didn't use any dates, so I'm not sure when he drew this page. I assumed it was well after his father left. He'd stopped drawing him, you see. That would have placed this after the murder. But now I think I might be wrong. He might have drawn this before the murder."

She flipped the page, and I was looking at Sammy again. A lot of Sammys. There were pictures of Sammy in front of the Michaels' house—drawn very accurately. Sammy walking up the driveway and entering the house. A young man cowering, face turned away. Sammy holding the gun out. The gun as it fires with a flare of flame. The young man lying in a pool of blood. Sammy, smiling.

"You thought this was fictional."

"I did. I didn't know this girl was real."

"She is. He's captured her perfectly."

"So you think this drawing is true? You think she killed Pete Michaels?"

After a long drag from her cigarette, her second since I'd sat town, she said, "Yes, I think that's what the drawing says."

I went back to studying the drawing. In addition to the images showing Sammy murder Pete, there was the word HURT. Why that word? He knew that Sammy killed Pete, but he probably didn't know why. She wouldn't have told him she was eliminating her competition. Andy might not have gotten her a gun.

She must have flirted with Andy, enticed him, to get the gun. Then, at this point she might have told Andy that Pete was hurting her. Then Andy would have felt like a hero just for getting her the gun.

It wasn't good that he didn't date this. I really needed to establish when this was drawn. I looked at Mrs. Showalter, and said, "May I?"

She nodded.

I carefully flipped back through some of the pages she'd skipped. I reached one that had a lot of imagery that seemed at first patriotic, but then on closer inspection, disturbing. An American flag with skulls instead of stars, a fife and drum corps made up of zombies, fireworks that were really bombs.

"Do you think this was July 4th? The bicentennial?"

"I think that's probably right," she said.

I began flipping back, passing the murder page and going two, three more, and I was at Halloween. It wasn't as disturbing as the Fourth of July, probably because Halloween is supposed to have skulls and zombies. I asked Mrs. Showalter, "The page with the murder on it, that was drawn sometime between Fourth of July and Halloween?"

"Yes."

"How long do you think it took your son to draw one of these pages?"

"I have no idea. I don't think he worked on them every day."

I decided to try to guess myself. I counted the pages between the Fourth and the murder. There were eight pages. Then I counted between the murder and Halloween. There were two pages. I wasn't sure that fit—there were ten weeks between the Fourth and the murder, and six between the murder and Halloween. That wasn't right proportionally—

But... no. The page that showed the murder would have been drawn after the murder, not on the day of the murder and not before the murder. It took more than a week to complete each page. Proportionally, it wasn't far off then. The page showing Sammy murdering Pete was drawn a week or two after the murder.

"Can I take this?"

"To copy it. You can take it to copy it. I'd like it back as soon as you're done with it."

"I can do that."

Honestly, I wasn't sure if I was lying. I had no idea how you copied something this big.

****

I slept most of Sunday, which was normal. You stay up until three in the morning and you sleep until at least noon. Around one, I went downstairs to make myself some breakfast. In the kitchen, I looked through the cupboard for some cereal and found some raisin bran. Box in hand, I walked over to the refrigerator. On the way, I glanced through the door into the dining room and saw Ronnie sitting there. Just sitting.

I changed course and walked into the dining room saying, "What's going—" I stopped when I noticed the rest of my money, my gun and Nick Nowak's ID sitting on the table next to him.

"Two things. Number one, did you really think I wouldn't stop in at The Hawk last night to see if you were working? And, number two, did you really think I wouldn't look around to see if there was any more money you were hiding?"

There was nothing I could say to that. I hadn't even thought about it. There had been too many other things on my mind to think of Ronnie. And that was wrong.

"I guess I was kind of stupid."

"No shit Sherlock. Why do you have this?" he asked.

"In case I need to leave in a hurry."

"In case you need to leave me. In case you need to leave me in a hurry. Why would you have to leave me?"

"That's not what I said. I might have to leave. That's not the same as leaving you."

"Except it is."

He looked incredibly sad and that broke my heart.

"You saved all this money?"

"I told you. I've been saving for years. Since before I met you, even."

"Nick Nowak. That's who you're going to be next?"

"Not for very long. Just until I find someone to sell me another identity."

"Were you ever going to tell me about any of this?"

"Probably not."

He stopped looking sad, now he looked angry. As angry as I'd ever seen him.

"Look," I said. "The only reason I would ever use it, the only reason I would ever leave was if my being here put you in danger."

"How is that logical?"

"I, I don't think I should explain that."

"Why not?"

"Because if you knew everything you'd be in danger."

"Why can't I go with you?"

"What?"

"I think that's the part that hurts the most. If you need to run away, if you need to go into hiding, ask me if I want to go with you."

"You have a life here. A life you love."

"I won't love it without you."

"And..."

"And? And what?"

"Well, we kind of stand out. I mean, we can change our names, but we'll still be a half-Asian kid with a white, old man boyfriend."

"Newsflash, we're not the only—"

"No, but we'll be the ones who are new in town and acting suspiciously."

"You have no imagination. We'll just tell people my family is Chinese Mafia, and they hate that I'm with you."

"If that were true, we'd never tell anyone."

"Normal people don't think that way."

"You're a normal person."

"I was. Until I met you."

That made me feel terrible. In fact, all of this conversation was making me feel terrible. What had I done to him? Why had I ever thought—

"I'm sorry," I said.

"That's not enough."

"What would be enough?"

"If you ever have to leave, promise you'll take me with you."

I hesitated for a moment, thinking about all the reasons I couldn't do that. And then I promised, knowing that someday I'd break that promise, but knowing I couldn't get through this any other way.

He stood up, and said, "I have a client in half an hour, I need to go."

"Can I hug you?"

"Later. Maybe."

"Okay."

"And while I'm gone put the gun in the Jeep. I don't want it in the house."

Without another word or a kiss goodbye, he walked out of the house. He was gone. And so was my appetite.

CHAPTER TWENTY-NINE

April 22, 1996
Monday

Christopher Robin died over the weekend. Not the Winnie-the-Pooh character, it's impossible to die once you've been trapped between the pages of a book. No, the real Christopher Robin Milne. The boy, recently a seventy-five-year-old man. who had apparently been haunted all his life by the animated alter ego his father created. It was on NPR as I drove to The Freedom Agenda.

Apparently, his father's decision to name a beloved character after his son had backfired and resulted in years of torture for the boy, creating an estrangement that lasted most of their lives. As the saying goes, no good deed goes unpunished.

I was early, having slept poorly. Ronnie and I had slept together in the same bed, but it felt adversarial. He was in his corner; I was in mine. At one point, I think he kicked me. I listened closely to see if he was awake. I mean, if he kicked me in his sleep that was one thing but—I decided he was asleep. Or at least I was pretty sure.

I thought I might beat Karen and Lydia into the office, but they were both there when I arrived. Carrying the sketch pad, I stopped at Lydia's office and asked if she had a minute. She did.

As I sat down, she said, "Edwin made it clear to Stu that he's fired as a client."

"They had their meeting already?"

"No, Edwin called him. He didn't want him in the office."

"How'd he take it?"

"He threatened to have Edwin disbarred. That amused Edwin."

"I'm sure it did."

"You know, you didn't need to come in today. Between the time you spent with Candy Van Dyke and then with Joanne, I think I owe you some paid time off."

"I want to talk to you about Larry Wilkes again."

I could tell she was trying hard not to roll her eyes. "You're stubborn, aren't you?"

I explained that I'd been neatening up the file to put it away, when I saw the discrepancy with the newspaper article. That led me back to Sammy Blanchard.

"So you think she's the murderer?"

"I know she's the murderer."

"She didn't confess though, did she?"

"No. She's too smart for that."

"We can't connect her to Pete. Or the murder scene. Or the gun—"

"I think we can connect her to the gun."

I explained to her about Andy Showalter's drawings. She was thoughtful for a moment, then asked, "His mother will testify that the drawings were done by her son and to the time period in which they were created?"

"Yes."

"If we can prove that Andy Showalter perjured himself and that his testimony was key to Larry's conviction, then we might get him a new trial."

"So you'll take the case?"

Instead of answering, she called out, "Karen!" It took only a moment for Karen to be in the doorway. "Karen, could you find someplace to copy these sketches. There must be places that do that, right?"

"I have a friend who works for an architect, she'll know."

"Dom, let Mrs. Showalter know that we can't give these back to her. We're going to need to give them to the DA handling this and get them into evidence. Karen, call their office in Downey, find out if the original prosecutor is still working and if not, who do they want to deal with the Larry Wilkes case."

Back to me, "Did you tell me you got the transcripts?"

"I did."

"Okay. Karen, I'm going to need two more copies of the transcripts, one for me, one for you. No. Make that three. One for Edwin. He's going to think I'm out of my mind. This guy might be out of prison before we can get to trial."

"Compensation for twenty-five years in prison," I said.

"Don't worry, I'll bring that up. Okay, let's get started."

I got up and walked out of the office. As I passed Karen, I said, "I'll start copying the transcripts. You focus on the other stuff."

"Thanks."

Our copy machine was an actual Xerox, which was about the best thing you could say about it. It was nearly a decade old and was a cast-off from a law firm in downtown LA, which meant it got a lot of use in that first decade. It sat in the back room opposite my makeshift desk and next to the coffee station.

The old workhorse broke frequently, and Karen was on a first-name basis with all the repair guys. She'd also learned enough about the machine that she'd started taking a chance on fixing it herself before she called them. She took care of the problem about fifty percent of the time.

I have to say I was pretty happy. We were taking the case, so I didn't have to feel bad about how things had worked out for Larry Wilkes. Even if we weren't able to get him out of prison before his sentence was up, the money would help him hold onto his greedy boyfriend Bryson. He'd be better off without him, but that wasn't my decision to make.

And then I realized, *we* wouldn't be taking the case. Lydia was taking the case and I would be taking a powder. This was really the last thing that had been keeping me from leaving. My happiness began to crumble. Don't think about it, I told myself. Just do it.

I'd brought the box full of Larry's transcript over to the Xerox and, after filling the copier with paper, began putting the transcripts into the machine about twenty pages at a time. It was supposed to be able to do more than that, but we found that it would jam if we didn't go slowly. So, we went slowly.

I'd refilled the paper trays twice when I heard the bell at the front go off. Someone had come in. At that time in the morning, it was frequently the FedEx guy. Sometimes it was a courier, but they showed up on and off all day long. Occasionally people dropped in to talk about their incarcerated—

Karen let out a little scream, which was odd. She didn't seem like the kind of girl—had she won the lotto? No, no, it wasn't that kind of scream. A moment later, I heard Lydia say in a clear, loud voice, "Stu, put the knife down."

I moved away from the copy machine and took two steps toward the front. Then I stopped. What did I think I'd be able to do? Stu had a knife; I had nothing. I turned and quietly walked out of the building. Once in the alley, I bolted down to the street, then around the corner to the rental car. I unlocked the driver's door, reached under the front seat, and pulled out the Beretta. Clicking off the safety, I ran back down the alley to The Freedom Agenda.

I slipped back into the building as quietly as possible. Creeping across the room, I could hear Lydia telling Stu, "You really need to think about what you're doing. You haven't done anything yet. What you're doing to Karen is assault, but if you stop now, if you stop hurting her, we can get that taken down to a misdemeanor."

"I thought you weren't my attorney anymore."

"You're right. I'm not. But I can get you someone. Someone good."

"Nah, don't bother. I'm gonna fuck you up, bitch. I'm gonna fuck you up good."

I was pressed up against the wall of Lydia's office. I could see her back, but I couldn't see Karen or Stu. From what was being said, I was pretty sure he had a knife to Karen's throat.

"Ladies, this is what we're going to do. Lawyer lady is going to take her clothes off or I'm going to slit the Black bitch's throat."

It was now or never. I stepped around the corner into a spot next to Lydia. Stu and Karen were seven or eight feet from us.

"No, Stu, that's not what's going to happen. You're going to drop the knife or I'm going to blow your fucking head off."

"You wouldn't take the chance. You could blow her head off instead."

That caused Karen to whimper a little.

"Don't worry, Karen, I used to be a police officer. I know what I'm doing."

"Bullshit," Stu said.

"I'm going to count to five," I said. "One, two, three—"

I could see the muscles in his forearm tense. He was about to slit her throat. I fired. A small hole appeared under his right eye. The knife fell out of his hand.

"Karen step away."

She backed into the door jamb, saying, "He was going to kill me. I could feel it. He was going to kill me."

Stu dropped to the floor. He looked pretty dead.

I felt Lydia reach out and take the gun away from me. Softly, she said, "Dom you need to leave. The police can't look closely at you."

"But—"

"No buts. Get of here." Then she fired the gun at the wall. Karen squeaked.

"What did you do that for?"

"I took two shots at Stu, the second killed him, okay?"

"But—"

"Okay?"

"Okay."

Lydia looked at me again, and said, "Get out of here. Now."

I did what she wanted.

****

Ten minutes later, I was at home climbing into the shower. There were tiny specs of gun powder residue on my forearm. That's why Lydia had to fire the gun. For the gunshot residue. I scrubbed my arms raw. After the shower, I wrapped a towel around myself and went down to the basement. I threw my clothes into the washing machine. As I started the washer, I realized I probably transferred residue from my clothes to my body. I went upstairs and took another shower.

I was nearly finished when I realized I was shaking. For the third time in my life, I'd killed a man. Each time had been in self-defense or in defense of others. I wish that made it easier. It didn't.

It was also the third time I'd killed a man and not stuck around to talk to the police. Honestly, I didn't trust them much. Actually, I didn't trust them at all.

I got dressed and then sat on the edge of my bed for a bit taking deep breaths. I had to do this. I had to go back down to The Freedom Agenda and act like I was arriving late for work. I didn't want to do it, but I had to help Lydia sell her story.

When I got down there, the street in front was full of emergency vehicles and squad cars. I parked a block away on a much quieter street behind The Freedom Agenda. I walked around the block. A young police officer stood on the sidewalk blocking the entrance to the storefront. In another time and place he'd have been a good candidate for Hitler Youth.

"I'm sorry, I can't let you pass," he said when I tried to go around him.

"But I work here. What's going on?"

"Who are you?"

"I'm Dom Reilly. I'm an investigator for Lydia Gonzalez. What's happened? Is Lydia okay?"

"I can't give you any information."

A young woman in a Goth get-up stood nearby. She'd been following the conversation. She leaned toward us, and said, "There's been a shooting."

"Oh my God, who was it?" I asked. "Was it Lydia? Was it Karen?"

"My friend thinks the victim was a man."

"But that doesn't make sense. I'm the only man who works there." That wasn't exactly true, it could have been Edwin. But I wasn't trying to sell accuracy here.

"It's probably best that you just go home and wait there," the police officer said. "There's really nothing you can do here."

"I can't talk to Lydia?"

"I'm afraid that's not possible."

"You're sure? She needs to know I was here. Dom Reilly."

"There's no way you're going to be able to talk to her right now. It's not going to happen."

I tried asking the question again, a couple of times, providing a few semijustifications; then gave up and walked away. None of that was necessary. I knew before he said anything he wouldn't let me in. I just wanted him to remember me.

As I walked around the block to the rental car my mind was hornet's nest of ideas and thoughts and emotions. Could I really run away now? Wouldn't it put Lydia in jeopardy? The story she was telling did not include me, so I wasn't exactly needed. But— if I disappeared it would raise all sorts of questions. Suddenly, I would be needed.

But I couldn't stay. That would put Ronnie and John and maybe even Junior in danger. For all I knew Hamlet Gilbody wouldn't wait for me to come out of the house. He might just burn it down with us in it. I was royally screwed. I couldn't stay and I couldn't go.

As I approached the rental, I took the keys out of my pocket. The car came with one of those remotes where you flick a button, and the doors all unlock. I hit that button and there was a beep followed by a thwap—the locks unlocking. I reached out to open the driver's door and someone behind me said, "Nick Nowak."

I turned around and there was the little round man still wearing his Army surplus jacket.

"Hamlet Gilbody." I said.

He smiled. I assumed he was about to pull a gun out of his

pocket and shoot me dead next to a green car that looked like a frog. Somehow that seemed a fitting end. I hoped they wouldn't make Ronnie identify my body. I'd hate for him to see—

"I work for Lackerby, Leone and Cooke. They represent—"

"Deanna Hansen, I know. I owe her money. I imagine she's quite angry about that."

"I suppose she is. But we don't represent her anymore."

"What? You don't?"

"The Leone boy took a suitcase of cash belonging to her. He ended up dead because of it—not her fault—but in the process the Las Vegas police kept the cash as evidence. You see where it might be difficult for her to claim it. After that she found a new law firm."

I was struggling to grasp all of this. Hard to do when you're standing there wondering why someone hasn't killed you yet. I mean, it sounded like maybe he wasn't there to kill—

"What do you want?"

"As I started to say, we represent the estate of Owen Lovejoy."

"Oh."

"I'm sorry. Did you not know that Mr. Lovejoy had passed away?"

"I heard that he'd died a of couple years ago. It was longer than that, though, wasn't it?"

"He died in eighty-nine."

"Yeah, that's what I heard. So, why have you gone to all this trouble just to tell me my old lawyer is dead?"

"You're mentioned in his will."

"I am?"

"We would have concluded this matter sooner, but his family contested the will. That took several years and a friendly judge. And you haven't been easy to find. I'm the third investigator they've put on it."

"There are good reasons I'm difficult to find."

"Yes. I've picked up on that. I'm only here about the Lovejoy estate though. I have no other business with you."

"How did you find me?" I asked.

"One of the regulars at The Hawk told me you lived on 2nd

Street. I've been staking out different parts of the street for more than a week."

"It's a long street."

"Yes, I learned that the hard way. I was driving by when you came out of your house this morning. I followed you down here. Do you have something to do with that mess going on a block away."

"No comment."

That brought a smile to his face. Then he reached into an inside pocket of the Army surplus jacket. I jumped even though it was clear he wasn't about to kill me.

"I have a check for a hundred thirty-six thousand four hundred twenty-two dollars and eighty-five cents. It's made out to Nick Nowak. Will you be able to cash that, Dom?"

I took the check and stared at it. Why had Owen done this? I guessed that the amount he'd left me was actually a hundred thousand dollars and the rest was simply interest that had accumulated since his death in eighty-nine. A hundred thousand dollars was the amount of money he allowed Deanna Hansen to put up for my bail. The amount I originally owed her. Had he been intending that I pay her back?

It was very unlikely she'd accept a hundred and thirty-six thousand dollars to pay things off. She was going to add interest. A lot of interest. Criminals tended to charge a higher rate than most banks. Maybe he thought she'd take the deal to stay on good terms with her attorneys. He wouldn't have known that relationship would all fall apart years before I could be found.

Of course, I *could* try negotiating with her. I could *try* to get her to take the money. And I might, if it weren't for Monroe White and Rita Lundquist. They'd still be after me.

"Can you cash the check?" he asked again.

"Yes, I can."

"Then I think our business is concluded." He reached into his pocket and took out a card. "Just in case you need anything."

"I won't."

"I hope that's true."

CHAPTER THIRTY

April 22, 1996
Later

I want to say that right and wrong are not the things we think they are. But that's not exactly what I mean. Sometimes, what's right is wrong and what's wrong is right. And other times, right and wrong are basically the same thing. Or rather, some things, some acts, some events, are wrong and right at the same time. Like killing Stu Whatley.

It is wrong to kill. I know that; I feel that. As I've said, Stu Whatley was the third man I'd killed. Each man I killed was to protect myself or others. Sometimes both. That makes it right. Except I can't help feeling that I should have been able to find ways to avoid killing and still find a way to protect myself and those I care about. I feel that I should, but then I can never find what that path should have been.

Life went on. Jackie-O's personal belongings were auctioned off for thirty-four million—a tad more than my things would bring; Clinton released a shitload of oil from our national stores to bring down gas prices, which had nearly reached a buck and a half a gallon; and Ronnie had gotten the cast album for *A Funny Thing Happened on the Way to the Forum* and sang along incessantly.

Of course, I gave him the money I'd been left, and we bought the co-op he wanted. He almost didn't take it.

"Where did it come from?"

"An old friend of mine passed away, quite a while ago actually. His attorney finally found me." Truthful, if not very specific.

"Why did he leave it to you?"

"We were involved for a little while," I said, also true. "But not long enough for him to leave me this much money. Honestly, I really don't know for sure why he wanted me to have it."

"You know when people start sentences with the word 'honestly' it generally means they're anything but," he said pointedly.

I wanted to say he'd been reading too many books on sales. That wouldn't have helped things though. Instead, I said, "I'm telling you the truth," as sincerely as possible.

He must have believed me, because he said, "I'll take the money on one condition. Your name goes on the deed."

"Okay," I agreed, still a bit reluctant. But the reality was, no one was looking for Dom Reilly. They were only looking for Nick Nowak. If they knew to do a property search for Dominick Reilly, then I was already sunk.

****

Lydia had to do several interviews with the police, but it was quickly obvious it wasn't going anywhere. No one wanted to prosecute an attorney for killing a rapist who was holding her assistant at knife point. And when Candy Van Dyke came forward and identified Stu Whatley as her rapist, well, that was the end of it.

It made the papers and then talk radio. Certain hosts believed that anyone arrested by the police should spend the rest of their lives in prison. They made it seem like Stu Whatley was evidence that Lydia's work was invalid, and she was doing little more than getting guilty men out of prison on a technicality.

Larry Wilkes' case was moving forward slowly. I'd gone back up to see him again, having reversed our decision. I also explained that it was Sammy Blanchard who'd killed Pete and not Coach Carrier.

"But, she was like sixteen," he said.

"I know. But you were all doing pretty adult things."

"But... do you think she's some kind of bad seed?"

"I don't know," I said. Of course, that made me wonder what might have happened to her that made her set her sights on an old man and then kill to get him. But I had no idea what that might be.

A month or so later, Ronnie dragged me to a fundraiser for the Long Beach Historical Association, a group which was fifty percent realtors. Candy Van Dyke was there. She looked fabulous. She saw me but didn't come right over. About halfway through the event—which was appetizers and booze—she came over and said hello.

"Hello Candy. You look well."

"I am well, thank you. Of course, most people are on three glasses of wine, aren't they?" She reached out and grabbed my wrist. "I want to say thank you."

"For?"

"Killing Stu Whatley."

"I didn't have anything to do with that," I replied.

"I don't think too many people believe that cockamamie story your boss is telling."

"It's true."

"Whatever you say. I just wanted thank you personally for what you did."

I had no choice but to say you're welcome.

EPILOGUE

August 1976

The two naked boys lay crushed together in Pete's tiny twin bed. Arms and legs entangled, sweating, sticking to each other. The room was small, on the opposite wall his brother's twin bed. Pete had tucked a chair under the doorknob, just in case.

No one would try the door though. His parents were on a bus tour to Laughlin, Nevada. His brother had a twenty-one-year-old girlfriend who had an apartment in Seal Beach. Still, Pete locked the door and stuck a chair under the knob. He wasn't ashamed of who he was, but he knew his family would be unhappy if they found out, and he didn't like making people unhappy.

They were happy to have the afternoon to themselves. Larry would be leaving for school in Santa Barbara soon. It weighed heavily on both of them.

"I don't want to go," Larry whispered. "I want to stay here with you. I want to stay naked with you forever."

"I don't want you to go, but you have to."

"No I don't. I can tell my parents I don't want to."

"If you can go to college, you have to."

"Do you want to go to college?" Larry asked, a bit doubtful. Pete had hardly been a stellar student.

"Maybe. I don't know."

"I thought your uncle was getting you into the longshoreman's union."

"Yes, he thinks he can do that."

"Then you're set. You'll always have money."

"And I'll only ever be one thing. I'll be twenty in a few months. I don't think I want my whole life decided for me."

"We're not going to see each other very much, are we?" Larry asked, clearly unhappy.

"We will. I'll come visit you. We'll have sex in your dorm room."

"I'm going to have a roommate."

"Then I'll get a hotel room."

"And then what?"

"Trust me. It'll be okay."

"It's four years."

"Four years ago you were, what, fourteen? Fifteen? Did you think you'd be in my bed, sticky with cum, thinking about how much you *loved* me."

"Don't make fun of me."

"I'm not making fun of you. Not really. I want you to love me. I love you."

"You do?"

"I do."

Larry thought for a moment. "When I was fourteen, I didn't think I'd ever love anyone. Didn't think I *could* love anyone. I didn't think queers did that."

"Well, apparently they do," Pete said, kissing him. "Don't worry about the future. Things will work out. I promise."

Desert Run

Full Release

The Ghost Slept Over

My Favorite Uncle

Femme

Praline Goes to Washington

Aunt Belle's Time Travel & Collectibles

Masc

Never Rest

Code Name: Liberty

The Less Than Spectacular Times of Henry Milch

Fathers of the Bride

Year of the Rat

A Fabulously Unfabulous Summer for Henry Milch

Marshall Thornton writes two popular mystery series, the *Boystown Mysteries* and the *Pinx Video Mysteries*. He has won the Lambda Award for Gay Mystery three times. His romantic comedy, *Femme* was also a 2016 Lambda finalist for Best Gay Romance, as was his romantic suspense novel, *Code Name: Liberty*. Other books include *My Favorite Uncle*, *The Ghost Slept Over* and *Masc,* the sequel to *Femme.* He is a member of Mystery Writers of America.

9 798990 239722